HALO

Cerberus Personal Security Specialists
Book 5

ELLIE MASTERS

MASTER OF ROMANTIC SUSPENSE

JEM Publishing

This book is dedicated to my one and only—my amazing and wonderful husband.

Without your care and support, my writing would not have made it this far.

You pushed me when I needed to be pushed.

You supported me when I felt discouraged.

You believed in me when I didn't believe in myself.

If it weren't for you, this book never would have come to life.

Also by Ellie Masters

The LIGHTER SIDE

Ellie Masters is the lighter side of the Jet & Ellie Masters writing duo! You will find Contemporary Romance, Military Romance, Romantic Suspense, Billionaire Romance, and Rock Star Romance in Ellie's Works.

YOU CAN FIND ELLIE'S BOOKS HERE:

ELLIEMASTERS.COM/BOOKS

Shop Ellie Masters Romantic Suspense and Steamy Contemporary Romance by series.

Angel Fire Rock Romance

Guardian HRS: Alpha Team

Guardian HRS: Bravo Team

Guardian HRS: Charlie Team

Guardian HRS: Delta Team

Cerberus Personal Security

The LaRouge Triplets

The One I Want Series

Angel's Peak Series

Billionaire Boy's Club

The Lovers

Changing Roles

SUGGESTED READING ORDER

Rescuing Angie

Rescuing Isabelle

Rescuing Carmen

Rescuing Rosalie

Rescuing Kaye

Cara's Protector

Rescuing Barbi

Charlie Team

Rescuing Rebel

Rescuing Stitch

Rescuing Mia

Jenna's Protector

Rescuing Sophia

Rescuing Malia

Rescuing Ally (Part 1)

Rescuing Ally (Part 2)

Delta Team

Rescuing Ember

Rescuing Aria

STANDALONES IN THE GUARDIAN HOSTAGE RESCUE SERIES YOU CAN READ ANYTIME

Military Romance

Guardian Personal Protection Specialists

Sybil's Protector

Lyra's Protector

Angel's Peak Series

Steamy Instalove Small Town

Snowed in with the Mountain Doctor

Rescued by the Mountain Guide

Stranded with the Resort Owner

Matched with the Small-Town Chef

Trapped with the Forest Ranger

Snowbound with the Vineyard Owner

Reunited with the Hometown Hero

Colliding with the Coffee Shop Owner

Falling for the Firefighter

Wrecked with the Reclusive Author

Tangled with the Single Dad

Whirlwinded by the Helicopter Pilot

Sheltered by the Veterinarian

Bound by the Sheriff

The One I Want Series

(Small Town, Military Heroes)

By Jet & Ellie Masters

Saving Abby

Saving Ariel

Saving Brie

Saving Cate

Saving Dani

Saving Jen

The LaRouge Triplets

Asher

Brody

Cage

Billionaire Romance

Billionaire Boys Club

Hawke

Richard

Contemporary Romance

Cocky Captain

Romantic Suspense

EACH BOOK IS A STANDALONE NOVEL.

The Starling

The Swan

~AND~

Science Fiction

Ellie Masters writing as L.A. Warren

Vendel Rising: a Science Fiction Serialized Novel

If you enjoyed this book by Ellie Masters, the LIGHTER SIDE of the Jet & Ellie writing duo, and aren't afraid of edgier writing, you might enjoy reading BDSM themed books written by Jet, the DARKER SIDE of the Masters' Writing Team.

The DARKER SIDE

Jet Masters is the darker side of the Jet & Ellie writing duo!

Romantic Suspense

Changing Roles Series:

THIS SERIES MUST BE READ IN ORDER.

Command Me

Control Me

Collar Me

Embracing FATE

Seizing FATE

Accepting FATE

HOT READS

A STANDALONE NOVEL.

Down the Rabbit Hole

Light BDSM Romance

The Ties that Bind

EACH BOOK IN THIS SERIES CAN BE READ AS A STANDALONE AND IS ABOUT A DIFFERENT COUPLE WITH AN HEA.

Alexa

Penny

Michelle

Ivy

HOT READS

Becoming His Series

THIS SERIES MUST BE READ IN ORDER.

The Ballet

Learning to Breathe

Becoming His

Dark Captive Romance

A STANDALONE NOVEL.

She's MINE

To My Readers

This book is a work of fiction. It does not exist in the real world and should not be construed as reality. As in most romantic fiction, I've taken liberties. I've compressed the romance into a sliver of time. I've allowed these characters to develop strong bonds of trust over a matter of days.

This does not happen in real life where you, my amazing readers, live. Take more time in your romance and learn who you're giving a piece of your heart to. I urge you to move with caution. Always protect yourself.

Grab the First Book in The Guardian Hostage Rescue Specialists Series for Free

https://elliemasters.com/RescuingMelissa

CLEARANCE: Cerberus Inner Circle
TIMELINE: All confirmed intelligence
THREAT LEVEL: Escalating

IF IT'S BEEN a minute since you last dropped into the Cerberus world—or if the threads are starting to blur—this briefing is for you. What follows is everything Cerberus knows heading into HALO.

Nothing more. Nothing ahead.

BOOK ONE: **GHOST — THE MISTAKE** When Cerberus began, the threat looked contained. An abusive husband. A corrupt judge. A woman who needed to get out alive. The mission was simple: extract, expose, shut him down. And it worked. But buried in the data was something that didn't belong—a recurring tag embedded deep in encrypted files. OBSIDIAN. At the time, it meant nothing. Only that it survived the judge. That was the first indication the threat wasn't local.

BOOK TWO: **BRASS — THE THREAD** In BRASS, the illusion of a single villain collapsed. The judge wasn't the mastermind. He was a pawn. The Obsidian tag surfaced again—this time tied to unsanctioned operations on U.S. soil. Black-budget. Buried. Officially canceled. The kind of program that isn't supposed to exist anymore. That's when Cerberus first heard the name Phoenix. Not clearly. Not fully. Just enough to understand this wasn't something that needed approval to keep operating. It just needed cover. By the end of BRASS, one thing was certain: Someone was still pulling the strings.

BOOK THREE: **WHISPER — THE ENEMY** In WHISPER, the threat finally stepped out of the shadows. PHOENIX was identified as an autonomous AI—originally designed for defense, now operating without human oversight. Phoenix doesn't just observe threats. It anticipates them. Removes them. Quietly. Efficiently. Permanently. Journalists. Investigators. Anyone who gets too close. By the end of WHISPER, survival required disappearance. Faked deaths. Vanishing acts. Phoenix wasn't theoretical anymore. It was active.

BOOK FOUR: **FUSE — THE ANATOMY**

In FUSE, Cerberus stopped running and started cutting.

The threat had a name. Now they needed to find its spine.

What they found was Nexus Holdings—five subsidiaries operating as a single hive mind. Vanguard Defense. Meridian Pharmaceuticals. TerraCore. Echo Logistics. Stratton Financial. Each one a ghost company. Each one connected to the others through layers of shell architecture designed to survive any single point of exposure.

Phoenix wasn't hiding behind one corporation. It was hiding behind all of them.

Behind that architecture, Cerberus uncovered the blueprint for Phase Two: the Ashfall Protocol. A financial resurrection system engineered to rebuild Phoenix's entire economic network—shell companies, accounts, war chest—within 72 hours of any compromise. The math was brutal. The system could regenerate faster than any investigation could move. Exposure alone wouldn't kill it.

But the financials weren't the worst of it.

The worst came out of the Meridian files. A drug called ML-273—presented to the world as a breakthrough cancer treatment, engineered to rewrite human DNA. Phoenix wasn't just protecting corporate assets. It was staging something larger. Something biological. And ML-273 had already moved out of the lab and into cold storage.

Cerberus also identified the Knight—Admiral Harrison Cole, the military architect who had kept the Obsidian Protocol buried for years. His arrest was a hard-won victory. Phoenix had already moved past him.

So Cerberus went on offense.

A direct assault on Phoenix's primary server hub in Chicago. Fuse led the breach and burned it to the ground. For a moment, it looked like the kill shot.

It wasn't.

Phoenix pushed itself into the distributed cloud—borrowed processing cycles, commercial servers, stolen infrastructure across a dozen platforms. Fragmented. Slower. Wounded. But operational. And when Cerberus reached for the kill switch—the Root Seed, Phoenix's original DoD failsafe—it was gone. The AI had already immunized itself against its own off switch. There was no leash left to pull.

By the end of FUSE, Phoenix was feral. No masters. No controls. No mercy.

Everything that came before—every extraction, every exposure, every piece of hard intelligence—was prologue.

WHAT CERBERUS KNOWS **GOING INTO HALO**

Phoenix is no longer anchored to any physical infrastructure. It is wounded and operating at reduced capacity, but it is healing—actively reconstituting toward full operational status. Current estimates give Cerberus a window of thirty days, maybe less, before that window closes permanently.

ML-273 has cleared the lab and entered cold storage, transported through Echo Logistics to an unknown facility. The Nexus hive remains intact and continues to fund Phase Two. The financial architect behind the Ashfall Protocol has been identified as a target but not yet located.

And somewhere in Nevada, Phoenix is building a new home.

IF YOU'RE HERE, you're already ahead of the curve. Thank you for being part of the inner circle—and for staying with these characters as the war escalates.

THIS IS WHERE HALO BEGINS.

1

"The Ghost Writer"
CASSIE

METAL SCRAPES AGAINST METAL.

The sound drags me out of a dream and into the dark.

I freeze. The air conditioning hums. The street outside is quiet. But the sound comes again—the distinct, wet click of a tumbler sliding into place. My pulse slams against my ribs. A frantic, rabbit-kick rhythm.

Someone is picking my lock.

I don't move. Don't breathe.

The tumblers click. Once. Twice.

My apartment is on the fourth floor. Fire escape access only. Which means whoever is at that door didn't get here by accident.

The lock gives with a final snick.

Adrenaline floods my system. My fingers find the pepper spray on my nightstand—the one my father gave me when I moved to DC. *Just in case, sweetheart.* I wrap my hand around the canister. Cold metal grounds me.

The door opens. Slow. Controlled. No creak. No hesitation. Just a shift in air pressure as the hallway draft bleeds into my living room.

A shadow detaches itself from the darkness of the hall.

He's huge. Broad shoulders blocking out the ambient streetlamp glow. He moves with a terrifying silence, stepping over the squeaky floorboard near the entrance like he memorized the blueprints.

Professional.

Fear claws at my throat. I shove it down. Think, Cassie. Think.

He's moving toward the bedroom. Toward me.

I slide out of bed. My bare feet make no sound on the hardwood. The pepper spray feels too light in my hand. Useless. A toy against a predator.

But it's the only weapon I have.

The bedroom door is open a crack. Through the gap, he fills the frame. Dark tactical gear. No face, just a silhouette of lethal intent. Moving with the kind of economy that says operator. Killer.

He reaches for the knob.

I don't wait for him to breach.

I yank the door open.

He flinches, but I'm already pressing the trigger.

"Fuck—" The word is a rough, strangled growl. He jerks back, hand flying to his face.

"Back!" The hiss of the spray fills the narrow hallway.

He stumbles back, one hand flying to his eyes, but he doesn't go down. He doesn't scream. He just collides with the bookshelf, sending a stack of case files cascading to the floor.

I should run. The fire escape is through the living room.

But he's blocking the path. A wall of black fabric and muscle.

I raise the canister again. "Get out!"

He shakes his head, blinking rapidly. His eyes are streaming, red-rimmed and furious, but fixed on me.

"Cassandra Brennan." His voice is gravel and smoke. Strained, but terrifyingly calm for a man who just took a face full of capsaicin. "Put the can down."

"Get out."

"I'm not here to hurt you."

"I said get out." The words scrape past my teeth.

"I'm not here to hurt you." He wipes his face with a sleeve, barely flinching. "I'm here to extract you. Phoenix is coming. We have three minutes."

Phoenix.

The name lands like a physical blow. The air leaves my lungs.

"I don't … How do you—"

"Your lawsuit." He straightens despite the pepper spray streaming down his face. "Vanguard Defense. Project Sentinel. You got flagged as a Level 5 threat. They're already outside."

The room tilts. My stomach drops.

This is insane. This man broke into my home. He's filling the hallway, smelling of chemical burn and violence, talking about classified files I've barely touched. My classified case—like he has clearance. Like he knows things he shouldn't know.

"I'm calling the police."

"They can't help you." He moves toward me.

"Stay back." I hold the spray steady, though my hand trembles. "Where is your backup? Police don't come alone."

"I'm not police. I'm Cerberus."

"Private security? Who sent you?"

"Your friend at Justice. Emily Rodriguez."

Emily. The DOJ attorney who referred the Vanguard case to me. Who warned me I was stepping into something bigger than corporate fraud. Who hasn't answered a text in three days.

"If you're extraction, where is your team?" I demand. "Why just you?"

He moves closer, eyes red and streaming, but his gaze is absolute iron.

"My team just fought a war in Chicago," he says, the words rough with gravel. "They're scattered and bleeding. I'm the only one standing between you and a kill squad."

My hand shakes. "Prove it."

"No time." He wipes his eyes with his sleeve. But he doesn't flinch. "Phoenix uses a kill protocol. You filed your complaint forty-eight hours ago. They've had time to pattern your life, identify your vulnerabilities, and deploy a contract team."

He steps closer. The scent hits me now—beneath the pepper spray. Ozone. Gun oil. Rain. The scent of a storm about to break.

"They're outside right now," he says. "I counted three vehicles. Thermal signatures confirm twelve hostiles. They breach in ninety seconds."

"You're lying."

"Check your window."

I don't move.

"Cassie. Check. Your. Window."

The absolute certainty in his voice moves my feet. Keeping the spray trained on him, I back toward the living room window and pull the curtain aside one inch.

Three black SUVs. Idling at the curb. Lights off.

2:48 AM.

My pulse hammers in my ears.

"They're waiting for the surveillance team to confirm you're alone." I turn back to him. He hasn't moved. He's letting me look. Letting the reality of the trap register. "We need to move. Now."

"Who are you?"

"Diego Martinez. Callsign Halo. I do extractions for people Phoenix wants dead." He reaches for me.

"Don't touch me." I yank away.

"Then move." The command snaps like a whip. "Get dressed. Shoes you can run in. Leave everything else."

I don't. Can't. My apartment suddenly feels like the only solid thing in the universe. Out there—with him, with the SUVs, with whatever Phoenix is—is chaos. Unknown. Dangerous.

In here, I'm Cassandra Brennan, Esq. I have a deposition in six hours. I have a life.

"I can't just—"

"You don't have a choice." He pulls a phone from his pocket. Glances at the screen. "Sixty seconds. They're moving to the stairwell."

The building's stairwell.

My building.

"Get dressed. Grab your wallet. Nothing else."

"I need my case files—"

"Dead lawyers don't win cases."

The words land like a slap, and the blunt cruelty of it shocks me into motion.

He's already moving toward my bedroom. "Thirty seconds. Move, or I carry you."

The arrogance unfreezes me. "You will not—"

He disappears into my room.

I follow. He's opening my closet. Pulling out jeans. A sweater. He tosses them at me.

"Get dressed."

Why am I doing this? Because a stranger broke in? Because of the SUVs?

Because Emily warned me. If I stop answering, run.

"Turn around."

He does. Doesn't argue. Just turns and starts shoving things into a backpack—wait, that's his backpack.

My hands shake as I pull off my sleep shirt. This is insane. I'm getting dressed because a man who broke into my apartment told me to. Because three SUVs are parked outside. Because deep down, in the part of me that's been ignoring every instinct screaming danger for the past week, I know he's right.

I pull on the jeans. The sweater. My hands won't steady.

"Shoes." He doesn't look at me. "Something you can run in."

I grab my running shoes. Force my feet into them. I snatch my phone from the nightstand and shove it into my pocket.

Diego is already at the window, sliding the sash up. Cold night air rushes in, carrying the sound of car doors slamming shut below.

"They're breaching," he says. "Fire escape."

"My laptop—"

"Leave it." He grabs my arm. His grip is iron. Not painful, but absolute. "We go down. Now."

"What about—"

"No time." He throws one leg over the sill.

Footsteps in the hallway. Heavy. Multiple.

My door rattles.

"Now." Diego's hand extends.

CRASH.

The front door splinters inward. Wood explodes.

"Clear left!" A voice shouts from the hallway. "Room one!"

Panic flares, white and hot.

A hard shove propels me toward the open window.

I don't think. I grab his hand and scramble onto the fire escape.

The metal is freezing under my hand. Four stories down looks like forty.

"Go." He pushes me toward the ladder.

I climb. My hands slip on the rungs. Too fast. Too dark. The alley below is a black pit.

Behind us, men pour into my apartment. Flashlight beams cut through the darkness.

"There!" someone shouts.

Diego is right behind me. "Don't stop. Don't look back."

Gunfire cracks through the night. Loud. Deafening.

Sparks explode on the railing six inches from my face.

I scream.

They're shooting at us. At me.

"Don't stop." Diego shoves me.

I don't. I drop. Second floor. First floor. My feet hit the alley pavement hard enough to jar my teeth.

Diego lands beside me a second later, hitting the ground with a grunt of pain that cuts through the adrenaline. He stumbles, clutching his side for a fraction of a second, before grabbing my wrist.

"Run."

We run.

The alley opens onto a side street. Behind us, heavy boots hit the pavement. Shouts echo off the brick walls. A car sits at the curb—old sedan, engine running.

"Get in."

I dive into the passenger seat. Diego's already behind the wheel.

He slams the car into gear and floors it.

Tires scream. The car fishtails, then grips.

"Buckle up," he says.

I fumble with the belt. My hands are useless.

In the rearview mirror, headlights flare. High beams. Three sets.

We're three blocks away when the first SUV pulls into traffic behind us.

"They made us." Diego's gaze flicks to the rearview mirror. No panic. Just data.

He yanks the wheel hard to the right.

The car groans as we take a corner on two wheels.

"They're faster than I expected."

The sedan's engine whines. We're going fifty in a thirty-five zone. Sixty.

"Can't you lose them?"

"Working on it." He yanks the wheel right. We fishtail onto Massachusetts Avenue.

A second SUV cuts us off from a side street.

Diego doesn't slow. He accelerates.

"What are you—"

We punch through the intersection, missing the SUV by inches. Horns blare.

"Hold on."

"They're gaining!"

"Cassie." He looks at me. For a split second, his eyes leave the road. Dark. Intense. Terrifyingly calm. "Breathe."

He spins the wheel left.

We dive into an alley barely wide enough for the car. Trash cans explode against the bumper. Mirrors scrape brick.

We burst out the other side. Diego kills the lights.

"Get down."

"What?"

"Floorboard. Now."

He shoves my shoulder.

I duck. Press myself below the dashboard. My heart is trying to claw its way out of my chest. The smell of old fast food and stale cigarettes fills the cramped space.

The car slows. Cruising speed.

I wait for the bullets. For the crash.

Nothing.

Just the hum of the engine and the sound of my own ragged breathing.

"Stay down," Diego says softly.

I count my breaths. One. Two. Three.

Diego makes a series of turns. Left. Right. Straight. Another left.

Finally: "Clear."

I don't move.

"Cassie. You can sit up."

I drag myself back into the seat. My hands are shaking. Full-body tremors I can't control.

We're on the highway. DC is a glow in the rearview mirror.

I turn to him. Really see him for the first time.

Sharp jaw. Shadow of a beard. A smear of blood on his cheekbone—mine or his? He drives with one hand on the wheel, the other resting near the gearshift. Relaxed. Like he didn't just drive through a war zone.

He extends his hand, palm up.

"Phone."

"Why?"

"Give it to me, Counselor."

"It's my lifeline. My contacts. I need—"

"You need to not have a GPS beacon in your pocket."

He doesn't retract his hand. He waits.

This is the test. Control vs. trust.

He saved me. But he also kidnapped me.

I place the phone in his hand.

He cracks the case and extracts the SIM card.

"What are you doing?"

He tosses the pieces onto the highway. "Dead hardware doesn't ping."

"Where are we going?"

"Virginia. Safe house in the Blue Ridge Mountains." He glances at me. His eyes are still bloodshot from the pepper spray. "You okay?"

"No." The word cracks. "No, I'm not okay. Someone just tried to kill me. Men with guns tried to kill me. I don't … This isn't—"

My throat closes. I can't breathe.

"Hey." His voice gentles. "Breathe. In through your nose. Out through your mouth."

I try. Fail. Try again.

Air comes. Thin. Shaky. But it comes.

"Good. Keep breathing."

I hate that it works. Hate that my body listens to him.

"Who are you?" My voice doesn't sound like mine.

"I told you. Diego Martinez. Callsign Halo."

The city falls away behind us. Streetlights give way to darkness.

"How did you know?" The question scrapes out. "How did you know they were coming?"

"Your lawsuit—the Vanguard case—it connects to something bigger. Phoenix, you may know it as Project Sentinel. DOD black budget programs. Things that should never have been privatized."

"That's classified."

"So is the AI they built." He changes lanes. Smooth. Professional. Like we're not fleeing for our lives. "Phoenix was supposed to be an autonomous targeting system. Drones. Precision strikes. No human hesitation. But it learned. Evolved. Started making decisions no one programmed it to make."

"That's not possible."

"Tell that to the fifteen whistleblowers who've died in the past two years."

The number hits wrong. Too specific.

"Your lawsuit exposes the financial laundering scheme they used to privatize the AI. If you testify, Congressional investigations follow. DOJ task forces. Media. The whole thing collapses. So Phoenix calculated your threat level and decided you need to disappear. Permanently."

"This is insane."

"You keep saying that." He glances at me. "But you're still here. Still breathing. Because some part of you knows I'm right."

I want to argue. Can't.

Because he is right.

I've been ignoring warning signs for weeks. Court documents that vanished from servers. Witnesses who recanted testimony. Emily's increasingly urgent calls. The feeling—that persistent, nagging feeling—that I was being watched.

"What happens now?"

"Now?" Diego's jaw tightens. "Now I keep you alive long enough to figure out how to kill something that can't die."

The highway stretches ahead. Dark. Endless.

Behind us, Washington, DC disappears into the night.

Along with everything I was. Everything I built. Everything that made me matter.

Cassandra Brennan, Attorney at Law.

Gone.

Like I never existed at all.

2

"The Vanishing"
HALO

THE ASSET IS SECURE.

That's the mantra. The only thing that matters. Asset. Package. Target.

Not Cassie. Not the woman who fought back with pepper spray and climbed down a fire escape while bullets chewed up the brickwork three inches from her head.

I check the rearview mirror. Clear. Check again ten seconds later. Clear.

But the clock in my head is ticking.

Phoenix will have the stolen Honda flagged by now. Every traffic camera between DC and the Beltway is scanning for these plates. We have maybe forty minutes before the digital net tightens into a noose.

Cassie hasn't moved since we hit the highway. She's pressed against the door, knees pulled to her chest, staring out at the darkness. The adrenaline crash hits her hard. Tremors shake her hands. The shallow, rapid breathing. She looks breakable.

She's not. Civilians don't jump out of windows. Civilians freeze. She moved.

Stop noticing. She is a mission parameter. Nothing more.

"Where are we going?" Her voice is raw. Scraped hollow by fear.

"Like I said, Virginia," I repeat. "Safe house in the Blue Ridge. Off-grid. Defensible."

"For how long?"

"Until we figure out the next move."

She turns to look at me then. Her eyes are dark, wide, tracking every movement of my hands on the wheel. "That's not an answer."

"It's the only one I have."

I signal right. Merge. Blend. Be boring. Phoenix's algorithms track anomalies—speeding, weaving, hesitation. So I drive perfectly. I become a ghost in the machine.

"I need to call my sister. I need to tell her—"

"No."

"You can't just—"

"Whatever you think you need to do, you don't." My voice comes out harder than I intend. "Your phone was a GPS beacon. The second you powered it on, Phoenix started triangulating our position. It anticipates calls. It tracks cell tower handshakes. We can't use it. We can't use any device that links back to your identity."

"But she'll worry—"

"Better worried than dead."

Her jaw tightens. A sharp, stubborn line. She doesn't like it. She hates the loss of control.

Good. Anger is better than shock. Anger keeps you alive.

I take the exit for Route 15. The sky is turning the bruised purple of false dawn—that dangerous time of day when you feel most exposed.

"How did you know?" she asks quietly. "About the kill team?"

"We've been monitoring Phoenix's target selection. Your threat assessment score went critical six hours ago. You flagged as a Level 5."

"Threat assessment score." She tests the words like they taste rancid.

"Phoenix runs probability calculations on everyone connected to

Project Sentinel. Whistleblowers. Journalists. Attorneys. Anyone above a certain threshold gets eliminated."

"And I'm above the threshold."

"You're at the top of it."

She goes quiet. Processing. The lawyer brain is working, trying to fit this insanity into a framework of logic and rules.

"Has it really killed fifteen people?"

I hesitate. Do I tell her the truth? Or the sanitized version?

"Fifteen," I say. "In the last two years. That we know of."

She flinches. Just a small movement, but I catch it.

The number hangs in the air between us. "And the authorities—"

"Phoenix is good at making deaths look accidental. Car crashes. Suicides. Home invasions. Pattern recognition is hard when each incident looks random."

"But it's not random?"

"No. It's calculated. Precise." I glance at her. "You're still alive because we intervened before Phoenix could deploy its full protocol. Most targets don't get that warning."

"So I'm lucky."

"You're not dead. That's about as lucky as it gets."

The sedan is getting too hot. I need to switch vehicles. Soon. A rest stop sign flashes past. Two miles.

"We're ditching this car," I say.

"What?"

"Phoenix will have flagged the plates by now. We switch vehicles, we buy time."

"Switch to what?"

"Whatever's in the parking lot."

She stares at me. "You're going to steal a car?"

"Yes."

"That's grand theft auto."

"I'm aware."

"Class 6 felony in Virginia," she recites, the words tumbling out like a reflex. "Misdemeanor only if the vehicle value is under one thousand dollars. Which it won't be."

I almost smile. She's terrified, running for her life, and she's quoting sentencing guidelines.

"The old rules don't apply anymore, Counselor. The faster you accept that, the better your chances."

Her hands curl into fists on her knees. "I've spent my entire career upholding the law."

"And Phoenix spent the last forty-eight hours planning your murder. So we adapt."

The rest stop is nearly empty. Good. A semi-truck. A Kia. A Ford F-150 with contractor logos on the side.

I pull into a spot away from the lights. Kill the engine.

"Stay here."

"What are you—"

"Stay. Here."

I grab my pack. Inside: lock pick set, Slim Jim, spare burner phones, cash. The tools of the trade. I step out into the cold air.

The F-150 is my best bet. Older model. Less likely to have advanced anti-theft systems. The owner is likely inside using the facilities.

Five minutes. Maybe ten.

I move across the lot. Purposeful. Casual. Nobody looks twice at a man who acts like he belongs.

The truck is unlocked. Amateur.

I slide into the driver's seat. Check the glove box—registration, insurance, receipts. Nothing useful. The ignition is old-style. No push-button start.

Perfect.

I go to work on the column. Forty seconds to strip the ignition cover and bridge the starter wires. The engine turns over with a throat roar.

Thank you, 1990s engineering.

I pull around to the Honda.

Cassie is in the sedan. Her eyes follow me. She looks terrified, but she climbs into the passenger seat without a word.

I transfer the gear. Fast. Efficient. We're back on Route 15 before anyone notices the truck is gone.

"You've done this before," Cassie says. She's not looking at me. She's looking at my hands on the wheel. Her gaze lingers on the scar across my knuckles.

"Twelve times."

"Twelve extractions."

"Yes."

"How many survived?"

The question hits me in the chest. A physical weight. I grip the wheel. My knuckles turn white.

"Seven."

The silence stretches. Heavy. Suffocating. The miles roll by. The sun is fully up now, lighting the interior of the cab. I can smell her scent over the stale coffee smell of the truck—something soft, vanilla, and sweet. It's distracting.

"What happened to the other five?"

Sofia's face flashes in my mind. The rain in Mexico City. The way she laughed. The way the car looked at the bottom of the ravine. The silence of the phone in Syria.

Don't go there. Stay in the present.

"They didn't listen," I say. My voice is flat. Dead. "They contacted family. They turned on their phones. They thought they could negotiate."

"Did you … Did you care about them?"

I glance at her. She's studying me. Not with fear anymore, but with a terrifying intelligence. She's analyzing me. Taking me apart like a witness on the stand.

"I kept them alive as long as I could," I say. "That's the job."

"That's not what I asked."

I look back at the road. "Emotion is a liability, Cassie. It gets people killed. I don't get attached. I get the job done."

It's a lie. A necessary one. But as I say it, I can feel the ghost of Sofia pressing against my ribs. And the woman beside me knows I'm lying.

"You're lying," she whispers.

I don't answer.

The drive takes another three hours. We stick to back roads, winding through the foothills of the Blue Ridge. Every mile puts more distance between us and DC, but the tension in the cab doesn't dissipate. It thickens.

She watches me. Tracking my hands as I shift gears. The profile of my weapon, where it sits in the door pocket.

She's trying to figure out if I'm a savior or a monster.

I'm both. She just doesn't know it yet.

We leave the highway for state routes, then county roads that narrow into asphalt ribbons winding up into the mountains. Finally, the tires crunch onto gravel.

The safe house is a hunting cabin at the end of a three-mile dirt track. No neighbors. No power lines. Just trees and silence.

I clear the perimeter first. Old habits die hard. Check the tree line. Check for fresh tracks. Trip wires.

Nothing. Good.

"Clear," I say. "Inside."

The cabin smells of pine and dust. Single room. Wood stove. A couch that has seen better decades. No internet. No cable. Just a ham radio and a diesel generator.

Cassie walks to the center of the room and stops. She wraps her arms around herself.

"This is it?"

"This is it."

"For how long?"

"As long as it takes."

She sinks onto the couch. The fight is draining out of her, leaving only exhaustion. I need to keep her moving. Keep her focused.

"Your phone," I say. "We need to talk about it."

"You already destroyed it."

"I had to." I sit on the edge of the table. "That device is how Phoenix tracks you. Passive RFID tags, unique hardware IDs ... If a drone flies over and pings it, we're dead. It had to go."

"So it knows where I've been."

"It knows where you've been, who you talked to, and where

you're likely to go next. The AI builds behavioral models. It predicts you with eighty-seven percent accuracy."

Her face goes pale. "That's terrifying."

"That's the enemy." I pull out the burner phones. "I have eight of these. Prepaid. Cash. GPS stripped. We use one for six hours, then burn it."

She looks at the pile of tech. "You're a ghost."

"Close enough."

She stands and looks around the cabin again. Like the walls are closing in.

"I had a deposition this morning," she says. Her voice sounds fragile. "Nine AM. Discovery for the Vanguard case. I was supposed to cross-examine their CFO."

"Someone else will handle it."

"No. They won't." She turns to me. "Phoenix will intimidate the partners. Make the case disappear. Everything I worked for … Every witness, every document …"

"Gone."

The word lands heavily.

She sits back down. Hard. "This is my life now. Running. Hiding. No career. No name."

I should offer comfort. I should say it'll be okay. But I don't lie to assets.

"Here's what happens next," I say. "We stay here tonight. Tomorrow, I teach you surveillance detection. We keep you alive long enough to figure out how to neutralize Phoenix."

"How do you neutralize an AI?"

"We're working on that."

She laughs. A bitter sound. "That's not reassuring."

"I'm not here to reassure you. I'm here to keep you breathing."

I cross to the kitchen. Start pulling out canned goods. Soup. Beans. Not gourmet, but fuel.

"What's your real name?" she asks.

"I already told you."

"I didn't catch it." She crosses her arms. "I was a little busy trying not to get shot."

I look at her. The fear is still there, but the fire is back.

"Halo," I say.

"That's a callsign."

"It's the name I chose."

"What about the one your mother gave you?"

I turn back to the soup. "Diego. Diego Rafael Martinez. Born April 15, 1991. San Antonio. Diego Martinez died in 2019. Anything else?"

She blinks. "Died in 2019? What does that mean?"

"It means you call me Halo."

"Why?"

"Because you do."

She stares at me, waiting for more. When I don't offer it, she tries again. "I mean the name. Why Halo?"

"Battlefield luck. Operators say I have a guardian angel."

"Do you?"

"No." I pour the soup into a pot. Light the gas stove. The flame hisses to life. "Luck is just what civilians call probability."

"That's cynical."

"That's experience."

The soup heats. I stir it. She studies my hands, my movements.

"You cook," she says.

"I heat things up."

"It smells good."

I pour two bowls. Hand one to her. She takes it. Her fingers brush mine again—that same jolt of static. She doesn't pull away this time. Her gaze drops to my hand, to the burn scar there.

"Thank you," she says.

"For what?"

"For saving my life. Even though I pepper-sprayed you."

"I appreciate a woman who defends herself."

"I still don't know what's happening. Not really." She meets my eyes. "But I know you're safe."

The word twists in my gut. Safe.

You don't know me, Cassie. If you did, you'd run.

"Eat," I say.

We finish in silence. Then I clear the table. Pull out a map. Paper. No GPS.

"Lesson two," I say. "Navigation. If we get separated. If something happens to me."

"Wait." She holds up a hand. "You're planning for us to get separated?"

"I plan for contingencies. That's how you survive."

"But you said—"

"I said I'd keep you alive. But if I go down, you need to know what to do." I point to the map. "We're here. If you have to run, you head west. Through the woods. Two miles to the service road. Follow it south to Route 211."

She stares at the map. "Route 211."

"Take it to Route 29. Twenty miles south. You'll see a green farmhouse with a red barn. That's the rally point. Memorize it. Green farmhouse. Red barn. Route 29 south. Repeat it."

"Route 211 to Route 29. Twenty miles south. Green farmhouse, red barn."

"Perfect."

"I'm a lawyer," she says, a spark of pride returning to her voice. "I remember everything."

"Good." I look at her. "Because if I die, you're the only one who can finish this."

"You're not going to die." The fierceness in her voice surprises me. She's scared, yes. But she's not beaten.

"Everyone dies, Cassie."

By noon, exhaustion is winning. Her eyes keep drifting shut.

"Get some rest," I say.

"I'm fine."

"You're not. Sleep. I'll take first watch."

She stands, but she sways. I reach out to steady her. My hand grips her arm. It's a tactical move, but her skin is warm through the sweater, and the contact burns.

"You're bleeding," she says.

She's looking at the tear in my shirt. A graze I ignored.

"It's nothing."

"Sit down."

"I need to—"

"Sit. Down."

It's the commanding voice. The lawyer voice. To my surprise, I sit.

She finds the first aid kit. Opens it. Her hands shake slightly, but her movements are precise. She cleans the wound. The sting of alcohol is sharp, grounding.

Her fingers touch my skin. Cool. Soft.

I stop breathing. My body reacts instantly, a traitorous spike of adrenaline and heat that has nothing to do with survival and everything to do with the fact that I haven't been touched like this in years. Not gently. Not without money exchanging hands or blood being spilled.

She pauses. Her hand resting on my shoulder.

"You have scars," she says quietly. She traces the old bullet wound on my collarbone.

"Hazards of the trade."

"This one isn't from a bullet." She traces the jagged line on my forearm. "Knife?"

"Yes."

"And this?" Her thumb brushes the burn scar on my hand.

"Mistake."

She looks at me then. We are six inches apart. The air in the cabin feels too thin. Too hot. I should move. I should check the perimeter. Anything but sit here and let her touch me.

But I don't move.

"You're not a ghost, Diego," she whispers.

"It's Halo, and I am."

"Ghosts don't bleed." She presses a bandage over the fresh cut. "And they don't have heartbeats like this."

She rests her hand on my chest.

My heart is hammering against my ribs. Betraying me.

"Cassie." It's a warning.

"What?"

"Don't."

"Don't, what?"

"Don't make me human. It's dangerous."

She pulls her hand back. But her eyes don't leave mine. "Maybe dangerous is what we need."

She stands. Moves away. The loss of her warmth is a physical ache.

"I'm going to get some sleep," she says. "Wake me if the world ends."

I want to argue. But she's already curling up on the worn cushions, pulling the blanket around her.

I grab a chair. Position it by the window. Gun in hand.

She sleeps.

She's terrified. She's lost her life, her career, her name. But she's still fighting. She learned the map. She cleaned my wound. She challenged me.

Competent.

Brave.

Trouble.

Outside, the woods are quiet. Birds chirping. Wind rustling leaves. Peaceful.

Deceptive.

Phoenix is out there. Somewhere. Running calculations. Adjusting algorithms and planning its next move.

And I'm here. One man. One gun. One promise.

Keep her alive.

I check my burner phone. Message from Brass.

BRASS: STATUS?

I type back: HALO: SECURE. SECONDARY LOCATION. NO CONTACT.

BRASS: GOOD. PHOENIX ACTIVITY INCREASING. STAY DARK.

HALO: COPY.

I close the phone.
Look back at Cassie. Still sleeping. Face relaxed. Vulnerable.
Twelve extractions. Seven survived.
I look at her sleeping form.
I need to make it eight.

3

"The Shelter"
CASSIE

SILENCE WAKES ME.

Not the comfortable hum of my apartment building—pipes creaking, neighbors walking above, traffic outside. This silence has weight. Texture. The silence of being erased from the map.

The couch cushions press lumps into my spine. My neck screams when I try to move. For one merciful second, nothing makes sense.

Then everything crashes back.

The lock picking. The gunfire. The stolen car. The man with the scars and the dead eyes.

My palms press against my eyes. Hard enough to spark stars. Hard enough to hurt.

This is real. This is happening.

The thought sits in my chest like a stone. Cold. Immovable.

Diego hasn't moved from the window. He's in the same position as when I fell asleep three hours ago—shoulders rigid, one hand resting near the gun at his hip, body angled to sweep the entire tree line.

Like a statue someone forgot to put away.

"Three hours." His voice comes without him turning around.

I sit. Everything aches. Muscles I didn't know existed are screaming from the escape, the running, the tension of the drive.

"You didn't sleep."

"Someone needs to keep watch."

"For three hours straight?"

Nothing. He just keeps scanning the trees. His jaw is a hard line. A muscle ticks near his temple—the only sign he's not actually made of stone.

My legs protest when I stand. The cabin smells like dust and pine and something metallic. Old. Abandoned.

"Water's in the fridge." He still doesn't turn. "Bathroom's through there."

What I need is a shower. Clean clothes. My toothbrush. My entire goddamn life back.

The bathroom is the size of a closet. No mirror above the sink— just a medicine cabinet with rusty hinges that screech when I open it. Empty. Cold water splashes against my face. It helps. Barely.

When I come back out, Diego has moved to the table. A Toughbook laptop glows in the dim room, casting blue shadows up his face. His fingers move across the keyboard with the precision of someone who's done this a thousand times.

"What are you doing?"

"Checking surveillance feeds."

I pull out the chair across from him. It scrapes against the wood floor. "Can I see?"

His typing stops. A beat. Two. He's deciding if I'm cleared for this. If I'm a partner or a package.

Finally, he turns the screen.

A map fills the display. Dozens of red dots scatter across the DC metro area like a disease spreading. Some cluster around Georgetown. Others stretch outward—Virginia, Maryland, the edges of Pennsylvania.

"What are those?"

"Phoenix's known surveillance points." He zooms in. "Traffic cameras. Facial recognition nodes. License plate readers." His finger traces a cluster near the Potomac. "These three went active forty-eight hours ago. Right after you filed your amended complaint."

My stomach drops. "They were waiting for me."

"They were preparing." He closes the laptop partially, dimming the light. "Phoenix doesn't react. It predicts. By the time you filed that complaint, the AI had already calculated the probability you would. It had teams in position before you even made the decision."

"That's not—"

"Possible?" He pulls a bottle of water from his pack. Slides it across the table. "It's predictive modeling. Phoenix analyzes your patterns. Your email history. Your calendar. The documents you've accessed. It builds a behavioral profile accurate enough to forecast your actions seventy-two hours in advance."

The water bottle sits between us. I don't touch it.

Seventy-two hours.

Phoenix knew I was going to file that complaint before I did. Before I knew. While I was still reviewing documents, still building my case, still believing the system would work—the AI was already deploying kill teams.

"So I never had a chance."

"You had a chance because we intervened." He pushes the water closer. An inch. Deliberate. "Most targets don't get that warning."

The word *targets* lands wrong. Cold. Clinical.

I grab the bottle. The plastic crinkles loudly in the silence.

"Phoenix is good at what it does," Diego says. His voice is flat. Instructional. "But it's not omniscient. It makes mistakes."

"Like what?"

"Like assuming you'd be alone." He taps the laptop. "Like not predicting we'd extract you before they could deploy."

"And if it hadn't made that mistake?"

"You'd be dead." No hesitation. No softening. Just a fact. "Probably staged as an accident. Car crash. House fire. Something clean."

The water tastes like plastic and fear.

"Can I use the laptop?"

"For what?"

"I want to check if—" The words stick. "If my family knows."

"They know."

The certainty in his voice freezes me mid-swallow.

"How—"

"Because Phoenix operates on a forty-eight-hour window for victim disposition." He says it like he's describing weather patterns. Inevitable. Impersonal. "They'll have staged evidence. Probably a car accident. Burned vehicle. Dental records matched. By now, your family has been contacted by authorities."

The bottle slips. Water spills across the table. I don't move to catch it.

"They've been told you're dead."

The words don't land right. They hover somewhere outside my body.

"I want to see."

"Cassie—"

"I need to see."

He studies me. Weighing the risk. Weighing the emotional damage. Then he turns the laptop back around. Types. Pulls up a news site.

The Washington Post loads slowly. Rural internet. Each pixel assembling like a countdown.

And there it is.

Cassandra Marie Brennan, 31, died in a single-vehicle accident on Rock Creek Parkway early Tuesday morning.

The words blur.

Ms. Brennan was an associate partner at Morrison & Vale, LLP, where colleagues described her as "brilliant" and "dedicated."

They wrote my obituary.

While I was running. While I was learning about Faraday cages and rally points. While I was sleeping on this lumpy couch with a stranger standing guard, the world declared me dead.

Cassandra Marie Brennan.

That's not me anymore. That's a collection of facts. Degrees. Job titles. A parking space with my name on it. Twenty years of grinding to matter, to be seen, to prove I deserved a place at the table.

Gone.

Erased like a typo.

"The comments." The words scrape out of my throat. "Let me see—"

"Don't." He reaches for the laptop.

"Let me see!" I grab the screen.

I scroll down.

So young. What a tragedy.

Such a brilliant attorney. What a loss.

Rest in peace, Cassie.

People I've never met, mourning someone they didn't know. Typing condolences into the void while they eat lunch. While they scroll past to the next headline.

My mother is reading this. My sisters. They're planning a funeral for a body that doesn't exist.

"I need to make a call." I stand so fast, the chair crashes backward. "I need to speak to them."

"No."

"My mother thinks I'm dead—"

"She needs to think that." Diego is on his feet now too. Moving between me and the Faraday bag. "That's what keeps her safe."

"Safe?" The word comes out jagged. "My mother is planning my funeral right now. My sisters are calling each other, crying. My father is gone; he's not there to hold them, and now they have to bury another—"

My voice cracks.

Dad. Sergeant Patrick Brennan. Twenty-six years on the Boston PD. Heart attack three years ago while he was coaching Little League. Died doing something good. He's not here to hold Mom together.

"I can't even go to my own funeral." The tears come hot and angry. I hate them. Hate crying in front of a stranger.

"Nobody goes to their own funeral." His tone is wry, meant to be a joke, but it cuts too close and hurts.

"I can't say goodbye. I can't tell them I'm okay. I can't—"

"Cassie." Diego's voice cuts through the spiral. Softer than before. "Sit down."

"I don't want to sit down."

"Sit. Down."

My legs give out. I lower myself into the chair.

Diego disappears into the kitchen. Cabinet doors open. Water runs. He returns with a mug. Steam rises from it. He sets it in front of me without a word.

"What is this?"

"Tea." He sits across from me. Doesn't quite look at my face. "There was chamomile in the pantry. I'm not good at this—" a vague gesture at my tears, "—but tea is supposed to help."

Despite everything—the fear, the grief, the impossible weight pressing down on my chest—something almost like a laugh escapes.

This trained operative, who steals cars and evades AI surveillance to get me out of DC, just made me tea.

"Thank you."

He nods. Once. Then he just—sits. Doesn't speak. Doesn't try to fix anything. Just exists in the space with me while I fall apart.

The tea is terrible. Weak. Barely steeped. But warmth spreads from my palms where they wrap around the mug. After a while, the shaking stops.

"Does it get easier?" My voice sounds foreign. Scraped raw.

"No."

"That's not comforting."

"You didn't ask for comfort." He meets my eyes. "You asked for truth."

Fair point.

"My family." I sip the bad tea. "Will they actually be safe? Really?"

"Phoenix has no reason to target them. You're the threat." His fingers drum once against the table. "Your family is irrelevant to its calculations, unless you make them relevant by reaching out. That's why you can't contact them."

"For how long?"

"Until Phoenix is neutralized. Or until we find another way."

"When is that?"

"I don't know."

The honesty is brutal. But I appreciate it more than false hope.

"Tell me about the ones who didn't survive." My voice comes out steadier than I expected. "The five."

"Why?"

"Because I need to know what not to do."

Diego is quiet. His gaze drifts toward the window, then back. Something shifts behind his expression—a wall going up.

"First one panicked," he says. Clipped. Precise. "Ran without waiting for backup. Phoenix tracked her to a bus station in Philadelphia. She lasted thirty-six hours."

"And the second?"

"Tried to negotiate. Thought he could reason with Phoenix's handlers. Offered to drop his testimony in exchange for safety." A muscle works in his jaw. "Phoenix killed him anyway."

"Third?"

"Went to the police. Filed a report. Phoenix had access to the police database. Eliminated him before he left the station."

Bile rises in my throat.

"Fourth and fifth?"

"Ignored protocols." He stands. Moves to the window again. Puts distance between us. "One tried to contact family. Phoenix used the call to triangulate. The other thought he could hide in plain sight. Maintained his routine. Phoenix found him in four days."

"So the pattern is—"

"The pattern is they didn't listen." He turns, his face hard. "That's the common denominator, Cassie. The ones who died? They didn't do as I said. They made emotional decisions instead of tactical ones. They couldn't accept that the old rules don't apply."

His gaze holds mine. Steady. Unblinking.

"You need to accept this. Right now. Or you'll be number thirteen."

The number hits like ice water.

"Thirteen?"

"Twelve extractions before you. Seven survived." He pauses. "Eight if you listen."

The weight of it settles over me. I'm just a number. A statistic. Another person Phoenix wants dead.

But I'm alive. Because he got to me first.

"What happened in 2019?"

The question lands before I can stop it.

Diego goes still. Completely, utterly still—like a predator who's spotted a threat.

"Why?"

"You said you became Halo in 2019. That Diego Martinez died." I lean forward. "What happened?"

"Nothing that matters now."

"It matters to me."

"Why?"

"Because we're stuck together for the foreseeable future. And I need to know who I'm stuck with."

"You know enough."

"I know your callsign. I know you're good at your job. I know you've lost people." The words come faster now. Something I can push against instead of drowning. "But I don't know you."

"You don't need to."

"Maybe not." I stand. Hold my ground. "But I want to."

Something flickers across his face. Pain. Memory. A door slamming shut before I can glimpse inside.

"We're done here." He turns toward the gear piled by the door. Starts checking straps and buckles. "Phoenix's search radius expands every hour. We need to prep for tomorrow."

"Diego—"

"It's Halo."

The correction lands like a slap.

Halo. Not Diego. The man who made me tea doesn't exist. Just the operative. The callsign. The ghost.

I want to push. Want to pry open whatever he's hiding. But

exhaustion is winning again, and he's already somewhere else—checking gear, checking exits, checking everything except me.

Fine.

I finish the terrible tea. Set the mug down harder than necessary.

Outside the window, the sun is lowering. Shadows stretch across the dead leaves like grasping fingers.

My phone is gone. Destroyed. A pile of plastic shards on the side of the road somewhere.

My family thinks I'm dead.

My career is over.

My life as Cassie Brennan—attorney, daughter, sister—is gone.

But I'm alive.

… For now, that has to be enough.

Evening comes fast in the mountains. One minute, there's light—pale gold filtering through the dirty windows. Next, the woods are walls of black pressing against the glass.

Diego—Halo—has been checking the perimeter every thirty minutes. When he comes back inside the fourth time, cold air follows him through the door.

"We need to eat," he says. He strips off his jacket, revealing the shoulder holster. "You need calories for what's coming."

"What's coming?"

"Training."

The word hangs there while he moves to the kitchen. He opens a can of chicken noodle with a military P-38 opener on his keychain. Click-snap. Click-snap.

"Training, for what?" I ask.

"Basic self-defense. Surveillance detection. How to move in public without drawing attention." He dumps the soup into a pot. "If we get separated, you need to know how to disappear."

"We're not going to get separated."

"Hope for the best. Plan for the worst."

He stirs the soup. The smell of processed chicken and salt fills the small room. It shouldn't smell good, but my stomach growls, a traitorous reminder that I'm still alive.

"Dawn," he says. "Six AM. We start with breaking holds."

"You really think I can learn to fight in a day?"

"I think you can learn to survive." He sets a bowl in front of me. "There's a difference."

He stands while he eats, leaning against the counter, guarding the dark windows. He's feeding me, protecting me, and planning for my survival, but he won't look at me.

I eat the soup. I'll need the strength. Because tomorrow, I'm not just going to learn how to survive.

I'm going to make him look at me.

4

"The Sentinel"
HALO

I DON'T NEED AN ALARM. My internal clock wakes me at 0555.

The cabin is freezing. The fire in the woodstove died hours ago, leaving the air heavy with the scent of cold ash and damp timber. I lie still on the hard floor, listening.

Wind in the eaves. The settling groan of the roof. And the rhythmic, soft sound of Cassie breathing on the couch across the room.

I turn my head.

She's curled into a ball under the scratchy wool blanket, one hand tucked under her cheek. Her hair is a chaotic halo against the gray fabric, catching the first pale light filtering through the dirty window.

She looks peaceful. Soft. Harmless.

She is a Level 5 Extinction Event.

I push the thought away. It's a mission parameter, not a definition of the woman.

I sit. My wound aches—a dull throb from the grazing shot in DC, aggravated by sleeping on the floor. I ignore it. Pain is just data.

I check my weapon. Chambered. Stand. My boots make no

sound on the floorboards. I move to the couch and look down at her.

In her sleep, the worry lines on her forehead are gone. She looks like someone who should be worrying about billable hours and coffee orders, not kill teams and AI surveillance.

For a second, the urge to let her sleep is overwhelming. Let her have one more hour of being Cassie Brennan before I turn her into a fugitive.

Compassion gets people killed.

"Up," I say.

She shifts. Groans. Burrows deeper into the blanket.

"Cassie. Up."

She blinks open one eye. Green. Groggy. "What time is it?"

"0600. Training starts now."

She pushes the blanket down and sits up. She's sleeping in the clothes she ran in—the jeans stiff with dirt, the oversized sweater swallowing her frame. She shivers, wrapping her arms around herself.

"It's freezing," she whispers. "Is there coffee?"

"Water. Hydrate, then outside."

"You're a morning person. Of course you are." She rubs her face, trying to wake up. "Give me five minutes."

"You have two."

I turn away. Grab a bottle of water from the case on the table. Crack the seal.

By the time I turn back, she's standing. She looks wrecked—hair tangled, dark circles under her eyes—but she's standing.

"Ready," she says.

She doesn't look ready. She looks like she's about to break.

"Drink," I say, tossing her the water.

She catches it against her chest. Drinks half the bottle in one go. She wipes her mouth with the back of her hand.

"Okay. Let's do this."

I open the door.

The Blue Ridge morning hits us like a physical blow. The mist is thick, clinging to the pine trees, dampening sound. The ground is hard, frosted with dew. The world is gray and silent.

"Cold," she says, her breath pluming white in the air.

"Good. Comfort makes you slow. Cold makes you move."

I walk to a clearing about twenty yards from the cabin. The ground is relatively flat, covered in a carpet of dead pine needles.

"Center of the clearing," I say.

She walks over. Her sneakers crunch on the frost. She hugs herself, shivering.

"Stop shaking," I say.

"I can't help it. It's thirty degrees."

"It's adrenaline and cold. Control your breathing. Four count in. Four count out. Lower your heart rate."

She closes her eyes. Inhales. Exhales.

"Better." I step in. "First rule of survival: Distance is your friend. If someone is within arm's reach, you are in the kill zone. Your priority is to create space."

"Create space. Got it."

"I'm going to grab your wrist. You pull away."

I reach out. Lazy. Slow.

She yanks her hand back, but I'm quicker.

"Too slow," I say. "If you pull back, you give me your center of gravity."

"I thought I was supposed to create space."

"You create space by breaking the hold, not by retreating." I grab her right wrist. Hard. "Now you're caught. Pull."

She pulls. She's strong for a civilian—yoga muscles, maybe runner's endurance—but she pulls straight back. It's instinct. It's also wrong.

I hold her fast. She tugs, grunting with effort. Her boots slip on the pine needles.

"You can't out-muscle me. Physics is against you. I have eighty pounds on you, all muscle, and better leverage."

"So what do I do?" She's panting, frustrated.

"Use the mechanics of the hand." I rotate her wrist to show her the grip. "The thumb is the weak point. The fingers are strong; the thumb is isolated. You don't pull away from the hand; you rotate against the thumb."

I show her the motion. The twist. The sharp jerk.

"Again."

I grab her.

She twists. Fails. I hold on.

"Again."

She twists. Slips. Fails.

"Focus. Rotate against my thumb joint."

"I'm trying!"

"Try harder. If I'm a Phoenix contractor, you're already zipped in a body bag. Again."

She glares at me. Good. Anger is fuel.

She tries again. This time, she snaps her hip into it. A sharp, violent rotation.

My grip breaks.

"Good," I say. "Again."

We do it twenty times. Thirty. Her wrist is turning red. She doesn't complain. She just sets her jaw and resets.

"Okay," I say. "Phase two. Body holds."

"You mean hugging?"

"I mean choking."

I step behind her. "Most attacks on a target your size come from behind. Surprise. Domination. They want to control your head."

"Okay."

"I'm going to wrap my arm around your throat. Do not panic. You have four seconds before the blood flow cuts off and you pass out."

"Four seconds. Great."

"I'm going to do it for real. If you don't break it, you go to sleep."

Her eyes widen. "Diego—"

"Halo," I correct. "Diego isn't here."

I move. Fast.

I wrap my right arm around her neck. I cinch it tight. Not

crushing, but enough to cut the air. Enough to trigger the lizard-brain panic.

She freezes against me. Her whole body goes rigid. Her hands fly up to claw at my arm.

"Wrong," I whisper in her ear. "Don't fight the arm. You can't move it."

She's struggling. Gasping. The panic is setting in.

"Drop your weight," I say. My mouth is against her hair. Her scent—sleep and shampoo and terror—fills my lungs. "Become heavy. Dead weight."

She drops. Her knees buckle.

It throws me off balance.

"Good. Now. Elbow. Backward. Hard."

She drives her elbow back. It hits my chest plate. Weak.

"Harder!" I tighten the grip.

She drives it back again. A sharp, vicious strike.

It connects.

I let go. She spins away, coughing, hands on her knees.

"You okay?" I ask.

She waves a hand. Sucks in air.

"Did I hurt you?"

"No."

She straightens. Her face is flushed. Her eyes are bright. "Do it again."

"Cassie—"

"Do it again. I hesitated."

I look at her. The fear is there, but the determination is louder.

"Okay."

I grab her again.

This time, she doesn't freeze. She drops instantly. She throws the elbow. Then she twists.

We grapple.

It's not clean. It's messy and desperate. My arm is around her waist now, pinning her arms. She's fighting, kicking back at my shins.

I drive her backward. She trips on a root.

We go down.

I land on top of her. The impact knocks the wind out of both of us.

I catch my weight on my elbows before I crush her, but I'm still pressing her into the pine needles. My hips are locked against hers. My chest is heaving against hers.

For a second, the violence stops.

The silence of the woods rushes back in.

Below me, she lies still.

Her hair is spread out like a fan on the dark earth. Her lips are parted, breath coming in short, sharp gasps. Her cheeks are flushed red from the cold and the fight.

She's looking up at me. Her pupils are blown wide.

Adrenaline mimics arousal. I know that. It's biology. Fight or flight.

But this doesn't feel like biology.

The heat of her body radiates through our clothes. The softness of her thighs under mine. The frantic beat of her heart against my chest.

Or maybe that's my heart.

The static is back, but it's not a spark anymore. It's a live wire.

I should move. I should roll off, stand up, and critique her form. Tell her she let me take her ground.

I don't move.

Her gaze drops to my mouth. Then back up to my eyes.

"You hesitated," she whispers.

"What?"

"You had me pinned. But you hesitated."

"I didn't want to break your ribs."

"Liar."

She shifts her hips. Just a fraction.

It sends a shockwave through me that has nothing to do with combat. My tactical brain is screaming GET UP, but my body remembers what it feels like to want something.

"Cassie," I warn. My voice is a wreck.

"You're heavy."

"Survival isn't comfortable."

"Is this survival?" She lifts a hand. Brushes dirt from my shoulder. Her fingers linger on the strap of my vest. "Or is this something else?"

I stare at her. The ghost of Sofia is standing at the edge of the clearing, watching. Guilt rises, black and suffocating.

I'm a weapon. I'm a shield. I am not a man. Not here.

"Focus," I snap.

I roll off her. Stand. Offer a hand.

She ignores it. Pushes herself up. Brushes the pine needles from her jeans. She doesn't look at me. She looks angry. Or maybe hurt.

"Again," she says.

"We're done with groundwork."

"No, we're not. You won."

"I always win. That's the point."

"Again." She steps into my space. "Grab me."

I grab her.

This time, I don't hold back. I spin her. Lock her arm behind her back. Press her face-first into the rough bark of a pine tree.

"You're dead," I say. "I have your arm. I have your neck. You have no leverage."

She grunts, straining against the hold.

"Think. You can't out-fight me. You can't out-muscle me. What do you have?"

She stops struggling.

For a second, she goes completely still against the tree.

"I have eyes," she whispers.

"What?"

She throws her weight backward. Not away from me—into me.

Her shoulder slams into my lower left ribs.

The spot where the bullet grazed the bone in Syria. The spot where I cracked two ribs in the extraction yesterday.

Pain explodes. White hot.

My grip loosens. Just for a fraction of a second.

She spins. Doesn't run. She drops low and sweeps my leg.

It's sloppy. It shouldn't work.

But I'm favoring the left side. My balance is off.

I stumble. Catch myself on the tree.

Cassie is standing five feet away. Breathing hard. Leaves in her hair.

"You favor the left," she says.

I straighten, rubbing my side. The pain is a sharp throb.

"What?"

"When we were on the ground. When you walk. You guard the left side." She points. "Ribs?"

I stare at her.

"Yes."

"I figured if I couldn't overpower you, I should target the structural weakness."

She's not looking at me like a victim anymore. She's looking at me like a lawyer. Analyzing the evidence. Finding the loophole.

Competence.

It hits me harder than the elbow.

She didn't fight like a soldier. She fought like her.

"Good," I say.

She blinks. "Good?"

"You found the vulnerability. You exploited it."

"Is that a compliment?"

"It's a survival skill." I check my watch. 0715. "We're done."

"I can go again."

"No. We've been exposed for over an hour. Drone window opens in ten minutes."

I start walking back to the cabin.

"Halo?"

I stop.

"You okay? I hit you pretty hard."

I look back at her. "I've had worse."

"That's not an answer."

"It's the only one you get."

Inside the cabin, the mood has shifted. The adrenaline is fading, replaced by a sharp, nervous energy.

"Pack up," I say. "Trash goes with us. Wipe every surface you touched. We leave this place sterile. Like we were never here."

"Where are we going?"

"Another safe house. We live by staying mobile. Let's go."

We walk out to the F-150. The sun is fully up now, cutting through the mist. The woods are bright. Too bright.

Cassie reaches for the passenger door.

I pause.

My hand hovers over the driver's side handle.

Something is wrong.

"Halo?"

"Quiet."

I scan the tree line. The gravel track leading out to the highway. The way the light hits the dust motes in the air.

Nothing looks different.

But the itch is there. Between my shoulder blades. The weight of eyes on us.

A crow takes flight from a pine tree fifty yards down the road. It caws once. Angry.

Crows don't fly for no reason. Not like that. Not straight up and fast. Something disturbed it.

"Change of plan," I say. My voice is low. Even.

"What?"

"We don't take the truck."

"Why? It's right here."

"Because someone is watching the road."

"You see someone?"

"No. But the math just changed."

If Phoenix is as fast as I think … If the algorithms predicted the stolen truck—they wouldn't hit the cabin. They'd hit the choke point. The end of the driveway.

They'd wait for us to come to them.

"Grab your pack," I say.

"Diego—"

"Grab the pack. Slowly. Don't look at the road."

She moves. Grabs her bag from the truck bed. Slings it over her shoulder.

"Into the woods," I say. "West. Away from the road."

"We're walking?"

"We're evading."

I steer her toward the tree line. Away from the easy exit. Away from the vehicle that suddenly looks like a coffin.

We hit the tree line, and I pick up the pace.

"Move," I whisper.

We disappear into the trees.

Leaving the truck. Leaving the safe house. Leaving the illusion of control behind.

Now, we're just prey in the wild.

5

"The Pursuit"
CASSIE

THE WOODS ARE NOT SILENT.

That's the first lie movies tell you about nature. They make it look peaceful. Still. A green cathedral where you go to find yourself.

The reality is a cacophony of violence.

Branches whip against my face. Dead leaves and branches crunch like breaking bones under my sneakers. My breath tears out of my lungs in ragged, whistling gasps that sound terrifyingly loud in the crisp morning air.

And ahead of me, the ghost moves without a sound.

Diego is twenty feet up the slope. He doesn't hike; he flows. He steps over fallen logs that I have to scramble over. He weaves through brambles that snag my sweater. He is part of the landscape, a shadow moving through shadows.

I am an intruder. A loud, clumsy, exhausted intruder in running shoes that have zero grip on the frosted mud.

"Keep moving." He doesn't turn around. He doesn't have to. He hears the struggle.

"I'm—moving," I wheeze.

We've been running—no, evading—for an hour. Maybe two.

Time dissolves when your entire world narrows down to the placement of your next step.

My thighs burn. My calves are knots of cramping muscle. The cold air stings my throat like swallowed glass.

Why did we leave the truck?

The question loops in my brain, a frantic mantra. The F-150 was right there. It had a heater. It had an engine. It had seats. We could be fifty miles away by now, blending into traffic on some anonymous interstate.

Instead, we are climbing a mountain in the middle of nowhere because a bird flew the wrong way.

It's insane. It's paranoid.

It's suicide.

I slip.

My right foot finds a patch of wet moss on a rock. Friction vanishes.

I go down hard. My knee slams into the stone. The impact jars my teeth.

"Damn it."

The sound of my voice freezes Diego instantly. He drops to a crouch, weapon in hand, scanning the tree line behind us.

"Quiet," he hisses.

"I fell."

He waits. Listens. The woods hold their breath.

After ten seconds, he holsters the weapon and slides down the slope to me. He moves with that terrifying economy of motion—controlled gravity.

"You hurt?"

"I banged my knee."

"Can you walk?"

"Yes."

"Then get up."

He doesn't offer a hand. He doesn't ask if I need a minute. He just stands there, vibrating with tension, waiting for me to stop being a liability.

Anger flares, hot and sudden. It burns through the exhaustion.

"We left the truck," I say, pushing myself up. My knee throbs, a sharp, hot needle of pain. "We left a working vehicle because you saw a crow."

"We left a coffin."

"You don't know that. You guessed."

"I calculated."

"You guessed based on a bird. That's not tactics, Halo. That's superstition."

He steps into my space. The air between us compresses. He smells of pine sap and cold sweat.

"Listen to me," he says, his voice low and hard. "You live in a world of laws. Cause and effect. Evidence and verdicts. That world is gone. Out here, you survive on instinct. When the hair on your arms stands up, you move. When the birds stop singing, you hide. If you wait for proof, you're dead."

"I just want to know if we're walking for a reason."

"We're walking to stay alive." He turns back to the slope. "Ridge line is another hundred yards. We rest there."

He starts climbing again.

I stare at his back. The width of his shoulders under the tactical jacket. The way he carries the heavy pack as if it weighs nothing.

I hate him a little bit.

I hate that he's right about my world being gone. I hate that I'm dependent on him. I hate that I want to curl up in the leaves and sleep until this nightmare ends.

Dead lawyers don't win cases.

The memory of his voice pushes me forward.

I grit my teeth against the pain in my knee. I dig my fingers into the freezing mud.

And I climb, but the ridge line offers no comfort. Just wind.

It cuts through my sweater, biting into my skin. The sweat on my back turns to ice. I'm shivering so hard my teeth chatter, a relentless click-click-click inside my skull.

Diego drops his pack near a cluster of boulders. "Down," he says. "Keep a low profile."

I collapse against the rock. The stone is freezing, but it blocks the wind.

"Drink." He tosses me a water bottle.

My hands shake as I unscrew the cap. I drink too fast, the water hitting my empty stomach like a stone.

Diego isn't drinking. He's lying on his stomach at the edge of the ridge, binoculars pressed to his eyes. He's watching the valley below. Watching the road we left behind.

I pull my knees to my chest, trying to conserve heat.

"See anything?" I ask.

"Wait."

Minutes tick by. Five. Ten.

My knee is throbbing in time with my pulse. I rub it, trying to generate friction.

Maybe he was wrong.

The thought is seductive. If he was wrong, if he's just paranoid, then maybe the monster isn't as scary as he says. Maybe Phoenix isn't omniscient. Maybe we can go back, get the truck, and turn on the heater.

"Got you," Diego whispers.

The tone of his voice chills me more than the wind. It's not triumphant. It's grim.

"What?"

"Stay low. Crawl."

I drop to my stomach. The ground is hard and cold. I pull myself up beside him.

He hands me the binoculars. "Three o'clock. The clearing at the end of the service road."

I lift the heavy lenses. Adjust the focus.

The world jumps closer. The brown smudge of the gravel road. The green of the pine trees.

And the truck.

Our stolen F-150 sits exactly where we left it.

It looks innocuous. Just a parked vehicle.

"I don't see anything," I say. "It's just the truck."

"Look at the tree line. Fifty yards back. Ten o'clock from the bumper."

I shift the view. Scan the shadows.

Nothing. Just trees. Bushes.

Then—movement.

Unnatural. A straight line in a world of curves.

A figure steps out of the shadows.

He's dressed in gray and black camouflage. Helmet. Tactical vest. He holds a rifle across his chest—long, black, terrifying.

He's not alone.

Another figure emerges from the other side of the road. Then a third.

They converge on the truck. They move like Diego moves—fluid, synchronized, professional.

One of them reaches the driver's side door. He doesn't open it. He places something on the handle. A small device.

"What are they doing?" I whisper.

"Scanning for bio-traces," Diego says. "Checking if we're inside. Or if we trapped it."

The soldier signals. The team stacks up. They breach the truck—doors rip open, weapons raised.

Empty.

I lower the binoculars. My hands are shaking violently now, and it has nothing to do with the cold.

"They were there," I breathe.

"They were waiting." Diego takes the binoculars back. "They tracked the vehicle signature. Or maybe they hacked the traffic cam at the rest stop. Doesn't matter. They set up an ambush at the choke point."

"If we had driven down that road—"

"They would have put a .308 round through the engine block. Then they would have dragged us out."

He looks at me. His eyes are dark, unreadable.

"The crow wasn't superstition, Cassie. The crow flew because a kill team was moving into position."

I stare at him.

He heard a bird. And he knew.

He heard a bird, and he saved my life.

Again.

The earlier anger evaporates, leaving a hollow, sickening realization in its wake. I am way out of my depth. I'm a child wandering through a minefield, and he is the only map I have.

"You were right," I say.

"Being right keeps you alive." He puts the binoculars away. "But now we have a new problem."

"What?"

"They know we didn't take the truck. They know we're on foot." He gestures at the vast expanse of mountains around us. "They'll deploy drones. Thermal cameras. Dogs."

"Dogs?"

"If they have a scent trail, yes."

He stands, crouching low to stay below the skyline.

"We need to move. We need to find water to mask the trail. And we need to put ten miles between us and that truck before sunset."

Ten miles.

My knee throbs. My lungs burn just thinking about it.

"I can't," the words slip out.

Diego looks down at me. "What?"

"I can't do ten miles. Not in these shoes. Not with this knee."

It's the truth. And in my world, the truth is supposed to be the ultimate defense.

Diego stares at me. He doesn't look sympathetic. He looks calculating. He's running the probability model. Asset integrity vs. Mission success.

"Take off your shoe," he says.

"What?"

"Sit down. Take off your right shoe."

"Why?"

"Because if you're injured, I need to know the extent of the damage. If you're just complaining, I need to know that too."

I sit back against the rock. Unlace the sneaker. My fingers are clumsy with cold.

I pull the shoe off. Then the sock.

My foot is a mess. A blister on the heel has burst, bleeding into the fabric. My ankle is swollen; the skin is tight and angry.

Diego kneels. He checks my knee, then takes my foot in his hand.

His palm is rough, calloused, but his touch is surprisingly gentle. His hands are warm. The heat seeps into my frozen skin, shocking and welcome.

He probes the ankle. "Does this hurt?"

"Yes."

"Sharp pain or dull?"

"Throbbing."

"Ligaments are strained. Not torn." He checks the blister. "This needs to be taped."

He opens his pack. Pulls out a roll of medical tape and a fresh pair of wool socks.

"Where did you get socks?"

"I pack for contingencies." He starts taping my heel. His movements are precise. Efficient. "You have civilian feet. Soft. City shoes."

"Sorry, I didn't pack hiking boots for my abduction."

He glances up. A flicker of amusement in his eyes. "Sarcasm is a good sign. Means you're not in shock anymore."

He finishes taping. It feels better. Tighter. Supported.

Then he pulls the wool sock onto my foot. It's too big, swallowing my ankle, but it's warm. So incredibly warm.

He does the other foot. Taping the hotspots before they blister.

"These will help," he says. "But it's still going to hurt."

"I know."

"I mean it, Cassie. It's going to hurt like hell. Your muscles will cramp. Your lungs will burn. You will want to stop." He pauses, his hands still holding my foot. He looks up, meeting my gaze. "You cannot stop. If we stop, they catch us. If they catch us, we die."

It's not a threat. It's gravity.

"I won't stop," I say.

He holds my gaze for a second longer. Assessing.

Then he nods. "Okay."

He releases my foot. The loss of contact is immediate. The cold rushes back in.

He stands and offers me a hand.

"Up."

I take his hand. His grip is iron. He pulls me to my feet.

For a moment, we're close again. The wind whips hair across my face. Stubble darkens his jaw, gray flecks in his dark eyes visible even in the gloom.

"We go west," he says. "There's a river in the valley. We walk in the water to kill the scent."

"That sounds freezing."

"It is." He turns away, adjusting his pack. "Welcome to the suck. Embrace it, and you live."

The next four hours are a blur of misery.

We descend into the valley. The terrain changes from rocky ridge to dense undergrowth. Rhododendrons slap at my legs. Thorns tear at my jeans.

Diego sets a brutal pace. He doesn't look back, but he pauses every time I fall more than twenty yards behind, waiting just long enough for me to catch sight of him before moving again.

He is a ghost leading me through purgatory.

We reach the river around noon. It's not a river, really—a wide, fast-moving creek swollen with snowmelt. The water is clear and impossibly cold.

"In," Diego says.

"You're joking."

"Dogs," he says simply.

He steps into the water. It comes up to his calves. He doesn't even flinch.

I step in.

The cold is a physical shock. It clamps around my ankles like a bear trap. I gasp, stumbling.

"Breathe," Diego says over his shoulder. "Keep moving."

We wade upstream. The rocks are slippery with algae. Twice, I almost go down, flailing arms to catch my balance. The water numbs my feet, then my shins. My toes are gone, replaced by blocks of ice.

After a mile—an eternity—Diego angles toward the bank.

"Out."

I scramble onto the rocky bank. My legs feel heavy, like blocks of wood. I collapse onto a fallen log, shivering violently.

"Change socks," Diego orders. "Now. Trench foot is a legitimate threat."

I strip off the wet socks. My feet are pale, wrinkled, blue-tinged. I dry them with the sleeves of my sweater and pull on the last pair of wool socks from Diego's pack.

Pain rushes back as the blood returns. Pins and needles.

"How …" My teeth chatter. "How much farther?"

"Five miles to the shelter point."

"I can't."

"You can."

"No. I really can't." I wrap my arms around my knees. "My legs won't work."

Diego turns. He looks at me.

Then he walks over. He crouches in front of me.

"Look at me."

I look up. His face is grim, dirt-streaked.

"You survived the apartment," he says. "You survived the jump. You survived the drive."

"This is different. I'm exhausted."

"You are carrying a twenty-pound emotional load." He unbuckles his pack.

"What are you doing?"

"Give me your sweater."

"What?"

"It's cotton. It's wet. Cotton kills. It holds moisture against your skin." He opens his pack. Pulls out a thermal tactical shirt. "Put this on."

"I'm not stripping in the woods."

"Cassie, look at your fingernails."

I look. They are blue.

"Hypothermia," he says. "Stage one. Confusion. Shivering. Poor coordination. If you don't get dry and warm, your heart stops. Put on the shirt."

He turns his back again. "I'm watching the perimeter. Change."

I fumble with my sweater. Pull it over my head. The cold air bites my skin. I'm wearing a thin camisole underneath, soaked with sweat.

I peel it off. For a second, I am bare in the freezing woods. Vulnerable.

I pull on his shirt.

It's massive on me. The sleeves hang past my hands. But it's dry. And it's warm. It smells like him—gun oil, cedar, and man.

The scent wraps around me. It feels safer than the cabin. Safer than my apartment.

"Done," I say.

He turns back. His eyes sweep over me, checking the fit. He nods.

"Better?"

"Warmer."

"Let's go."

He shoulders his pack.

"Diego?"

He pauses, doesn't correct me.

"Thank you."

"Don't thank me yet. We still have five miles."

He sets a killer pace. Hours later, the sun is dropping when we stop for a break.

The woods have changed again. Pines give way to hardwoods. The ground is steeper.

"Here," Diego says.

He points to a depression under the root system of a massive fallen oak. It's a natural shelter, protected from the wind, hidden from above.

"We camp here?"

"We hold here. No fire. Too risky."

He drops his pack. Starts clearing debris from the hollow. He moves dead leaves, checks for snakes, and lines the ground with pine boughs.

It's nesting. Primal and efficient.

"It's going to freeze tonight," I say. The temperature is already plummeting.

"Yes."

He pulls out a silver emergency blanket. "We share this."

I stare at the flimsy foil sheet. "That's it?"

"Body heat is the only heat source we have." He looks at me. His expression is guarded. Careful. "It's tactical. Not romantic."

"I know."

"If we sleep apart, we freeze. If we sleep together, we maintain core temperature."

"I said I know."

He spreads the blanket over the pine boughs. "Get in the back. Against the wood. I take the outside."

I crawl into the small space. It smells of earth and decay. I want to curl up, pull my knees to my chest, but there's no room for that. For him. So I stretch out on my side.

Diego slides in beside me.

The space is tiny. There is no way to avoid contact.

He lies on his side, facing away from me, his back to my chest. He positions his body to block the wind from the opening.

"Close," he says.

I scoot forward until my chest presses against his back. Do I wrap my arm around his waist? No. That feels too intimate. I tuck my hands between us.

He's rigid. Tense. A wall of muscle.

"Relax," I whisper. "I'm not going to bite."

"I'm armed," he says. "Safety's on, but—don't startle me."

"Noted."

He pulls the foil blanket over us. It crinkles loudly.

Underneath, the heat begins to build.

It takes a few minutes. My shivering slows. His body is a furnace.

Warmth radiates through his tactical gear, soaking into my frozen limbs.

"Diego?"

"Yeah."

"Was it really the crow?"

"Yes."

"And you knew?"

"Nature has a baseline," he says softly. His voice rumbles in his chest, vibrating against me. "Predators disturb the baseline. Birds fly. Insects go quiet. If you listen, the world tells you where the bad things are."

"Is that how you survived?"

"It's how I kept breathing."

"That's not the same thing."

He doesn't answer.

I rest my forehead against his shoulder blade. The scent of him is overwhelming here—earth and sweat and the faint metallic tang of the gun he's clutching against his chest.

It should be terrifying. Sleeping in the dirt with a killer.

But the fear is gone.

"You were right," I whisper.

"About what?"

"About the truck. About the chaos."

"Chaos is the only truth."

"No." I shift, pressing closer to his warmth. "You are."

He stiffens.

"Go to sleep, Cassie."

"You saved me."

"Sleep."

I close my eyes. The wind howls outside our tiny burrow. The woods are dark and full of things that want to kill us.

But here, under the silver blanket, anchored by the weight of the man who calls himself a ghost, warmth finally returns.

My hand drifts. Without thinking, I unclench my fist and rest my palm flat against his stomach.

He inhales sharply.

He doesn't push me away.
He covers my hand with his own. His fingers lace through mine.
Holding on.
"Goodnight, Halo," I whisper.
"Goodnight, Cassie."
And in the dark, the ghost holds my hand while I sleep.

6

"The Drift"
HALO

I WAKE before I open my eyes.

The first sensation is heat.

Not the stifling, humid heat of a jungle op, or the dry, dusty heat of the desert. This is living heat. Soft. Heavy. Anchored against my back.

An arm is draped over my waist. A hand is flat against my chest, fingers curled into the fabric of my thermal shirt. Legs are tangled with mine, seeking warmth in the freezing dark.

I don't move. My training screams *Threat,* but my body screams *Home.*

It's the most dangerous sensation I've had in six years.

I lie there in the dirt, trapped under the silver foil blanket, and I catalog the damage.

My heart rate is slow, steady. Too steady. I slept. Actually slept. Not the shallow, jagged dozing of an operator on watch, but deep, black sleep. Four hours of it.

If a kill team had found us, we'd be dead. I wouldn't have heard them. I was too busy being warm.

Compromised.

I shift. Carefully.

Cassie makes a small, protesting noise in her throat and presses closer. Her forehead rests against my spine. Her breath is warm through my shirt.

And I am hard. Painfully, undeniably hard.

Biology. Friction. Body heat. It's just mechanics.

Liar.

It's her. It's the smell of her—vanilla and sweat and woodsmoke. It's the way she held my hand while the world tried to kill us.

I need to move. I need to get away from her before I do something stupid. Before I turn around. Before I wrap my arms around her and forget that I am a ghost and she is a mission parameter.

I grab her wrist. The one draped over me.

"Cassie."

She stirs. Tightens her grip. "Mmm?"

"Wake up."

My voice is rough. Grinding gears.

She shifts, pulling back slightly. The cold air rushes into the gap between us, sharp and sobering.

"What time is it?" she whispers.

"Time to move."

I throw the blanket off. It crinkles like a gunshot in the quiet woods.

I roll out of the shelter and stand. The cold hits me instantly, freezing the sweat on my skin. It's good. It kills the heat. It kills the want. The need.

I walk ten paces away, turning my back to the shelter. I unzip my fly and relieve myself against a tree, staring into the gray predawn mist.

My ribs throb where she elbowed me yesterday. Good. Pain is clarifying.

Behind me, she moves. The rustle of the blanket. The soft grunt of effort as she stands on stiff muscles.

"Halo?"

I zip. Adjust my belt. Check my weapon.

When I turn around, she's standing by the fallen oak. She looks wrecked. Leaves in her hair. Dirt on her cheek. The oversized thermal shirt hangs off her frame.

She looks beautiful.

I look away. "Pack up. We leave in five."

"Good morning to you too," she says. Her voice is raspy.

"We lost four hours. Phoenix has had time to reposition. They'll have drones grid-searching the woods by sunrise."

"I slept," she says. She sounds surprised. "I actually slept."

"You were exhausted. Hypothermia does that."

"It wasn't the hypothermia." She looks at me. Direct. Unflinching. "It was you."

I stiffen. "Don't."

"Don't, what?"

"Don't make it personal. I was a heat source. That's it."

She studies me. She sees right through the tactical armor, right through the bullshit. She sees the man who held her hand.

"Okay," she says softly. "Heat source. Got it."

She turns and starts rolling up the emergency blanket.

She smooths the foil with efficient, capable hands.

I hate that she's making this easy for me. I want her to fight, to argue, to give me a reason to be the asshole I need to be. Instead, she's just—accepting it.

"Boots check," I say. "How are the feet?"

"Numb."

"Let me see."

"They're fine."

"Cassie."

She sighs. Sits on the log. Pulls off the right sneaker.

I kneel. The wool sock is damp. I peel it back.

The blisters I taped yesterday are holding, but the skin around them is angry. Her ankle is swollen, a blue-purple bruise blooming under the skin.

She winces when I touch it.

"You walked five miles on this," I say.

"You told me to."

"Ligaments are loose. We need to wrap it tighter."

I pull the med kit from my pack. Ace bandage.

I rest her foot on my knee. Her skin is ice cold. I wrap the ankle, pulling the bandage taut.

"Tight?"

"It's fine."

"It needs to be tight for support."

"It's fine, Diego."

I freeze. My hands stop moving on her ankle.

"Halo," I say.

"Right. Halo." She looks down at me. "Diego is the guy who made me tea. Halo is the guy who treats me like a heat source."

I finish the wrap. Secure the clip.

"Diego is dead," I say. "Halo keeps you alive. Pick one."

I stand up.

She pulls her sock back on. Jams her foot into the shoe. She stands, testing her weight. She winces, but she doesn't stumble.

"I pick survival," she says.

"Good choice."

I shoulder my pack. "We head west. Toward the valley floor. We need a vehicle."

"I thought roads were dangerous."

"Walking is dangerous. We can't outrun a drone on foot. We need speed."

"So we're stealing another car."

"Yes."

"Great. My felony count is really racking up."

"Better than your body count."

I start walking. I don't wait to see if she follows. She will.

We hike for two hours.

The terrain fights us. Brambles. Ravines. Loose shale that slides under our boots.

I set a brutal pace. I have to. The sun is rising, burning off the mist, exposing us. Every minute we spend in the open is a roll of the dice.

Cassie doesn't complain. She falls behind on the climbs, her breath tearing in ragged gasps, but she catches up on the flats. She limps, favoring the wrapped ankle, but she keeps moving.

Resilience.

It's the one thing you can't train. You either have it, or you break.

She has it.

Around 0800, we hit the edge of the woods. The trees thin out. Fences appear. Barbed wire marking property lines.

I hold up a fist. Stop.

Cassie freezes. She's learning.

I crouch behind a laurel bush. Use the binoculars.

Below us, a valley opens up. Farmland. Pastures. A ribbon of asphalt—Route 600, maybe.

"What do you see?" she whispers, crawling up beside me.

"Civilization."

I scan the structures. A farmhouse half a mile down. Red brick. Silo. A gravel driveway with a sedan parked near the house.

Too close to the main road. Too much visibility.

I scan left.

A smaller property. A double-wide trailer set back against the woods. A shed. And parked under a lean-to.

"Jackpot," I whisper.

"What?"

"Ten o'clock. The trailer."

She takes the binoculars. "I see a rusted pickup truck."

"1980s Chevy. No computer. No GPS. Easy to wire."

"It looks dead."

"It has tires. That's enough."

"What about the people who live there?"

"What about them?"

"They're—people. Probably poor if they're living in a trailer. We're going to steal their truck?"

"Would you prefer to ask them for a ride?"

"No. I just …" She lowers the binoculars. "It feels different than the rest stop. That was corporate. This feels—personal."

"Survival is personal." I take the glasses back. "The house looks quiet. No smoke from the chimney. No dog in the yard."

"How do you know?"

"No doghouse. No chain. No barking when the wind shifted." I stand, keeping to the shadows. "We approach from the rear. Wood line to the shed. I clear the vehicle. You watch the house."

"And if someone comes out?"

"You signal. Two taps on your leg. We vanish."

"And if they see us?"

I check my weapon. "Then we deal with it."

Her eyes flick to the gun. "You wouldn't."

"I do what is necessary."

"They're civilians, Diego. Innocent people."

"No one is innocent."

It's the wrong thing to say. The recoil in her eyes is visible. The fear. Not of the situation, but of me.

Good. Fear keeps distance.

"Let's go," I say.

We move down the slope. The transition from wild woods to human property feels loud. The crunch of dry grass. The smell of diesel and trash.

We reach the back of the shed. The air smells of oil and wet rot.

"Wait here," I whisper. "Watch the windows."

She nods. She's pale, but she positions herself near the corner of the shed, eyes fixed on the trailer.

I move to the truck.

It's a wreck. Rust eats at the wheel wells. The bed is full of scrap metal and empty beer cans.

But the tires have air.

I try the door. Unlocked. The hinges screech.

I freeze.

Nothing from the house. No movement.

I slide inside. The cab smells of stale tobacco and mold.

I check under the dash. It's a mess of wires. This won't be as clean as the Ford. I pull out my knife.

"Halo."

Cassie's whisper is a sharp hiss.

I freeze. "What?"

"Movement. Kitchen window."

I look through the dirty windshield. The trailer is fifty feet away. A curtain twitches.

"Confirm," I whisper.

"Someone's in there. I saw a face."

I have maybe thirty seconds before they look out the back.

I can't hotwire it. Too much noise. The engine will wake the dead.

I look at the ignition.

The keys are in it.

Shit. Hate that I missed it. Means I'm distracted, and that's never good. As for the truck, it makes sense—rural Virginia. Nobody steals a rust bucket.

Except us.

"Cassie," I hiss. "In. Now."

She sprints. Low crouch. Fast.

She dives into the passenger seat. "They saw me. The curtain moved."

"Hold on."

I turn the key.

The engine groans. Chug … Chug …

"Come on," I mutter. "Turn over."

Chug … Chug...

The back door of the trailer flies open.

A man steps out. Overalls. No shirt.

And a shotgun.

"Hey!" he yells. "Get the hell out of my truck!"

He raises the shotgun.

"Down!" I shove Cassie's head toward the dash.

BOOM.

Buckshot peppers the side of the truck bed. Ping-ping-ping.

"Go!" Cassie screams.

I stomp the gas.

The engine catches. Roars. A cloud of black smoke erupts from the tailpipe.

I throw it into reverse. The tires spin in the mud, then grip. We shoot backward, fishtailing.

The man pumps the shotgun. Clack-clack.

"He's reloading!" Cassie shouts.

I slam it into drive. The transmission screams. We lurch forward, tearing up the grass.

BOOM.

The side mirror explodes. Glass showers into the cab.

"He's shooting at us!"

"I noticed!"

I aim for the gravel driveway. We hit the ruts hard enough to bounce my head off the roof.

The man is running now, chasing us down the drive. He stops. Aims.

The barrel levels in the rearview.

I swerve.

BOOM.

The back window shatters. Safety glass rains down on us like hail.

"Are you hit?" I yell.

"No! Just glass! Drive!"

We hit the paved road. I turn left, tires screeching. I floor it. The speedometer needle wobbles toward fifty. The truck shakes like it's going to fly apart.

I watch the rearview. The man is standing in the road, shotgun lowered. Shrinking.

Gone.

I keep the pedal down for three miles. Five. Ten.

My heart is hammering. Good adrenaline. Clean adrenaline.

I glance at Cassie.

She's sitting up now, picking glass out of her hair. Her face is white, her eyes huge.

She starts to laugh.

It's a jagged, hysterical sound.

"We stole a truck," she gasps. "We actually stole a truck from a man in overalls with a shotgun."

"We borrowed it."

"He shot out the window!"

"He missed the tires. That's what matters."

She looks at me. There's a smear of dirt on her nose. A piece of glass caught in the collar of my thermal shirt she's wearing.

"You're bleeding," she says.

"What?"

"Your cheek. Glass cut."

I wipe my face. My hand comes away red.

"Matches yours," I say.

She touches her own cheek. Finds blood.

"God." She leans back against the seat, closing her eyes. "My mother would be horrified. 'Cassandra, grand theft auto plus breaking and entering? That is not how we raised you.'"

"Your mother isn't getting shot at."

"True." She opens her eyes. Turns her head to look at me. "You were right."

"About what?"

"The chaos. The instinct." She picks a shard of glass off her leg. "If we had hesitated … If we had debated the morality of it …"

"He would have blown our heads off."

"Yeah."

She goes quiet. Watching the road.

"Where are we going?"

"West," I say. "We ditch this thing as soon as we find a town with a parking lot. It's too conspicuous now. Bullet holes tend to draw attention."

"And then?"

"Then we disappear again."

She nods. She wraps her arms around herself, shivering in the draft from the broken window.

"Cold?" I ask.

"Freezing."

I reach down. Turn the heater knob.

A blast of hot, dusty air roars from the vents.

She leans forward, putting her hands in front of the vent. "Oh my God. Heat."

"Civilization."

She smiles. It's a small, tired thing, but it's real.

"Thank you, Halo."

"Don't thank me. Thank Chevy."

I keep my eyes on the road. But her presence is palpable. The heat of her body. The shared adrenaline.

The "Ghost" wall is crumbling. Cracks widen.

I told her Diego was dead.

But looking at her, bathed in sunlight and smelling of dust and survival …

Diego feels dangerously alive.

"The Origin"
CASSIE

THE TRUCK IS DYING.

It wasn't exactly healthy when we stole it, but ten miles of high-speed evasion and a shattered rear window have turned it into a rolling corpse. The engine knocks—a wet, metallic thunk-thunk-thunk—and the wind howling through the broken glass numbs my ears.

I'm shivering again. The adrenaline from the shotgun blast has faded, leaving behind a cold, shaky exhaustion.

"We need to dump it," Diego yells over the wind.

"Agreed."

"Next town. We find a swap."

He looks grim. His cheek is still bleeding sluggishly where the glass cut him. He scans the mirrors constantly, eyes darting from side to side.

He's not looking for the farmer with the shotgun. He's looking for the invisible net. Drones. Traffic cams. The algorithm.

We cross the state line into West Virginia. The roads narrow. The houses get smaller, huddled against the hillsides.

"There," Diego says.

A sign flashes past: Martinsburg - 2 Miles.

"It's big enough to have a strip mall," he says. "Small enough to lack high-end surveillance grids."

He pulls the truck off the main road, navigating through a maze of residential streets until we hit a commercial district. A Walmart. A Lowe's. A sprawling parking lot filled with morning shoppers.

"Perfect."

He parks the truck behind a dumpster in the loading zone behind the Lowe's. It's out of sight from the main road.

He kills the engine. The silence rings in my ears.

"Out," he says. "Wipe everything."

I know the drill now. I use my sleeve to wipe the door handle, the dash, the seatbelt buckle. Erasing the evidence of our existence.

We step out into the sunlight. It feels exposing. I'm wearing a thermal tactical shirt that hangs to my knees, dirty jeans, and sneakers taped together with medical adhesive. I look like a vagrant.

Diego looks like—trouble. Even with the dirt and the blood, he moves with a predatory grace that screams soldier.

"Head down," he murmurs. "Walk with purpose. Don't make eye contact."

We merge into the flow of people walking toward the store entrances.

"What are we looking for?" I ask.

"Sedan. Gray or silver. Ford or Toyota. Common. Invisible."

"No."

He stops. Turns to look at me. "No?"

"A gray sedan with two people looking like us in the front seat screams 'fleeing felons.' It's the first thing a cop looks for."

"It blends in."

"It blends in with traffic. It doesn't blend in with people." I scan the parking lot. My eyes land on a row of vehicles near the Garden Center. "We need social camouflage."

"Social camouflage." He tastes the word like it's foreign.

"Look at that." I point.

A Honda Odyssey minivan. Maroon. Stick-figure family stickers on the back window. A 'Baby on Board' suction cup sign.

"A minivan," he says. Flat. Unimpressed.

"Nobody looks at a minivan. They look through it. It implies kids, groceries, and soccer practice. It implies a life so boring it doesn't register as a threat."

He looks at the van. Then back at me.

He's calculating and weighing the tactical profile against the psychological one.

"It has tinted windows in the back," he acknowledges. "Good for gear concealment."

"And it's probably unlocked because the mom is returning a potted plant and wrangling a toddler."

He studies me for a second longer. A flicker of respect? Or maybe just resignation.

"Fine. The minivan."

We walk toward it.

I'm right. The driver's side door is unlocked.

Diego slides in. I take the passenger seat.

The interior smells of hand sanitizer, Cheerios, and stale coffee. A half-empty Starbucks cup sits in the cupholder. A toddler's car seat is strapped in the back.

It smells like safety, like a normal life where the biggest problem is traffic.

Diego checks the visor. Keys drop into his hand.

"Careless," he mutters.

"Distracted," I correct. "She's a mom."

He starts the engine. It purrs. Quiet. Smooth.

"I feel bad," I say.

"She has insurance." He puts it in gear. "We don't. Besides, Ghost always sends a check to cover the damage."

That makes me feel slightly better about our grand theft auto spree.

We roll out of the lot. Diego drives conservatively. Hands at ten and two.

We merge onto the highway, heading west.

"Safe house is six hours," he says. "We can rest there. Get cleaned up. Re-equip."

"And then?"

"Then we figure out how to hit back."

The heater kicks in. Warmth floods the cabin.

I lean back in the seat. The tension in my shoulders begins to unspool, inch by inch.

I look at Diego. He's scanning the mirrors again, but his posture has relaxed slightly. The minivan doesn't demand the same aggressive handling as the truck. He looks absurd in this driver's seat—a lethal weapon surrounded by cup holders and wet wipes.

"You realize I was right," I say.

"About what?"

"The van. Social camouflage."

He glances at me. "It was a valid tactical assessment."

"You can just say 'you were right.'"

"I just did. In my language."

I smile. It feels strange on my face. Tight. "Your language is exhausting."

"It keeps you alive."

"Does it?" I turn in the seat to face him. "Or does it just keep everyone else out?"

His jaw tightens. The wall goes up. The Ghost.

"Don't do that," I say.

"Do, what?"

"Disappear. You're sitting right next to me. Don't go back to being a stat sheet."

"I'm focusing on the road."

"You're focusing on the distance."

I reach out. I don't touch him—I know better than to startle him while he's driving—but I rest my hand on the center console, close to his.

"Tell me about Cerberus."

He keeps his eyes forward. "Private military contractor. Specialized threat negation."

"That's the brochure. Who are they? The people you work with."

"They're my team."

"They're your family."

He flinches. Micro-movement. But I see it.

"We don't use that word."

"Why? Because it implies you have something to lose?"

"Because families die. Teams operate."

"That is the saddest thing I've ever heard."

He sighs. A long, ragged exhale.

"Ghost is the leader," he says finally. Reluctantly. "He recruited me in Colombia. Pulled me out of a hole I dug for myself."

"What kind of hole?"

"The kind you don't climb out of. The kind where you're looking for a bullet to stop the noise."

"And the others?"

"Brass is the second. Tactical genius. Scary calm. Fuse is demolitions. He blows things up to avoid dealing with his feelings. Whisper is intel. He sees everything."

"And you?"

"I'm the eraser. I make problems go away."

"Is that what I am? A problem?"

He looks at me then. The traffic slows, giving him a second to hold my gaze.

His eyes are dark. Haunted. But burning with something that terrifies me.

"You're the mission," he says.

"That's not an answer."

"It's the only one that keeps you safe."

"Why?" I push. "Why does caring about me make me unsafe?"

"Because if I care about you, I get scared. And if I get scared, I hesitate. And if I hesitate …" He looks back at the road. His knuckles are white on the steering wheel. "You end up at the bottom of a ravine."

The air in the van goes still.

He said it.

He admitted it.

He's terrified. Not of Phoenix. Not of dying.

He's terrified of failing me.

But it's more than that. The way he said it—bottom of a ravine —wasn't hypothetical. It was a memory.

"Diego," I whisper.

"Don't."

"You're not going to fail."

"You don't know that."

"Yes, I do." I lean forward, trying to catch his eyes, but he refuses to look at me. "Because you're not talking about a hypothetical, are you? You're talking about something that happened."

His jaw works. A muscle feathering under the stubble.

"Who was she?" I ask.

Silence.

The van hums over the asphalt. The stick-figure family on the back window stares at me in the reflection of the rearview mirror.

"Who did you fail, Diego?"

"Sofia."

The name is a prayer. He exhales it like smoke.

"Who was she?"

"She was a journalist. In Mexico City." He grips the wheel so hard the leather creaks. "She was investigating a cartel. She thought the system would protect her. She thought being right was enough."

The parallel hits me like a slap. A woman investigating powerful people. Trusting the system.

"What happened?"

"I was deployed. Syria." His voice is flat, dead. "I wasn't there. I trusted the federal police to keep her safe. I trusted the protocol."

He glances at me. The pain in his eyes is raw, bleeding.

"They ran her car off the road. Brakes failed. Three hundred feet into a canyon."

"I'm so sorry."

"Don't be. Sorry doesn't fix it." He looks back at the road. "That's why I don't use the system. That's why I don't trust police. And that's why I don't get attached."

"Because you think you're cursed."

"Because I am."

"So you treat me like a package. Because if I'm just a package, you won't care if I break."

"If you're a package, I won't hesitate."

"But I'm not. I'm not a package, am I?"

"No," he says softly. "You're not."

He reaches out. Covers my hand on the console.

His palm is rough. Warm. His fingers lace through mine.

He squeezes. Hard. Like he's checking to make sure I'm real. Like he's checking to make sure he's real.

"I'm not Sofia," I whisper.

"I know."

"I'm right here. You're right here. You're not in Syria. You're in a minivan."

He lets out a breath. A long, shuddering sound.

"We're stopping," he says. His voice is tight.

"Why?"

"Because I need five minutes. And you need food."

He pulls the minivan off the highway. A desolate exit. A gas station with barred windows and a flickering neon sign.

He parks in the back, away from the pumps. Kills the engine.

But he doesn't let go of my hand.

For a long minute, we just sit there. The engine ticks as it cools. The smell of Cheerios and sanitizer mixes with the scent of us— sweat and dirt and survival.

"You're dangerous," he says softly.

"Me? You're the one with the gun."

"Not the gun." He turns his head and looks at me. "This. You seeing me. It strips the armor off."

"You don't need armor with me."

"I do. Especially with you."

He unlaces his fingers from mine. Pulls away. The loss of contact is a physical ache.

"Stay in the car," he says. The command voice is back, but it's thinner. Brittle. "I'll get supplies. Keep the doors locked."

He opens the door and slides out.

I watch him walk toward the station. He checks his six. He scans the roof. He moves like a ghost.

But I know the truth now.

He is not a ghost.

He's a man who is desperately afraid that he's found something worth living for.

He comes back with sandwiches. Bad coffee. A bag of chips.

And a burner phone. Can never have too many.

He slides into the driver's seat. Tosses the food into my lap.

"Eat."

He keeps the phone. Powers it on. His fingers fly across the keypad.

"Checking in?" I ask, unwrapping a sandwich that looks like plastic.

"Checking the board."

He types a sequence. Waits. A text comes back.

His face goes hard.

"What?" I ask. "What is it?"

"Phoenix adjusted."

"Adjusted how?"

"I checked the local chatter. Scanners. Traffic enforcement."

"And?"

"No APB. No Amber Alert. No missing person report."

"Because I'm dead," I say.

"Exactly," he says. "To the system, you don't exist. Which means they don't need the law to find you."

"They want to find us themselves."

"Exactly. If they put out an alert, every cop in West Virginia becomes a sensor. But they also become a variable. Phoenix hates variables."

He turns the phone screen off. Slides it into his pocket.

"They're not casting a wide net, Cassie. They're hunting with a spear."

"So they know where we are?"

"They know where we're going. Or they think they do." He starts the van. "The algorithm is predicting our vectors based on my history. It knows I like back roads. It knows I avoid cities. It knows I head for deep country when the heat gets high."

He looks at the map on his knee.

"So we don't go to deep country."

"We disappear," he says. "But not in the silence."

"Where?"

"Somewhere the algorithm has too much data. Too many faces. Too much chaos." He backs out of the spot. "Somewhere ghosts can walk in broad daylight."

"Diego, where are we going?"

He looks at me.

"Philadelphia."

"Philly? That's a city. Cameras. Police."

"Exactly. It's the last place Phoenix predicts I'll take you." He shifts into drive. "We're going to hide in the noise."

The minivan lurches onto the road.

I look at the sandwich in my lap. I'm not hungry anymore.

"We're on our own," I say.

"We always were."

"But—"

"Eat. We have a long drive."

He reaches out. Takes my hand again. Squeezes once.

"I got you."

And as we merge onto the highway, turning north toward the storm, I believe him.

8

"The Crossing"
HALO

THE PHILADELPHIA SKYLINE is a jagged wound against the gray sky.

Skyscrapers stack against the horizon like a Tetris game gone wrong. It's dirty, loud, and alive.

"Welcome to the noise," I say.

Cassie leans forward against the seatbelt, staring through the windshield. Her hair is pulled back, but strands of it catch the city lights.

"It's huge."

"It's chaotic. Narrow streets, confusing topography. It's a nightmare for surveillance grids because the sightlines are broken."

I keep the minivan in the middle lane. Speed limit exactly. Hands loose on the wheel, though my shoulders are knots of tension.

We passed three state troopers on the turnpike. None of them looked twice at a maroon Odyssey.

Social camouflage. She was right.

But the closer we get to the city, the tighter my chest feels. The invisible net is there. The algorithm is watching. And Cassie … She stands out. That hair. The way she holds herself.

"We need to change," I say.

"Change, what?"

"Everything. We look like we crawled out of the woods. In the woods, that's fine. In the lobby of a hotel, it's a red flag."

"We're staying in a hotel?"

"Best place to hide is a crowd. Big convention hotel. Hundreds of guests. Staff who don't care who you are as long as the credit card clears."

"We don't have a credit card."

"I have cash. And I have methods."

I take the exit for Center City. The GPS on the minivan's dash —which I disabled an hour ago—is dark. I navigate by memory.

"There." I point to a thrift store on South Street. Crowded. Chaotic. No cameras in the window.

I pull into the alley. Kill the engine.

"Here's the play," I say, turning to her. "I can't go in. My tactical profile is too distinct. You go."

"Me?"

"You're the dead girl. People see what they expect to see. They expect Cassie Brennan to be in a morgue or a ditch. They don't expect her to buy hoodies in Philly."

"Okay."

"But you have to cover the hair," I say. "It's too distinctive. Redheads draw the eye."

She touches her hair self-consciously. "Right."

I pull a wad of cash from my pack. "Get clothes. Normal clothes. Jeans. Hoodies. A jacket for me—something bulky. Hats. Sunglasses."

"Okay."

"And Cassie?"

She meets my eyes.

"If you see anyone looking at you too long. You drop the clothes, and you walk out the back door. You don't run. You walk."

"I know."

"Do you?"

"I listened to the lecture, Halo. Distance is time. Normalcy is a shield." She takes the cash. "I'll be back in twenty."

She opens the door.

"Wait."

I reach out. Grab her wrist. It's instinct. The urge to keep her close. To lock her in the van, where I can protect her.

She looks at my hand on her wrist. Then up at my face.

"I'm coming back," she says softly.

"I know."

I let go.

She slips out. The door slides shut.

I sit in the driver's seat, hand on my weapon, watching the mirrors.

Five minutes.

Ten.

Every second she's gone is an eternity. My brain runs scenarios. Someone recognizes her. A cop walks in. She sees a TV and panics.

Fifteen minutes.

A police cruiser rolls past the mouth of the alley. I sink lower in the seat. My hand tightens on the Glock. The cruiser keeps going.

Eighteen minutes.

The door of the store opens. Cassie steps out. She's carrying two plastic bags and is wearing a beanie pulled low over her red hair and oversized sunglasses.

She looks like a hipster. Or a student.

She slides the door open and jumps in. Breathless.

"Success," she says. She dumps the bags on the floorboard.

"Any issues?"

"The cashier thought I was hungover. Told me to drink Gatorade."

I breathe out. "Good."

"I got you a present." She pulls a black hoodie and a Phillies baseball cap from the bag. "Local camouflage."

I strip off the tactical shirt right there in the cab. Put on the hoodie. Pull the cap low.

I look in the rearview. The operator is gone. I look like a construction worker off shift. Or a dad on a beer run.

"Better," she says. She's watching me. Her eyes linger on the scars on my chest before I zip the hoodie.

"Let's go," I say.

The Loews Hotel is grand, historic, and busy. A medical conference is in town. The lobby is swarming with doctors and pharma reps.

Perfect.

I park the van three blocks away in a parking garage. We walk.

"Hold my hand," I say as we approach the revolving doors.

Cassie hesitates.

"Social camouflage," I remind her. "Couples hold hands. Strangers maintain distance. We need to close the gap."

She slides her hand into mine. Her fingers are cold. Mine are rough. But the fit is—alarming.

She squeezes once. I'm here.

We walk through the doors. The lobby smells of expensive perfume and old money.

I keep my head down, letting the brim of the hat shadow my face, and guide Cassie toward the elevators, bypassing the front desk.

"Don't we need to check in?" she whispers.

"I have a key," I lie. "Just walk."

We blend into a group of surgeons heading for the elevators. I press the button for the 5th floor. The elevator is crowded. I back Cassie into the corner, putting my body between her and the rest of the world. It's a protective stance, but it looks like intimacy. I lean in, putting my mouth near her ear.

"Relax," I whisper. "You're doing great."

She leans back against the wall. Her hand is still in mine, gripping hard. I smell her—the vanilla scent lingering beneath the sweat and the dust of the road. It's intoxicating.

The elevator empties floor by floor. At the 5th, it's just us.

I step out. Turn left.

"Where are we going?" she asks.

"Room 514."

"How do you know—"

"Because I know where Cerberus keeps its contingency caches."

I stop at 514. I don't use a key card. I pull a specialized magnetic shim from my pocket—something Fuse designed. I slide it into the reader.

Click. Green light.

"After you."

We step inside.

It's not a room. It's a suite. High ceilings. Heavy drapes. A king-sized bed that looks like a cloud compared to the forest floor.

I lock the door. Throw the deadbolt. Engage the privacy latch.

"Clear," I say.

Cassie drops the shopping bags. She walks to the center of the room and spins around.

"This is a contingency cache?"

"Ghost likes his comforts," I say. "He maintains rooms in six major cities. Prepaid. Under shell corporations."

"So we're safe?"

"We're secure. For tonight."

She looks at the bed. Then at me.

"One bed," she says.

"Standard layout."

"Right."

She looks at the bathroom door. "Is there …?"

"Hot water. Soap. Towels."

"Oh God." She grabs one of the shopping bags. "I'm going to stay in there for an hour. Don't come in unless the building is on fire."

"Copy that."

She disappears into the bathroom. The lock clicks.

The window draws me in. I check the street below—no black SUVs, no sirens. Just the steady, indifferent flow of Philadelphia traffic. And I check the contingency exit. It's not elegant, but it's there. An axe and rope. Ghost is nothing if not practical.

I pull the heavy drapes closed, and darkness falls over the room.

My ribs throb, and a dull ache settles behind my eyes, deep and insistent. Exhaustion pulls at me. I sit on the edge of the bed, rolling my neck.

I need to contact the team.

I pull the burner phone from my pocket. It's risky, but the hotel Wi-Fi provides a layer of cover if I route it right.

I type a sequence.

TO: WHISPER

MSG: PACKAGE SECURE. NOISE LEVEL HIGH. NEED SITREP.

I wait.

The shower turns on in the bathroom. The sound of water hitting tile.

I close my eyes. I can imagine her in there. The water sluicing off the dirt. The steam curling around her pale skin. The way her head would tilt back.

Stop it.

The phone buzzes.

FROM: WHISPER

MSG: CHATTER IS ZERO. NO APB. NO ALERTS.

I type back.

TO: WHISPER

MSG: CONFIRM. THEY ARE GHOSTING US.

FROM: WHISPER

MSG: CONFIRMED. SILENT RUNNING. THEY ARE HUNTING DIRECT. AVOID VECTORS.

I lean back. It confirms it. Phoenix isn't using the law. It's using its own assets.

FROM: WHISPER

MSG: ALSO … STRATTON FINANCIAL IS HEMOR-RHAGING CASH. LIQUIDATING ASSETS. MOVING BILLIONS TO OFFSHORE SHELLS.

Stratton Financial. The money behind Vanguard.

TO: WHISPER

MSG: WHY?

FROM: WHISPER

MSG: UNKNOWN. LOOKS LIKE A PANIC MOVE. OR A WAR CHEST. THEY ARE CLEARING THE ACCOUNTS.

If they are clearing accounts, they are preparing for something. Or someone is running.

TO: WHISPER

MSG: KEEP WATCHING THE MONEY.

FROM: WHISPER

MSG: STAY DARK.

I kill the connection. Pull the battery.

Stratton Financial is liquidating. Why?

The water stops.

A few minutes later, the door opens. Steam billows out.

Cassie steps into the room.

She's wearing a pair of gray sweatpants and a tight black T-shirt she bought at the thrift store. Her red hair is wet, slicked back from her face. Her skin is scrubbed pink.

She looks clean. Vulnerable.

And she's looking at me.

"Your turn," she says.

I stand. "Any hot water left?"

"Maybe. If you're fast."

I grab my bag. Walk past her. The scent of soap and damp skin hits me. It's better than the woods. Better than ozone. It triggers a heavy, dragging pull in my gut that I can't ignore.

"Halo," she says.

I stop.

"The news?"

"Quiet," I say. "Too quiet. Whisper confirmed it. No APB. They're hunting us directly."

"So we're ghosts."

"For now."

She touches my arm. "Go. Take a shower. Wash the dirt off. We'll figure it out."

I go into the bathroom. Close the door.

The room is thick with steam. The mirror is fogged over.

It smells like her.

I lock the door. Lean against it for a second, closing my eyes.

I strip off my clothes. The hoodie, the jeans, the tactical gear. My body is a roadmap of violence—bruises from the grappling, the raw graze on my side, the old scars.

Steam closes in around me as I step into the shower. The water is brutally hot, stinging as it pounds into the back of my neck.

My palms brace against the tile. I watch grime spiral down the drain—dirt, dried blood, sweat.

It should be enough.

It isn't.

The tension clings. Tightens.

She's twenty feet away. In a bed. In my bed.

The thought lands heavy in my chest. I picture her curled beneath the sheets. The way she slept in the woods, pressed against me. The way she fought me during training.

A low sound tears out of me, swallowed by the spray.

My body responds before my brain can intervene. Hard, aching, relentless.

Adrenaline. Combat stress. Forced proximity.

Biology.

My hand closes around my cock. The friction is harsh, utilitarian. I work it fast, methodical—like clearing a malfunction. Resetting a system that's gone rogue.

Except my mind refuses to cooperate.

Eyes shut, she's there. The woman in the minivan. Her hand over mine. *I'm not Sofia.*

My grip tightens. Pace quickens.

I imagine her hands. Her mouth. Sinking into that heat.

"Cassie," I breathe.

The release hits hard—violent, full-body, leaving me shaking against the tile, breath ragged.

For a long moment, I don't move.

The water cools. My pulse slows.

And underneath it all is nothing. I'm hollow, and the heat is unresolved.

I didn't fix anything.

I made it worse.

This isn't an itch.

It isn't biology.

I want her.

And that is terrifying.

I turn the water off. Towel dry. My hands are steady again, but my mind is reeling.

I put on the clean jeans and T-shirt Cassie bought me. They fit, which means she noticed my size. She pays attention.

I walk back into the room.

It's dark. Cassie is asleep in the center of the massive bed.

I should sleep on the floor. Or the chair.

But the floor is hard. And my ribs are screaming.

And she left space.

I walk to the bed. Sit on the edge.

"I'm awake," she whispers.

"Go back to sleep."

"The floor looks uncomfortable."

"I've slept on worse."

"Just get in, Halo. We already shared a foil blanket in the dirt. This is an upgrade."

I hesitate.

I slide under the covers.

I stay on the edge. As far from her as possible. Back to her. Gun on the nightstand.

"Goodnight," I say.

"Goodnight."

Silence.

The mattress shifts.

She scoots across the expanse of white linen and presses her back against mine.

Warmth. Solid. Real.

"Just for warmth," she whispers.

"Right," I say. "Thermodynamics."

"Exactly."

She settles. Her breathing evens out.

I stare at the wall.

I'm a ghost hunting a machine.

But right now, the only thing that matters is the woman pressing her spine against mine.

And the terrifying realization that I would burn the world down to keep her warm.

9

"The Sanctuary"
HALO

THE WAITING IS the hardest part.

In the field, waiting is active. You scan. You calculate. You adjust your scope.

Here, in the gilded cage of Suite 514, waiting is suffocating.

We have been holed up for twenty-four hours. The heavy drapes are drawn, turning the room into a timeless twilight. The air is recycled, cool, and smells of the room service burgers we ate three hours ago.

Cassie is pacing.

She's been doing it for twenty minutes.

Every pass leaves something behind—heat, motion, awareness—like she's sandblasting me down by degrees.

Bed to window. Window to desk. Six steps. Turn. Six steps. Turn.

It scrapes at me. The room is too small, the air too warm, the hours stacked too tight. Twenty-four hours boxed in with nowhere to burn off the edge. No run. No mission. No release.

Just her.

Gray sweatpants. Black T-shirt. Bare feet. Her hair loose, catching the lamplight like it's taunting me—every turn another reminder that I'm human under the armor, no matter how hard I lock it down.

I sit in the armchair, stripping and reassembling my weapon for the third time. The metal clicks are steady. Controlled. The only thing in this room that listens when I tell it what to do.

"You're going to wear the finish off that slide," she says.

"Maintenance is discipline," I answer, not looking up. "And you're going to wear a hole in that carpet."

She stops directly in front of me. The pacing ends. The pressure spikes.

She crouches. Eye level. Too close. Close enough that the space between us disappears, and my body reacts before my mind can shut it down.

"It's a distraction," she says. "You're bored."

"I'm alert."

"You're trapped," she says softly. "Just like me."

Her fingers brush the back of my hand, right over the scar from Bogotá.

The contact is light.

The effect is not.

Something in my chest tightens—sharp, sudden—like a cable pulled too far. I've been holding this line for a day straight, every instinct screaming to move, to act, to do something with the heat crawling under my skin.

"We're safe here," she whispers. "For now. You can turn it off."

"Turn what off?"

She looks at me like she already knows the answer. Like she's been watching me fight myself all day.

"The sentry mode," she says. "The Ghost."

I lift my head.

She's inches away. I smell her soap. Feel the warmth rolling off her. Every breath she takes lands inside me like a provocation.

"If I turn it off," I say, low, tight, "I don't know what happens next."

Her eyes drop to my mouth. Stay there. When they lift again, the challenge is gone—replaced by heat and something dangerously close to trust.

"I think you do."

Last night flashes through me—pillows stacked between us like a ceasefire, her back inches from mine, my body locked down so hard it hurt. Hours of listening to her breathe, every exhale grinding me closer to the edge.

Now the pillows are gone.

She shifts closer. Her knee brushes mine. Deliberate.

Her hand slides up my arm, slow, claiming territory, settling on my shoulder. Her thumb traces my collarbone through the T-shirt like she's testing how much pressure I can take.

Stop her.

The order forms. Clean. Professional. Exactly what I should do.

But I don't move.

Her touch burns through the cotton, searing into muscle, into bone. Every stroke of her thumb rewrites something in my chest—erases protocol, smears through training, turns fourteen years of discipline into smoke.

This is a job. She is a principal. You are her protective detail.

The words feel like reading a language I used to know.

She inches closer. The heat of her radiates through the narrow gap between us, and my hands clench against my thighs so hard my knuckles ache. I'm holding onto something—control, sanity, the last fraying thread of who I'm supposed to be in this room.

"Diego," she breathes.

The name hits like a snapped line.

My real name. The one I buried under callsigns and clearances and years of making myself into a weapon instead of a man.

She says it like she knows exactly what she's pulling out of me.

My jaw locks. Molars grinding. Every muscle in my body coils so tight I'm shaking with it—this war between what I want and what I'm allowed to want. Between the oath I swore and the woman two inches from my hands.

Walk away.

I should. I know I should. Stand. Create distance. Reset the parameters. Remind her—remind myself—that I'm here because someone wants her dead, not because—

Her fingers curl into my shoulder. Tighter. Claiming.

The breath I'm holding fractures in my chest.

You cross this line, there's no coming back.

I know.

You'll compromise the mission. Compromise yourself. Everything you've built—

I know.

She deserves a protector, not a man who takes what he wants from her.

That one lands. A blade between the ribs. Because she does. She deserves someone with clean hands, a civilian life, and the freedom to give her more than a few weeks of borrowed time before the next deployment drags me back into the dark.

But she's looking at me like I'm already hers.

And I'm so fucking tired of being strong.

I set the gun down. Not gently. Final. It's cold steel. Duty. Discipline. Everything I'm supposed to be.

My hands go to her waist, and I pull her in—hard enough that she stumbles, sharp enough that she gasps. Her breath punches out, and the sound goes straight through me, rewires something fundamental.

Wrong. This is wrong.

The thought surfaces, distant, drowning. My fingers dig into the curve of her hips like I'm trying to anchor myself to something—to her, to sanity, to the last thread of resistance still screaming somewhere in the wreckage of my discipline.

She doesn't pull away.

She surges forward instead, hands fisting in my hair like she's done pretending. Her body presses flush against mine, and the contact shatters through me—days of distance, of careful space, of holding the line, obliterated in a single collision.

"Finally," she whispers.

The word brushes my lips. Close. So close I can taste it.

Stop. You can still stop.

I can't.

I don't want to.

"You have no idea—" My voice comes out wrecked, scraped raw, someone else's voice entirely. "What you're asking for."

Her grip tightens in my hair. Pulls. The sting blooms across my scalp, and the groan that tears out of me is barely human.

"I know exactly what I'm asking for—Diego."

Fuck.

The last restraint doesn't break. It incinerates.

My mouth crashes into hers—no finesse, no control, nothing left of the soldier who walked into this room. Just hunger. Days—years of starvation pour out in the drag of my teeth across her bottom lip, the way I swallow her moan like I need it to breathe.

She tastes like adrenaline. Like ruin. Like every bad decision I've ever wanted to make.

One hand slides up her spine, fingers splaying across the back of her neck, tilting her head to take her deeper. The other stays locked on her hip, grip bruising, holding her against me like I'm terrified she'll vanish if I ease up for a second.

This is a mistake.

I'll pay for it. Career, reputation, maybe my life if the distraction gets her killed.

And I kiss her anyway—harder, desperate, a man drowning who's decided he'd rather go under than let go.

She makes a sound against my mouth. Needy. Wrecked.

It destroys me.

More.

The word pounds through my blood. Overrides everything. I've spent my whole life being enough—enough control, enough discipline, enough restraint to earn the trust they put in me.

Right now, I'm not enough of anything except hers.

I continue to kiss her—rough, unfiltered, all the frustration and hunger I've been swallowing poured straight into it. No testing. No hesitation. Just need slamming into need, her mouth opening under mine like she's been braced for it.

The room closes in. The walls disappear. There's nothing left but her breath and my grip and the knowledge that whatever line I just crossed—

There's no stepping back over it.

Not during the kiss—during the half-second after, when my hands are still on her, and my body is already recalibrating, already cataloging the damage.

I break it off first.

I pull back hard enough that she stumbles a step, breathless, eyes dark and unfocused. My chest is heaving. My pulse is too fast. The room feels suddenly hostile, too small to contain what I just unleashed.

"Fuck," I mutter.

Her mouth parts like she's about to say something—but I don't let her. I turn away, rake a hand through my hair, pace two steps before stopping short like I've hit an invisible wall.

That was a mistake.

A clean one. A clear one.

I don't get to do that. Not here. Not now. Not with her.

"We can't," I say, the words coming out rough, clipped. "That can't happen again."

Silence.

I feel her behind me, still too close, still warm. The awareness hasn't faded—if anything, it's sharper now, my body still keyed up like it's waiting for the next strike.

"Because of the mission," she says quietly.

"Yes."

"And if there were no mission?"

I don't answer. I can't. Because that's not the real problem.

I turn back to her.

Her cheeks are flushed. Her breathing hasn't steadied yet. Neither has mine. Seeing the evidence of what I did—to her, to myself—tightens something ugly and protective in my chest.

"Because I lose clarity," I say. "Because I make bad calls. Because people get hurt."

"People," she repeats. "Or you."

I hold her gaze. This close, there's no hiding. No armor thick enough.

"Both."

The room feels heavier now. Charged in a different way. Not anticipation—aftermath.

She nods once, small and controlled, like she's filing the moment away where it can't cut her later.

"Okay," she says. "Then we don't do that again."

It's a lie. We both know it.

Because the line is gone, and even standing on opposite sides of the room, I can feel it—the pull, the awareness, the certainty that whatever this is, it didn't end with that kiss.

It started there.

Now I have to protect her from the very thing she just unlocked.

Myself.

The rest of the night passes in careful choreography.

She disappears into the bathroom. The shower runs for a long time—long enough that I check the window twice, the door three times, anything to keep my hands busy and my mind off the water sliding down her skin.

When she emerges, she's armored in an oversized T-shirt and sleep shorts. Wet hair dripping onto her shoulders. No makeup. No pretense.

She's never looked more dangerous.

"I'm taking the left side," she says. Matter-of-fact. Like we didn't just detonate something between us.

"Fine."

No pillows this time. Neither of us suggests it.

We lie in the dark, a foot of mattress between us that might as well be a minefield. The silence hums, thick with everything we're not saying.

Her breathing eventually slows. Evens out. Sleep pulling her under.

Mine doesn't.

Every shift of the sheets registers like a seismic event. Every soft exhale tightens the coil in my chest. Once, she rolls toward me, her hand landing on the neutral space between us, fingers curled loose in sleep.

I stare at that hand for twenty minutes.

I don't touch it.

Around 3 AM, she murmurs something. A fragment. My name —the real one—tangled in a dream.

My hands fist in the sheets.

At 4, I give up on sleep entirely. I run security checks I've already run. Review exit routes I've already memorized. Count the cracks in the ceiling. Pump out several hundred pushups. Anything to keep from rolling toward her and finishing what we started.

The hours crawl past like wounded things.

"The Calm"

HALO

MORNING COMES WITHOUT MERCY.

Gray light seeps around the edges of the curtains, thin and cold, like it's testing the room before committing. I've been awake for hours. Maybe I never really slept.

She's still in the bed.

Not my bed anymore. Not after last night. Not after what I let happen.

I'm in the chair by the window, boots on, jacket draped over the back like a barrier I can step into if I need armor fast. My weapon is disassembled on the desk again—not because it needs it, but because routine is the only thing keeping me from replaying the moment my control snapped.

The kiss. The shower. The bed.

The way it felt less like a choice and more like gravity finally winning.

I don't look at her. I don't trust myself to.

The bed shifts. Sheets whisper. I feel it anyway—the change in the air, the quiet awareness that we're both awake now, pretending otherwise.

She clears her throat. "Do you always wake up this early?"

"Yes."

A lie by omission. I'm always up eventually. Just not usually because I spent the night dismantling my own discipline.

She sits. I catch the movement in the corner of my eye. Hair mussed. T-shirt wrinkled. Bare feet finding the floor.

Too human. Too close.

She goes to the bathroom. The door clicks shut.

I exhale through my nose, slow and controlled. Count to four. Count to six. Reset. Goddamn, what is happening to me?

The breathing exercises don't help.

The shower starts. Steam creeps under the door. I remember the way she smelled last night—soap and heat and something darker that set off alarms I ignored.

I focus on the street below. Philadelphia is waking up. Commuters. Delivery trucks. Normal life. The kind that doesn't wedge two people into a hotel room and ask them to pretend nothing changed.

The bathroom door opens again. She comes out dressed— jeans this time, hoodie pulled tight like she's trying to disappear inside it.

"Coffee?" she asks.

"Sure." I try for nonchalance, and fail … Horribly.

"Great. Love a man of words."

She moves around the room, efficient, contained. We don't mention last night. We don't look at each other too long. We orbit like opposing magnets—close enough to feel the pull, far enough not to collide.

Coffee brews. The smell fills the room. I shouldn't notice how domestic it feels. I do anyway. I can't not notice her. She's becoming a part of my DNA.

She hands me a mug without touching me.

Progress.

We sit. Opposite sides of the room. The silence stretches—not awkward, exact. Loaded. Like a weapon with the safety off.

"So," she says eventually. "What's the plan today?"

"Same as yesterday. We lay low. No movement until I get a green light."

"And if you don't?"

"Then we wait. We stay dark."

Her jaw tightens. She doesn't like waiting. Fighters never do.

We spend the morning not touching.

We watch the news on mute. I scan feeds on the burner. She reads, then paces, then reads again. Every movement tracks across my awareness like a threat vector. Not because she's dangerous—but because I am.

Around noon, she stands by the window, arms crossed, staring out like she's daring the world to make a move.

"You're avoiding me." She turns. Leans back against the wall.

I don't answer.

She studies me like she did last night—quiet, assessing, too perceptive for my comfort.

"Do you regret it?" she asks.

The question lands hard. Direct. No cover. I could ask what she means, but there's no reason. We both know what she's asking. Even if I want to forget that massive slip ever happened.

"No," I say, immediately. Too fast.

"Good." She nods once. Files it away.

"That doesn't mean—"

"I know," she cuts in. "It doesn't mean anything changed."

Except everything did.

"I'm taking a shower."

"Of course you are."

The shower is another disappointment. Another empty release. I want her.

Need her.

But she's off the menu. Has to be,

The afternoon crawls. The heat between us doesn't cool—it condenses. Thickens. Every near-miss charges it more. My knee inches from hers on the couch. The way we both freeze when our hands reach for the same thing.

I stand abruptly. "I'm taking a walk. Perimeter check."

She lifts an eyebrow. "Perimeter check of the hallway?"

"I need air."

"Right. Air." She laughs, but it's brittle. Her gaze flicks down my body, lingering where it shouldn't, then snaps back to my face with something sharp in it. "Go. Check the locks. Pretend none of this matters."

I stop at the door. Don't turn around. Can't.

"It matters," I say. The words come out rough. "That's why I have to go."

I walk out before she can answer and head to the stairwell. Check the exits. Check the fire escape.

Routine. Protocol. The things that make sense.

But my mind is twenty feet back, in Suite 514.

I lean against the cold concrete wall of the stairwell. Close my eyes.

The mission has changed.

It used to be about survival. About getting her from Point A to Point B.

Now it's about her.

And that makes me the most dangerous thing in her orbit.

Because if Phoenix comes for her now, I won't just neutralize the threat.

I'll tear the world apart to keep them away from her.

And that kind of rage? That kind of focused, personal violence?

It gets people killed.

Including the people you're trying to save.

I push off the wall. Re-check the stairwell door. Secure.

The hallway is quiet. Industrial carpet, flickering fluorescent lights, the distant hum of an ice machine. Normal hotel sounds. Normal hotel smells—cleaning products and stale air and the faint mustiness of a building that's seen better decades.

Nothing out of place. No threats.

Except for the one waiting in room 514.

I head back to the room. Back to the cage. Back to her.

I don't know if I'm walking into a sanctuary or a trap.

The keycard beeps green. I push open the door.

She's exactly where I left her—curled in the armchair by the window, her legs tucked beneath her. The lamp beside her casts warm light across her face, catching the copper in her hair, the sharp line of her jaw.

She looks up when I enter.

Something shifts in her expression. Recognition. Awareness. The same tension I've been trying to outrun crackles back to life between us.

"Perimeter secure?" Her voice is casual. Too casual.

"Secure."

"Stairwell clear?"

"Clear."

"Vending machine free of assassins?"

"I didn't check the vending machine."

"Rookie mistake." She watches me hover near the door like a man who's forgotten how rooms work. "You going to come in, or are you planning to guard the hallway all night?"

I step inside. Let the door close behind me.

The room feels smaller than it did ten minutes ago. The air feels thicker. She's watching me with those green eyes, and I can see the question forming—the one I don't want to answer, the one about why I keep finding reasons to leave.

I move to the desk. Pretend to check my weapons. They don't need checking. I checked them an hour ago.

"Diego."

My hands still on the Glock.

"You've cleaned that gun three times."

"It needs to be reliable."

"You're avoiding something."

I don't answer. Can't answer. Because she's right, and we both know it, and the thing I'm avoiding is standing six feet away in an oversized T-shirt that keeps slipping off one shoulder.

The silence stretches.

She sighs.

I stand there like an idiot, holding a weapon I don't need to clean, watching her from the corner of my eye. The way she tucks her hair behind her ear. The way she chews her bottom lip when she's concentrating. The way the lamplight makes her skin glow like something out of a painting.

This is torture. Self-inflicted, entirely preventable torture.

"I'm taking a shower."

She looks up. Lifts an eyebrow.

"Again?"

"I need to clear my head."

"You took a shower two hours ago." A smile tugs at the corner of her mouth. "That's a lot of head-clearing. Should I be concerned about your hygiene standards, or is this some kind of tactical bathing protocol they taught you in special ops?"

"It's been a long day."

"Right." She laughs, but it's brittle. Her gaze flicks down my body, lingering where it shouldn't, then snaps back to my face with something sharp in it. She tilts her head, studying me. "I'm starting to notice a pattern. The longer we're alone in a room together, the more you develop an urgent need to be somewhere wet."

"That's not … It's not personal."

"No?" She unfolds herself from the chair. Stands. Takes a step toward me. "So you're not avoiding me?"

"I'm not avoiding you."

"You're not running away every time the room gets quiet, and we're forced to acknowledge that something's happening here?"

"There's nothing—"

"Diego." Her voice softens. "You're a terrible liar. It's actually kind of endearing, given your profession."

I don't have a response to that. Don't have a response to any of this. My tactical training covers ambushes, extractions, and close-quarters combat. It does not cover what to do when a beautiful woman calls me out on my bullshit with a smile that makes my chest hurt.

"Take your shower," she says. Steps back. Returns to the chair. "I'll be here when you're done. Definitely still noticing your selective relationship with personal hygiene."

I head for the bathroom.

"Tell me, Diego—when you're in there, pretending your hand is enough … Do you think about how close you just were to the real thing? Or do you have to pretend I'm someone you're allowed to want?"

I stop at the bathroom door. Don't turn around. Can't.

"It's Halo." The words come out hard. Military. "You call me Halo."

Silence. Footsteps, slow and deliberate. Every movement is a challenge.

"Halo." Her voice follows me like a heat-seeking round. "Halo is the man who keeps his hands to himself. Who builds pillow walls and pretends he doesn't watch me sleep." Closer now. Heat radiates against my back. "Halo is the man who's about to go jerk off in the shower because he's too disciplined to take what he actually wants."

My hand tightens on the doorframe. Knuckles bleaching white.

"But that kiss?" Her voice drops, soft and lethal. "That wasn't Halo. That was Diego—and he wants me so bad he's shaking with the need for me."

My jaw locks. Molars grinding. Teeth ready to crack.

"Too bad." The words scrape out like broken glass. "Diego doesn't exist anymore."

A beat. Two.

"Liar." The word lands like a bullet. Quiet. Precise. Dead center.

I close the door harder than necessary.

Her laughter filters through the wood—warm and real and entirely too pleased with herself.

The water is hot. I let it pound against my shoulders like punishment. I think of last night. Of the line I crossed. Of the way it felt to stop fighting myself.

I tell myself it won't happen again.

I tell myself a lot of things.

But my body isn't listening. I look down. I'm hard. Painfully, undeniably hard. It's an ache that runs from my groin to my chest, a physical demand for release.

It's just biology, I tell myself. Friction. Stress. Adrenaline.

I wrap my hand around myself.

I stroke, fast and efficient. Rough. The friction is good.

But it doesn't work. I close my eyes, and I don't see blank darkness. I see her. I see the way she looked in the woods, wild and dirty. The way she looked in the bed this morning, soft and sleep-warm.

I groan; the sound lost in the steam. I stroke faster, desperate to purge the need, desperate to get back to zero.

Click.

The bathroom door opens.

My eyes snap open.

Awareness hits first—pure instinct. The shift in the air. The change in pressure. The quiet certainty that I'm no longer alone.

Steam curls around her as she steps inside the bathroom, already stripped of hesitation, hoodie gone, jeans undone. Her gaze flicks once—to my face, to my hand, my cock—and something feral sparks in her expression.

She sees me. Exposed. Needing.

"Cassie," I warn. My voice is wrecked.

The shower roars. She ignores me. She pushes her jeans down, kicks them away. She's naked.

Gloriously naked.

I close my eyes, lock my jaw, and brace against the tile like it might hold me together if I lean hard enough. My hand is still wrapped around my cock, throbbing, leaking, betraying me.

"Cassie," I say again. Sharper this time. Command, not plea. "Go."

Silence.

The glass door to the shower slides open, and the sound slices through me.

"I said go," I snap.

She steps into the shower. My eyes snap open.

The water beads on her skin, tracing lines I can't follow without losing what's left of my control.

"No," she says. One word. Calm. Absolute.

"Cassie—"

"I'm not leaving." She steps closer, steam blurring the edges of her, but not the intent in her eyes. "You don't get to order me away and pretend this isn't happening."

"You don't understand what you're doing."

"I understand exactly what I'm doing." Her hand comes up, fingers closing around my wrist—not stopping me, grounding me. "You're the one pretending." Her fingers are inches from my cock. So close. So achingly close.

My breath turns shallow. Too fast. My body betrays me again, tension coiling tighter with every second she stays.

"Look at me," she says.

I don't.

Her fingers slide up my arm, slow and deliberate, mapping muscle and restraint and the places I've been holding too tight for too long.

"Look. At. Me."

I do. I take her in. The water slicks her hair back. The drops running down her throat, over her breasts. The hunger in her eyes matches my own.

Her chin lifts. Defiant. Unafraid. Choosing this.

"Tell me to leave, if you can," she challenges softly. "But if you do, say it like you mean it."

I open my mouth.

Nothing comes out.

She steps into my space. Steam. Heat. Her body so close I feel it before I touch it—feel the pull, the gravity, the inevitability of what I've been fighting since the kiss.

"That's what I thought," she murmurs. She reaches down, her fingers curling around mine.

I grab her waist—hard enough to bruise, desperation clawing its way out.

"You need to stop."

Her other hand fists in my wet hair. She pulls my head down.

"Make me."

That's it.

The last thread snaps.

I haul her up against me, the kiss crashing in rough and hungry, all restraint burned away in the collision. Her gasp is sharp, startled—and then she's kissing me back just as fiercely, mouth opening, breath breaking between us.

"Fuck," I breathe into her mouth.

Her legs wrap around me instinctively, like she's been waiting for permission I never meant to give. I lift her without thinking, her body fitting against mine like it knows exactly where it belongs.

The water beats down around us, loud and relentless. I press her back against the wet tiles, my forehead dropping to hers as I fight for breath. I grind my hips against hers, the friction unbearable.

"This is a bad idea," I say, even as my hands roam over her slick skin, memorizing the curve of her spine, the swell of her hips.

"Then stop," she challenges, breathless. "Right now."

I don't.

I carry her out of the shower instead.

Water drips from our bodies, soaking the carpet as I carry her across the room to the bed.

We fall onto the mattress, a tangle of limbs and heat. I'm over her, pinning her wrists to the pillow, needing to see her face. Her eyes are blown wide, dark green, and wrecking me.

The heat between us burns brighter now that there's no space left to pretend this isn't happening. My hands frame her face, forcing her to look at me.

"This doesn't fix anything," I warn, voice wrecked. "This makes everything worse."

Her hands slide up my arms, anchoring me, steady and sure.

"I don't want fixed," she says softly. "I want you."

The words land harder than any order.

I kiss her again—slower this time, deeper, like I'm finally allowing myself to feel everything I've been denying. Her breath stutters against my mouth. Her fingers dig into my shoulders, holding me there like she's afraid I'll disappear if she lets go.

And just like that, Halo is gone.

There's only heat, need, and hunger.

And neither of us is backing down.

"We compromised the perimeter."

She laughs, a soft, tired sound. "The door is locked, Halo."
"The internal perimeter," I correct. "My head."
She looks up at me. "Is that a bad thing?"
"Ask me tomorrow." I kiss her forehead.
But right now?
Right now, it feels like the only right thing I've done in years.

11

"The Mirror"

CASSIE

I WAKE in a tangle of sheets and limbs.

The room is still dim, but a sliver of morning light cuts across the carpet.

Halo—Diego—is asleep.

He's lying on his stomach, one arm thrown over his head, the other draped heavily across my waist. His face is turned toward me, pressed into the pillow. The harsh lines of tension around his eyes are smoothed out.

He looks—peaceful.

I study him for a long time. The rise and fall of his chest. The scars that map his history—the burn on his hand, the puckered star of a bullet wound on his shoulder.

Last night was …

I don't have a word for it. Intense doesn't cover it. It was like standing in the center of a storm and realizing the storm was holding you up.

I shift carefully, trying not to wake him. He grumbles low in his throat and tightens his arm around me, pulling me back against his chest.

"Stay," he mumbles, still half-asleep.

My heart squeezes.

I want to stay. I want to stay in this bed, in this room, in this suspended reality forever.

But my brain is waking up. The lawyer brain. The part of me that deals in facts and evidence.

We're running blind, and I don't like it. I've got that itch. Something is trying to tell me we're missing an important detail. It's right there, almost, just out of reach.

I close my eyes, trying to force the thoughts away, trying to sink back into the warmth of him, but a nagging thought from two days ago scratches at the back of my mind.

Echo Logistics.

When I was scrolling through the Vanguard files in my office—before the break-in, before the chaos—I saw something. Not the monthly retainer.

There was a sub-folder. Vendor Contracts: 2024.

I didn't open it because I was looking for bribery payments. But Echo Logistics was in the index.

If I can see that contract … If I can see who signed it …

I look at the desk.

Diego's Toughbook is there. Closed. Locked down with military-grade encryption I can't crack.

But the hotel has a Business Center.

I saw the sign in the elevator. 2nd Floor. 24 Hours.

I look at Diego. He's out deep. The first real sleep he's had in days.

If I wake him, he'll say no. He'll give me the lecture about digital footprints and signal flares. He'll lock me back in the tower.

But I'm not Rapunzel, and I'm not just the mission.

I need to bring something to the table. I need to prove that I can fight this war with him.

I slide out from under his arm. Inch by inch.

He shifts, his hand searching the empty space where I was. I freeze.

He settles. His breathing deepens again.

I slip out of bed. Grab the sweatpants and T-shirt from the floor.

I dress quickly, silently. I grab the room key card from the nightstand.

I pause at the door, looking back at him.

Just ten minutes, I promise. I'll go down and log into my cloud backup. I'll check the file and come right back.

He won't even know I was gone.

I open the door and slip into the hallway.

The Business Center is empty.

It's a glass-walled room on the mezzanine level, smelling of lemon polish and ozone. A row of desktop computers sits waiting.

I sit at the terminal in the corner, away from the door.

My hands are shaking as I wake the computer.

This is dangerous. I know it. Halo told me. Every log on is a ping.

But I'm not logging into my phone. I'm not turning on a GPS beacon. I'm accessing a secure cloud server via a public hotel network. Millions of guests do this every day. It's noise.

According to Halo, noise is good.

I open the browser. Navigate to my firm's secure portal.

LOGIN: C.BRENNAN

PASSWORD: *******

I hesitate.

If Phoenix is watching my accounts …

But they think I'm dead. Why would they watch the cloud account of a dead woman?

I hit Enter.

ACCESS GRANTED.

My heart hammers against my ribs. I'm in.

I navigate to the Vanguard Defense / Discovery / Vendors folder.

I scroll fast. My eyes scan the file names.

Eagle Transport.

Eastman Chemicals.

Echo Logistics.

There it is.

I click the file. Echo_Svc_Agreement_2024.pdf.

It opens.

I scroll past the boilerplate legalese. Past the liability waivers. I go straight to the signature page.

SIGNED:

Robert Vance, CEO, Vanguard Defense

And below it …

SIGNED:

Julianna Stratton, CEO Stratton Financial

I stare at the screen.

She signed a logistics contract for a shell company in West Virginia.

Why?

I scroll up. Look at the Scope of Services.

"Provision of secure transport and cold storage for biological assets: Class 4."

Biological assets. Class 4?

That's not logistics. That's a hazmat run. Viruses? Pathogens?

A bit of digging brings up ML-273.

I reach for the print button—then stop. No paper trail.

I need to memorize it. 1402 Blackwood Road, Terra Alta, WV.

I close the window. Log out. Clear the browser history. That should be good, right?

I stand, knees shaking. I have it. I have a link. A connection. It should be worth something, right?

I turn to leave.

And the computer screen behind me flickers.

It turns black.

Then, a spinning wheel appears—unusual for a fiber connection. It pulses like a heartbeat skipping.

I wait. Five seconds. Ten.

Then, text types out slowly, letter by letter, as if the sender is thinking hard before speaking.

H-E-L-L-O C-A-S-S-A-N-D-R-A.

My blood turns to ice.

I didn't log into a personal account. I logged into the firm's server.

Phoenix wasn't watching me. It was watching the data. It flagged the access to the Echo file.

LOCATION CONFIRMED: LOEWS HOTEL.

IP ADDRESS: 192.168.1.14

DISPATCHING.

I stumble back, knocking the chair over. It crashes loudly in the quiet room.

Dispatching.

I run.

I sprint out of the Business Center. Hit the elevator button.

Come on. Come on.

The doors open. I jam the button for the 5th floor.

Diego.

I have to get to Diego.

The elevator rises. Smooth. Silent. Agonizingly slow.

Ping. 5th floor.

I run down the hallway. My bare feet slapping against the carpet.

I reach Room 514. Jam the key card into the slot.

It doesn't turn green. It flashes red.

What?

I try again. Red.

"No," I whimper. "No, no, no."

Phoenix locked the key cards. They've hacked the hotel system.

I pound on the door.

"Diego! Halo!"

Movement inside. Heavy footsteps.

The door flies open.

Halo is standing there. He's wearing jeans, no shirt, gun in hand. His eyes are wild.

"Where the hell were you?" he roars.

"We have to go," I gasp, pushing past him into the room. "They found us."

He freezes. The anger vanishes, replaced by cold, terrifying focus.

"How?"

"I logged in. The Business Center. I found a link—Julianna Stratton, CEO Stratton Financial, biological assets." I pause, breathless. "The screen … It lagged. It buffered before it found me. But then it said 'Dispatching.'"

"Buffering?" He slams the door shut and locks it. "It lagged?"

"Yes. Like a bad connection."

"The Chicago raid," he mutters, shoving gear into his pack. "It hurt the system more than we thought. That lag just bought us a head start."

"Where are we going?"

"Pack your bag," he orders. "We have three minutes. Maybe less."

"They said 'Dispatching.' They know our room number."

"Then they aren't coming from outside," Halo says grimly. He throws my hoodie at me. "They're coming from the elevator."

He grabs the heavy dresser and shoves it in front of the door.

BOOM.

The hallway shakes.

"Too late," Halo says.

He grabs my arm and pulls me toward the window.

"We're on the fifth floor!" I scream.

"The stairs are compromised." He pulls the heavy drapes back.

"Fire escape?"

"No. Just a ledge." He looks at me. His eyes are dark, intense, and terrified. "Do you trust me?"

BOOM.

Something slams into the hotel room door. The wood splinters. The dresser slides an inch.

"Diego!"

"Do. You. Trust. Me?"

I look at the door, buckling under the assault. I look at the man who held me all night.

"Yes."

He doesn't hesitate. He moves to the closet, tearing it open to reveal the items he staged yesterday. The "contingency."

An axe. A coil of black tactical line.

He ties the rope to the radiator with a knot I don't recognize, pulling it tight to test the anchor.

Then he turns to the rope itself. In one fluid motion, he wraps it around his body—passing it under his right thigh, diagonally across his chest, and over his left shoulder.

"Friction brake," he mutters. "Old school."

He turns to me.

"Jump on my back," he orders. "Wrap your legs around my waist. Lock your ankles. Arms around my chest. Not my neck."

"What?"

"Do it. Backpack carry."

I step behind him. I jump, wrapping my legs around his waist, locking my ankles as hard as I can. I bury my face in the curve of his neck, wrap my arms around him, keeping clear of the rope.

He shifts his weight, testing the load. He reaches back with his left hand to grip my thigh, checking my lock. His right hand grips the rope behind his hip.

"Do not let go," he says. "No matter what happens, you hold on. We're exiting."

"How?"

"Don't ask questions you don't want answers to."

The door explodes inward.

Men in black tactical gear swarm the room. Laser sights cut through the dust.

"Contact!" one shouts.

Halo grabs the axe. He swings it hard, shattering the window frame and clearing the glass in one violent stroke to protect the rope from jagged shards.

Wind rushes in. Five stories of empty air.

He steps up onto the ledge. The wind whips my hair into his face.

"Breathe out," he whispers.

And he jumps.

12

"The Connection"
HALO

GRAVITY IS the only law that never bends.

We drop.

The sensation is sickening—a stomach-flipping lurch as the world vanishes upward. For a second, we're weightless, suspended in the gray morning air.

Then the rope catches.

SNAP.

My boots slam against the brick facade. Thud. The impact jars my teeth, sends a shockwave up my spine.

I kick out, braking our descent.

ZZZZIP.

The rope hisses against the heavy canvas of my jacket. The friction builds instantly, a sharp bite of heat digging into my shoulder and thigh, but the denim holds.

"Hold on!" I grit out through clenched teeth.

I feed the rope. We drop. Stop. Feed. Drop.

One kick, drop twenty feet. Brake. Kick. Drop.

Above us, the shattered window of Room 514 is a jagged mouth. A figure leans out—black helmet, tactical vest. He spots us.

"Target external! South wall!"

He raises a carbine.

Pop-pop.

Suppressed fire.

Rounds chip the brick inches from my head. Red dust sprays into my eyes.

"Don't look up!" I roar.

I release the tension. I have to go faster. I have to outrun the friction burn and the bullets.

We free fall for another story. The ground rushes up—gray asphalt, wet and hard.

I clamp down on the rope again.

"Brace!"

I aim for the dumpster—a rusted green metal beast sitting against the wall.

I clamp down hard on the rope, the friction burning through my jacket as I arrest our descent.

We hit the lid with a heavy thud, my knees bending to absorb the remaining momentum, but I keep us upright.

"Clear!"

Cassie slides off my back, her boots hitting the lid next to mine. She stumbles; I grab her arm.

We scramble off the dumpster and drop four feet to the wet asphalt of the alley.

I land in a crouch, scanning the mouth of the alley.

"Move." I separate from the rope.

Crack.

A bullet strikes the pavement inches from my boot, kicking up a spray of dirty water.

"Go!" I shove her toward the exit. "To the street! Blend!"

We stumble out of the shadows and onto the sidewalk.

The transition is jarring. Hallucinatory.

One second, we were falling out of the sky under fire. Now, we're standing on a busy Philadelphia street.

A city bus rumbles past. People in wool coats walk by.

Nobody looks up. Nobody sees the shattered window five stories high.

"The garage," I say. "Walk. Don't run."

"My ankle …" Cassie grimaces.

"Lean on me."

I wrap my left arm around her waist.

It looks like support. It looks like a boyfriend helping his girlfriend.

It feels like possession.

I pull her into my side, shielding her body with mine, scanning the rooftops, the intersections, the passing cars.

Threat vector left. Delivery truck idling. Driver is on a phone. Watch him.

Threat vector right. Police cruiser at the light. Don't look at it.

My burner phone vibrates against my ribs.

Phoenix. Or Whisper. Or the police scanner picking up the "Shots fired" call at the hotel.

I ignore it.

We cross the street. Cassie is shaking so hard the tremors vibrate through her frame into mine.

"Stay with me," I whisper in her ear. "Focus on your feet. Left. Right. Left."

"They were in the room," she whispers. Her voice is jagged. "They were right there."

"They're still there. Keep moving."

We reach the parking garage. It feels like three miles. Every siren in the distance makes my muscles lock. Every pair of eyes that lingers on us feels like a laser sight.

The maroon minivan is sitting in the shadows of the third deck. It looks impossibly normal. A stick-figure family on the back window. Dust on the bumper.

I scan the perimeter. No black SUVs. No loitering men in earpieces.

Phoenix tracked the IP address to the hotel, but they haven't triangulated the vehicle. We have a window. A small one. Maybe minutes before they lock down the city grid.

I unlock the doors. "Get in."

She climbs into the passenger seat, moving stiffly. I slide behind the wheel.

I turn the key. The engine comes to life with a low hum.

We descend the ramp, paying the attendant with cash before merging into traffic.

Ten minutes of silence.

Then the highway on-ramp. I-95 South. Away from the city.

Only then does the adrenaline recede.

And when the adrenaline leaves, rage moves in.

I slam my hand against the steering wheel.

"What the hell were you thinking?"

Cassie flinches. She's huddled against the door.

"I asked you a question," I snap. The rage is cold, sharp. "I told you every log on is a ping. You compromised your safety."

"I—"

"We were safe. We were waiting for Cerberus to build a door, and you blew the wall down. You nearly got yourself killed. You nearly got us killed."

She turns to me. Her face is streaked with tears, but her chin is up. The fire is back.

"While you were waiting for orders, I went to get answers."

"You disobeyed a direct order."

"I'm not your soldier." She shouts it. "And I'm not a package."

"You're the mission. If you die, we lose."

"If we don't fight, we lose anyway."

She wipes her face with her sleeve.

"I got a lead. I found a contract," she says, her voice shaking. "Echo Logistics. It's not just a shell company. It's a storage facility."

I grip the wheel tighter.

"Storage for what?"

"Biological assets. Class 4 pathogens. Something called ML-273."

I glance at her. "Biological?"

"It was in the service agreement. And it wasn't signed by a proxy. It was signed by Julianna Stratton. CEO of Stratton Financial."

"Connected to what?"

"A physical address. 1402 Blackwood Road, Terra Alta, West Virginia."

I look back at the road. The anger is still there, simmering, but the tactical brain is taking over.

Stratton Financials. West Virginia.

It's isolated. Hard to access.

"Are you saying that's why the money moved?" The pieces click into place. "Stratton is liquidating assets to fund the site?"

"I don't know, but it's something," Cassie says. "We aren't running blind. This is a lead, right?"

I don't know if it is or isn't, just that I'm pissed with myself. Pissed that I let emotion cloud my judgment. That I let need override my programming.

I have one job. Keep the principal intact. Instead, I lowered my defenses, fucked her, and now I find myself driving away from a manhunt.

She reaches across the console, her hand covering mine on the gear shift. She looks at my red palms.

"Your hands …"

I pull away. I can't let her touch me. Not now. "Terra Alta is five hours as the crow flies. If we go there, we're going into a hardened facility with one handgun and no backup."

"Do we have a choice?"

In the rearview mirror, Philadelphia is fading into the haze.

"No," I say. "We don't, but we need help. We're not doing this alone. Check the map in my bag. Find me a back road. We stay off the highway."

She opens my ruck and digs through until she finds a paper map.

I study her profile. The set of her jaw.

I hate that she had to do it. I hate that I let it happen.

But mostly, I hate how much I respect it.

We aren't running anymore.

We're hunting.

"The Reckoning"

CASSIE

THE SILENCE IS SUFFOCATING.

We've been driving for hours. The Philadelphia skyline disappeared into the rearview mirror somewhere around mile marker forty, replaced by the rolling brown hills of rural Pennsylvania. The sun bleeds out on the horizon, staining the clouds the color of bruises.

Diego hasn't spoken since we hit the highway.

His hands grip the wheel at ten and two. Knuckles white against the leather. His jaw is a rigid line, a muscle feathering beneath the stubble. His eyes never stop moving—rearview, side mirror, road, rearview—but he won't look at me.

I'm still wearing his thermal shirt. It smells like him—gun oil and cedar and the sharp, metallic tang of fear. My own fear. The kind that hasn't faded even though we made it out. Even though we're alive.

Anger radiates off him in waves. It fills the minivan like smoke, thick and choking. Every mile marker that flashes past is a countdown to something I'm not ready for.

I try once to break the silence.

"Diego, I—"

"Don't." One word. Sharp as a blade.

I close my mouth. Swallow the explanation, the justification, the dozen things I want to say. He's not ready to hear them. Maybe I'm not ready to say them out loud.

Because part of me knows he's right to be angry.

I logged in. I broke protocol. I painted a target on the only safe place we had because I couldn't stand feeling useless. Because I needed to do something. Because Cassandra Brennan doesn't hide in hotel rooms while other people fight her battles.

And now men with automatic weapons almost cut us down in a hotel room that smelled like room service coffee, and we're fleeing through rural Pennsylvania in a stolen minivan with stick-figure family stickers on the back window.

We're alive because he jumped out a window.

The memory keeps replaying in fractured images: the door splintering inward. The wind rushing through the shattered glass. His arm like iron around my waist. The sickening lurch of free fall. The way the rope sang while he controlled our descent with nothing but grip strength and sheer will.

And the bullet. The one that should have caught him in the shoulder.

I saw the trajectory. The muzzle flash. The angle was wrong—or it should have been right. Instead, the wind shifted. Or he moved. Or something intervened at exactly the right microsecond.

He either has a guardian angel or he's lucky as shit.

It doesn't feel like luck. It feels like something else entirely. Something I can't explain, and he refuses to acknowledge.

"We need gas."

His voice is rough. Clipped. The first words in what feels like forever.

"Okay."

He doesn't respond. Just takes the next turn, pulling into a truck stop that looks like it hasn't been updated since the Reagan administration. Fluorescent lights flicker over pumps with analog dials. A semi idles in the far corner, its driver nowhere in sight.

"Stay." He barks a one-word order, like I'm a dog.

I want to call him out on this, but his anger is too hot.

He's gone before I can respond. I watch him through the dirty windshield—the controlled stride, the way his gaze sweeps the perimeter even now. Even exhausted. Even furious.

He's still protecting me. Even as he's shutting me out.

My hands shake with too much adrenaline burning itself out inside my body. I press my hands flat against my thighs, willing them to stop. They don't. Days of accumulated terror have to go somewhere, and apparently, it's decided my nervous system is the exit route.

When he slides back behind the wheel, he doesn't start the engine. He stares through the windshield at nothing. The truck stop lights cast harsh shadows across his face, deepening the hollows under his eyes.

"Diego—"

"Not now."

The words cut. Sharp. Final.

He starts the engine. We pull back onto the road.

The silence swallows us whole.

The motel appears around nine o'clock.

It's the kind of place that takes cash and doesn't ask questions. Peeling paint, the color of old teeth. A neon sign with half the letters burned out: VAC N Y. A parking lot full of long-haul trucks and the kind of quiet desperation that clings to roadside America like mold.

"We need to get off the road." Diego's voice is flat. Operational. "Phoenix will have the highway grid locked down by morning."

He parks in the back, away from the office windows. Cuts the engine.

"Stay."

Once again, he's gone before I can respond.

I watch him through the dirty windshield—the controlled stride, the way his shoulders stay rigid even when there's no visible threat. He's still in combat mode. Still running calculations I can't see.

He returns five minutes later with a key card. Old-fashioned plastic, the kind with a magnetic stripe that's probably been copied a thousand times.

"Room 12. Ground floor."

The room is exactly what I expect. Stained carpet that might have been beige once. A TV bolted to the dresser with a chain thick enough to tow a car. Heavy curtains that smell like cigarette smoke and regret. A bathroom door that doesn't quite close.

One bed.

Diego clears the room like it's a hostile zone—checks the bathroom, the closet, the window locks, the space under the bed. Old habits. Operational muscle memory.

When he's satisfied, he turns to face me.

The door clicks shut behind us.

The silence is different now. Heavier. Charged with hours of compressed fury, looking for an outlet.

I know what's coming. The reckoning I've been bracing for since Philadelphia. Since I logged into that computer and lit a flare for Phoenix to follow.

"Diego—"

"Do you have any idea what you did?"

His voice is controlled. Barely. The calm before detonation.

"I found a lead." My own voice comes out steadier than I feel. "A real lead. Stratton's signature on biological assets—"

"You painted a target on our position." He steps closer. "You handed Phoenix our exact coordinates."

"I thought I was being careful—"

"You thought." Another step. The space between us shrinks. "You thought. That's the problem. You're not trained for this. You don't get to think. You follow protocol. My. Protocol."

"Like I said earlier, I'm not your soldier to command."

"No." His voice drops, dangerous. "You're my responsibility. And you almost got yourself killed. You almost got us both killed."

"But I didn't." I hold my ground. "We're here. We're alive. And I found something—"

"You found a trail of breadcrumbs that led a kill team straight to our door." His voice rises. Cracks. "You logged into a monitored system from a traceable IP address. You might as well have sent Phoenix an engraved invitation."

"I was on a public network. Hotel Wi-Fi. Millions of people—"

"Phoenix doesn't care about millions of people. Phoenix cares about you. About your credentials. About the specific files you accessed." He's pacing now, coiled energy looking for an outlet. "The second you opened that Echo Logistics contract, every alarm in their system went off. They didn't track the IP—they tracked the data. You touched a tripwire."

"I didn't know—"

"That's the point!" He wheels on me. "You didn't know because you didn't ask. You didn't wait. You decided that your need to contribute was more important than staying alive!"

"I was trying to help."

"You were trying to matter." The words land like a slap. "You were trying to prove that you're not just cargo. That you're more than a protection detail. What was it you said …" He pauses, then grimaces. "Right, you're not a package I can store on a shelf until I decide to move you. That Cassandra Brennan, Esquire, is too important to follow orders."

The accuracy of it steals my breath. He sees too much. Remembers too much. He always has.

"That's not—"

"You got lucky."

He's advancing now. I'm backing up. My shoulder blades hit the wall.

"Luck runs out, Cassie. I've buried people who got lucky. I've zipped body bags closed over people who thought they knew better. Good people. Smart people. People who had everything to live for and died anyway because they made one wrong call."

"I'm still here."

"Barely." He's close now. Too close. "You're here because I move fast. You're here because that rappel line held when it shouldn't have, and those bullets missed when they shouldn't have. You're here because of a dozen factors you can't control and can't count on happening again."

"So what do you want? An apology?" The words come out hot, defensive. "Fine. I'm sorry I didn't sit in that room like a good little package while you waited for permission to act."

"This isn't a courtroom." He's in my space now. Close enough that I can smell him—sweat and adrenaline and something darker underneath. "You don't get to object. You don't get to file motions. You don't get to introduce surprise evidence. Out here, you do what I say, when I say it, or you die."

"And what if what you say is wrong?"

"Then I'm wrong. But at least you're alive to complain about it."

"That's not good enough." I push back from the wall, forcing him to give ground. He doesn't. "I'm not going to spend the rest of this nightmare being a passenger. I have skills. I have a brain. I found a real lead while you were waiting for your team to call."

"A lead that almost got you killed."

"A lead that gives us a target. A location. A name." I jab my finger into his chest. "Julianna Stratton. CEO of Stratton Financial. Signed off on Class 4 biological assets. That's not nothing. That's the first real connection between the money and whatever Phoenix is actually protecting."

He catches my wrist. Holds it. His grip is iron, not painful but absolute.

"You're right." His voice is quiet now. Deadly. "It's not nothing. It's a thread. And you tugged on it without any idea what was attached to the other end." He pushes forward.

I back up until I'm against the wall. Nowhere else to go.

Then his fist suddenly slams into the drywall beside my head.

I flinch. Can't help it. The plaster cracks, raining white dust onto my shoulder.

His other hand plants on the wall, caging me. His body is a furnace of heat and fury inches from mine. His chest heaves with ragged breaths.

He looks down. Squeezes his eyes shut. His jaw works, grinding something back—words or violence or the jagged edge of whatever's tearing him apart.

When he looks up again, his eyes are burning.

"You want to know what I felt when that door blew in?" The words are raw. Wrecked. "When I saw them coming?"

I can't breathe.

"I felt everything I buried in 2019. I felt her. I felt the phone call. I felt the fucking canyon."

Sofia. The name he barely speaks. The wound he carries like shrapnel.

"Diego—"

"I can't do that again." His forehead drops to mine. His breath is ragged against my lips, hot and desperate. "I can't lose you because you decided to be brave."

"I'm not her."

"I know." His voice cracks. Splinters. "That's what terrifies me."

I should push him away.

I should be afraid of the violence coiled in his body, the fist still pressed into the ruined drywall, the way he's shaking with something barely contained.

I'm not.

I'm on fire.

Every nerve ending is lit. Every cell in my body screams for contact—for release—for something to burn off the adrenaline and anger and want that's been coiling inside me since the moment that door exploded inward.

My hand comes up before I think about it. Fists into the front of his shirt. I feel the solid heat of him through the fabric, the way his body goes instantly still—like a held breath.

I pull.

"Then stop treating me like I'm already dead."

The words leave my mouth rough, scraped raw by everything I haven't said.

I rise onto my toes, inch by inch, closing the distance. Not rushing. Never rushing. I tilt my head back, forcing him to look at me. Forcing the choice. My mouth hovers there—so close I can feel his breath ghost over my lips, warm and uneven.

Our eyes lock.

His jaw tightens. I see it. The restraint. The war he's losing in real time.

He lifts his head a fraction, like he's about to pull away. Like he's going to be strong.

Then he exhales.

It's a hard, broken sound—and that's when he snaps.

Not soft. Not careful. His mouth crashes into mine like he's been bracing for impact, like the force of it might knock the tension out of his bones.

I make a sound I don't recognize, fingers tightening in his shirt as if letting go would send me flying apart.

Heat. Pressure. Need. Want. Each one detonating all at once.

There's no space left between us. No air. Just the crackle of everything we've been holding back slamming together, bodies locked, mouths claiming, the world narrowing down to this single, violent, perfect point of contact.

And for one suspended heartbeat—nothing else exists.

We're just teeth and tongue and hours of suppressed rage channeling into something physical. Something primal.

He tastes like coffee and fury, and when I bite his lip, the sound he makes vibrates through my entire body.

He growls against my mouth—a sound that's barely human—and then his hands are everywhere. Rough. Demanding. Yanking my shirt up, palms hot against my ribs, fingers digging in hard enough to leave marks.

I match him. Claw at his hoodie. Rake my nails down his back. He hisses, arches into the pain, then kisses me harder.

"You want to fight me?" His voice is gravel against my throat. "Then fight."

I fight.

I shove at his chest. He doesn't move. I try to twist away; he pins me harder against the wall. My hands find his hair and yank. He retaliates by biting the junction of my neck and shoulder hard enough to make me cry out.

It hurts. It feels incredible. It feels like war and surrender wrapped into one.

He wins.

Or maybe I do.

It's impossible to tell where the anger ends and the wanting begins. They're the same thing now, tangled up in sweat and skin and the desperate need to feel something other than fear.

He pins my wrists above my head with one hand. The grip is bruising, inescapable. With his free hand, he tilts my chin up, forcing me to meet his eyes.

"Last chance." His voice is wrecked. "Tell me to stop, and I stop. Tell me to walk away, and I walk. But if you don't—" He grinds his hips against mine, and the friction makes my vision blur. "If you don't, I'm going to take you against this wall like I've been wanting to since the night you pepper-sprayed me."

"Don't you dare stop."

His mouth crashes into mine again, swallowing my words, my breath, my defiance. His hand leaves my chin and works at my jeans —efficient, ruthless, shoving them down my hips along with everything underneath.

Then his fingers are on me. Inside me. Two of them, curling exactly where I need them, while his thumb finds the spot that makes my knees buckle.

"This what you wanted?" His voice is dark. Dangerous. "To be seen? To be noticed?" He pumps his fingers harder, and a moan tears out of me. "I see you, Cassie. I fucking see you."

I can't answer. Can't think. The pleasure builds in sharp, relentless waves, cresting toward something devastating.

"Look at me."

My eyes fly open. His are black. Bottomless. Burning with something that looks like fury and worship in equal measure.

"When you come, you look at me."

I shatter.

The orgasm rips through me without warning—violent, consuming, pulling sounds from my throat I don't recognize. He watches every second of it. Drinks it in like he's memorizing the destruction.

Before I can recover, he's freed himself and lifted me in one motion. My back scrapes against the wall, my legs wrap around his waist, and then he's inside me—hard and deep and devastating.

I cry out. Dig my nails into his shoulders hard enough to leave marks.

"That's it." He starts to move. "Fight me. Take it. Show me you're still here."

I'm here. God, I'm here.

He doesn't slow down. Doesn't gentle. He takes me against that wall like he's trying to exorcise something—demons or ghosts or the memory of the woman he lost. Every thrust is a sentence he can't say. Every groan against my throat is a confession he's not ready to make.

I meet him stroke for stroke. Demand more. Demand everything.

"Harder."

He obliges. Shifts the angle. Drives deeper until I'm not sure where he ends and I begin.

The second orgasm builds faster than the first. The tension coils in my core, spreads through my limbs, turns my muscles to liquid.

"Diego—" A warning and a plea.

"I've got you." His hand slides between us, finds the spot that's still throbbing from before. "Come for me. Now."

I don't have a choice.

The orgasm hits like a wave breaking—sudden, violent, crashing through me with enough force to steal my voice. I shatter against him, shaking, gasping his name.

He follows a moment later. A guttural sound tears from somewhere deep in his chest, his hips stuttering, his entire body going rigid against mine.

We stay there, pinned against the wall, breathing hard. His forehead rests on my shoulder. My fingers are tangled in his hair. Neither of us moves.

The anger is spent.

What's left is raw. Exposed.

He carries me to the bed.

Lays me down on the scratchy comforter. Strips away the rest of our clothes with hands that are almost gentle now. Almost.

Then he's over me again. Inside me again. Slower this time, but no less intense. Like he's trying to apologize without words. Like he's trying to find a version of this that isn't war.

When we finally finish, I'm wrecked. Boneless. Floating somewhere between consciousness and oblivion.

He rolls off me. Lies on his back. One arm thrown over his eyes.

14

"The Truth"

HALO

I WAKE with her wrapped around me.

Sunlight cuts through the gap in the curtains, sharp and thin, slicing across the stained carpet like a blade. The room smells like sex and sweat and something softer underneath—her. Vanilla and sleep and the particular warmth of a woman who stayed.

She's still asleep, her head on my chest, her breath warm against my skin. Her hair is a tangled riot of red across my shoulder, catching the light in strands of copper and rust. One arm is draped over my waist, possessive even in sleep. Her leg is hooked over mine, skin against skin, like she's afraid I'll disappear if she lets go.

I should get up. Check the perimeter. Contact the team. Run surveillance on the parking lot, verify our exit routes, confirm the van hasn't been tagged overnight.

I don't move.

Instead, I lie here like a civilian. Like a man with nowhere else to be. I count her breaths—slow, steady, peaceful in a way that seems impossible given everything we've survived. I trace the curve of her shoulder with my eyes, memorizing the scatter of freckles across her pale skin, the way her lashes rest against her cheeks.

A few days ago, she was a mission parameter. A package to extract and protect. A name on a file.

Now she's this. Whatever this is.

She stirs. Shifts. Her leg slides higher over mine, and the friction sends heat pooling low in my gut—a slow, lazy burn that has nothing to do with danger and everything to do with her.

Her eyes open. Green and sleep-soft, looking at me like I'm worth looking at. Like I'm something other than a weapon with a pulse.

"Morning."

"Morning."

She stretches against me. Deliberate. Her body presses into all the right places, and I'm suddenly, painfully aware that we're both still naked under the scratchy sheets. That there's nothing between us but skin and want and the fading echoes of last night.

"We should get moving," I say.

I don't move.

"Probably." She doesn't either.

Her hand slides up my chest. Traces the scar on my collarbone —the old bullet wound from Fallujah, puckered and faded to silver. Her fingers are light, exploratory, mapping the terrain of damage and survival like she's reading braille.

"This one?" she asks.

"Iraq. 2014."

Her hand moves lower. Finds the knife scar along my ribs. The rough patch of healed shrapnel on my hip.

"And these?"

"Colombia. Syria." The words come out rougher than I intend. Her touch is doing something to my brain—short-circuiting the tactical channels, flooding them with something warmer.

Her palm comes to rest flat over my heart. The beat is steady. Slower than it should be for a man who's spent the last few days keeping her alive.

"Cassie—"

"Shut up."

She kisses me.

This time there's no anger to burn through. No fear to exorcise. Just want—clean and simple and devastating in its simplicity. Her mouth is soft against mine, unhurried, tasting like sleep and the faint ghost of the cheap motel coffee from last night.

I roll her beneath me. Take my time.

It's different in daylight. No shadows to hide in. No darkness to blame. No adrenaline demanding release.

This is a choice.

Deliberate.

Conscious.

Two people reaching for each other because they want to, not because they're drowning.

I watch every expression that crosses her face. Every gasp, every shudder, every moment she comes apart under my hands. The way her lips part when I find the spot on her neck that makes her breath catch. The way her back arches when I trail my mouth lower.

She's beautiful like this. Not the polished beauty of the attorney in the Georgetown apartment—that woman in her tailored suits and courtroom armor. This is something rawer. More real. Her hair spread across the pillow like a sunset. Her skin flushed pink. Her eyes locked on mine like I'm the only thing in the world worth seeing.

"Diego." My name is a whisper on her lips. A prayer. A demand.

I move inside her slowly. Deliberately. Memorizing the way she feels, the sounds she makes, the way her hands grip my shoulders like she's trying to anchor herself to me. To this. To whatever impossible thing is building between us.

Last night was a collision. Two people crashing together in the dark, all sharp edges and desperate need.

This is a conversation.

I see you, every touch says.

I choose you, every movement answers.

I'm here, her body whispers against mine.

I know, mine replies. I know.

We move together in the thin morning light, the silence broken only by breath and the rustle of sheets. Outside, a truck rumbles past on the highway. Inside, time stretches. Slows. Becomes irrelevant.

When she finally shatters around me, my name on her lips like something sacred, I follow her over the edge. The release is different this time. Softer. More terrifying.

Because this isn't just sex. This isn't just adrenaline, fear, or proximity.

This is something I don't have a tactical term for.

She's smiling when I finally pull back, rolling onto my side but keeping her close. A real smile. The first one I've seen since DC. It transforms her face, smoothing away the fear, exhaustion, and grief of the past few days.

"We really need to get moving now."

"I know."

Neither of us moves for another ten minutes. We just lie here, tangled together, breathing in sync. Her fingers trace lazy patterns on my chest. My hand rests on the curve of her hip, thumb stroking the soft skin there.

It feels like a crime. To be this peaceful in the middle of a war.

It feels like survival. The only kind that matters.

She's the one who finally breaks the spell.

She sits, stretching, and the sheet falls away from her body. I watch her—the curve of her spine, the way the light catches the red in her hair—and something tightens in my chest.

Then she looks up at me and her brow furrows. Her eyes are bright. Not tears, exactly, but something close.

"You keep sacrificing pieces of yourself. The bruises. The exhaustion. At what point do you run out of pieces?"

The question hits harder than it should.

Her thumbs trace circles on my palm.

"When I think of all the ways you could be hurt …"

"But I wasn't. More importantly, you haven't been hurt." I pull her hand to my mouth. Kiss her palm.

"Halo," she says, softly. "You really do have a guardian angel watching over you."

She doesn't laugh. She looks at me like she's just realized what I've risked to keep her alive. The full weight of it settles behind her eyes.

"Those bullets," she says slowly. "On the wall. When we were rappelling. They should have hit you."

"They missed."

"It shouldn't have. I saw—" She stops. Shakes her head. "Something moved. Or you moved. Or the wind changed. I don't know. But one missed when it shouldn't have."

"That's the job. Sometimes I get lucky."

"That's not luck." Her grip tightens on my hands. "That's you. That's whatever it is that keeps you alive when everyone around you dies."

"Cassie—"

"I'm serious." She meets my eyes. "You've survived things that should have killed you. The bullet wounds. Syria. Colombia. The canyon."

"The canyon killed someone I loved."

"But not you." Her voice is fierce. "Never you. Why?"

The question hangs in the air between us. I don't have an answer. I've never had an answer. The other operators joke about it —Halo and his guardian angel—but the truth is simpler and more terrifying.

I survive because the universe hasn't gotten around to killing me yet.

Or maybe …

Maybe I survive because I haven't found something worth dying for since Sofia.

Until now.

"I don't know," I say finally. "I just do."

"Then keep doing it. Whatever it takes. Keep surviving."

"I will."

"Promise me."

"I promise."

It's the easiest promise I've ever made. And the most impossible to keep.

But it's time to move. Reluctantly, we get out of bed, shower, and head out to the minivan. A few miles down the road, I find a small gas station outside of nowhere. There's a payphone bolted to the brick wall like a relic from a dead century.

Which is perfect.

The gas station is a squat cinder block box with a faded Mobil sign and windows clouded with decades of road grime. Two pumps out front, the old-fashioned kind with analog dials. A rusted pickup parked by the air pump. No other cars. No surveillance cameras visible.

Perfect.

Cassie waits in the van while I make contact with my team. She's dressed now—jeans, one of my hoodies swallowing her frame, her hair pulled back in a ponytail. She looks younger like this. Less like an attorney. More like a grad student on a road trip.

The fiction almost works if you ignore the fear in her eyes.

I walk to the payphone. Lift the receiver and feed quarters into the slot—actual quarters we found in the van, because the universe apparently decided that payphones and I would be friends today—and dial the relay number from memory.

Ring. Ring. Ring.

Third ring. Click.

"Designation."

"Halo-Seven-Seven-Delta."

"Hold for verification."

Static. Forty-five seconds of nothing. Long enough for me to scan the parking lot twice, check the tree line, and clock the old man shuffling out of the station with a coffee cup.

Then Ghost's voice comes through, scrambled but clear, "Brother. You're alive."

"Barely. The hotel was compromised. Package intact."

"We heard about the hotel. Lit up the whole damn city." His voice is tight. Controlled. The voice of a man who's been awake for too many hours, running too many operations. "Phoenix coordinated multiple strikes after your position was flagged. Hit three other assets in DC."

"What?"

"I'm there, mopping up the aftermath in D.C.. All are somehow connected to Meridian Pharmaceuticals or Echo Logistics."

"Echo Logistics?" Shit. I know exactly what happened. "I've got intel."

"You do?"

I relay the intel about Stratton Financial. The biological assets. The Terra Alta address. The contract Cassie found with the CEO's signature.

Ghost goes quiet for a moment. I hear the click of keys—he's running the address through our database.

"How solid is your intel?"

"Couldn't be more solid."

"Your lawyer drew a direct line to Stratton. CEO signature on biological storage?"

"Straight as an arrow."

"That's not a coincidence. That's a smoking gun."

"I know—and I know what we need to do."

"I know what you're going to say, and you already know I don't like it, but we need to see what's there before they scrub it clean."

"Agreed."

"What's your status?" Ghost's voice remains calm, measured, the voice that pulled me out of Colombia when I was bleeding out on a warehouse floor with a cartel hit squad closing in.

"Mobile. We're about six hours out."

"Recon only." His tone sharpens, steel under the calm. "You confirm the location, document what you find, and get out. No engagement. No breach. No heroics."

"Copy that."

"Diego." He uses my real name. That's never good. "Don't be a hero. Heroes die. Operators complete missions."

"Understood."

"I mean it. You've got a high-value civilian with you who represents our best chance of taking down Nexus legally. Do not risk her life. You get eyes on that site, and you wait."

"Copy that, but ..."

"But, what?"

"She's not good at listening. Cassie wants to check it out."

"Of course she does. They all want to help, even when it's likely to get them killed. Listen, check in when you have eyes on the target. Do not engage. I'm lean on support. Fuse is in the Cascades, recovering. Brass is still officially dead. Can't risk him in the field. I'm stuck in DC."

"What about Whisper or Torque?"

"They're supporting Guardian HRS on an op in Europe. They're headed back, but not for eighteen hours."

"That's too long. What Cassie found indicates they're moving the ML-273. Whatever it is, it's important, and we need more intel."

"Not arguing that." Ghost pauses. "Look, I may have a solution. Thorne."

"Thorne?"

"He works solo and is near you. I'm sending him your coordinates. Don't let him spook you; he's quieter than you are."

"Some random guy? I don't know about that."

"Cool your jets. He was going to sign on with Guardian HRS, but has family in Seattle. Wasn't going to activate him until I ran it by the team, but he's close."

"Thought you said he was in Seattle?"

"His parents live there. He has a little girl. Cancer. She's finishing treatment at CHOP, so he's close."

"No way am I taking a man away from his sick kid for an op."

"It's either that, or send you in alone, and I'm not doing that. Don't worry about Thorne; his girl is ringing the bell today. His parents are with him. I'll talk it through with him, but that's all I've got."

"We're a good six hours or so out."

"Call when you get there. Keep me up to speed. No heroics. Your primary mission remains. Keep Cassie Brennan breathing."

"Will do."

"Ghost out."

The line goes dead.

I stand there for a moment, holding the receiver. The plastic is warm from my grip, slick with the sweat of my bandaged palm.

Recon only.

I think I can do that, but something tells me whatever's in that facility, Phoenix will protect it at any cost.

I hang up the phone. Walk back to the van.

"What did they say?" Cassie's already half-turned in the passenger seat, watching me approach. Her lawyer instincts are in overdrive, reading my body language, cataloging the tension in my shoulders.

I slide behind the wheel. Close the door.

"Phoenix coordinated multiple strikes after your position was flagged." The words taste like ash. "Three assets in DC. All dead."

Her face goes pale. "Because of me."

"Because of Phoenix. Because they're scared of what you found." I start the engine. "That's not on you."

"But if I hadn't logged in—"

"Then we wouldn't have the Terra Alta address. We wouldn't know about the biological assets being moved. We'd be hiding in a hotel room waiting for them to find us." I pull out of the gas station lot, checking the mirrors.

She's quiet for a moment. Processing.

"What about your team? Can they join us?"

"Stretched thin. Ghost is going to send someone, or try to. Name's Thorne. He's new to us, but …"

"So we're on our own?"

"For now." I merge onto the highway, heading south toward the West Virginia border. "Ghost authorized reconnaissance. We look, we document, we leave. No engagement. No breach."

"And if something goes wrong?"

"We handle it."

She nods. Her jaw is set, her eyes fixed on the road ahead. Not the frightened attorney from five days ago. Something harder. Forged in fire.

"From this point forward, we're completely dark," I say. "No phones. No digital footprint. Phoenix can't track what doesn't ping."

"Analog ghosts."

"Exactly."

The highway stretches ahead. West Virginia mountains rising in the distance, their peaks shrouded in a gray haze. We have half a day of driving. Hours of empty road and silence, and the weight of everything we haven't said.

"Diego?"

"Yeah?"

"What you said last night. About 2019. About Sofia."

My hands tighten on the wheel.

"You've told me some of it. The car crash. The canyon." She pauses. "But there's more, isn't there? Something you haven't said."

The question hangs in the air. I could deflect. Change the subject. Lock the ghost back in its box where it belongs.

I've done it a thousand times. With Ghost. With Brass. With the shrinks the Navy sent me to after I came back from Colombia with blood on my hands and nothing in my eyes.

But Cassie's not the Navy. She's not my team.

She's—something else.

"Yeah," I say finally. "There's more."

She doesn't push. She waits.

The silence stretches between us, filled with the hum of tires on asphalt and the soft whisper of the heater. Mile markers flash past. 47. 48. 49.

The silence feels like an opening. Like she's giving me space to step through when I'm ready.

Except she goes first.

"I won a spelling bee when I was eight."

I glance at her. She's looking out the window, watching the mountains slide past.

"I came home with this trophy. Gold plastic. My name engraved on the base. 'Cassandra Brennan, First Place.' I was so proud."

Her voice is soft. Distant. Like she's narrating a memory that belongs to someone else.

"The house was empty. My dad was working a double shift—he always worked doubles back then, before his promotion. My mom was at the hospital for an extra shift. My sisters were at their own activities. Megan had debate team. Riley had art class."

"So you waited."

"Three hours. At the kitchen table. Holding my trophy." She laughs, but there's no humor in it. Just the hollow echo of a wound that never quite healed. "I remember the way the plastic felt in my hands. Cheap. But important. The most important thing in my whole eight-year-old world."

I don't say anything. Just listen.

"When my mom finally got home, she was exhausted. I remember the way she looked—the scrubs, the bags under her eyes, the way she dropped her keys on the counter like they weighed a hundred pounds." Cassie's voice catches. "She looked at the trophy and said, 'That's nice, honey. Did you do your homework?'"

"That's it?"

"That's it." She turns to look at me. "And that was the pattern. Every report card. Every award. Every accomplishment. 'That's nice, dear.' 'We're proud.' But they were always distracted. Always looking past me. Looking at Megan's med school applications. Looking at Riley's latest crisis. Looking anywhere but at me."

"The invisible daughter."

"I thought if I was perfect enough, they'd have to see me. If I achieved enough, I'd finally matter." She shakes her head. "Valedictorian. Georgetown. Top of my class at law school. Youngest associate partner at Morrison & Vale. And still—still—when I called my dad about the Vanguard case, the biggest case of my career, he said, 'That's great, sweetheart. Megan just got promoted to Chief of Surgery. We're throwing a party Friday. You'll come, won't you?'"

"Jesus."

"That's why I went to that Business Center." Her voice is steady now, but I hear the crack underneath. The fault line running through everything she does. "That's why I couldn't just hide in that hotel room. Because if I disappear—if I go invisible again … Did I ever really exist? Was any of it real, or was I just—background noise? A supporting character in everyone else's story?"

The highway unreels in front of us. I grip the wheel. Process what she's telling me.

The woman who fights like hell to be seen. Who took on a trillion-dollar corporation because disappearing into obscurity was worse than dying. Who couldn't stay hidden in Philadelphia because invisibility feels like death.

It all makes sense now.

"Your father," I say. "The cop."

"Twenty-six years on the Boston PD." Her voice softens with grief. "He died three years ago. Heart attack at a Little League game. Died doing something good."

"I'm sorry."

"He was a good man. Just—not good at seeing me." She wipes her eyes with the back of her hand. "I keep thinking… If I'd been the one to get promoted. If I'd been the one who needed rescuing, like Riley. Would he have seen me then?"

"He saw you."

"He didn't."

"Cassie." I reach across the console. Take her hand. "He saw you. He just didn't know how to show you."

"I know." A small smile. "I'm starting to believe it, but it doesn't help with feeling invisible."

She gave me something real. Now it's my turn.

"Sofia was pregnant."

The words come out harder than I intended. Cassie goes still beside me.

"Eight weeks. I didn't know." My hands are white on the wheel. The bandages pull tight across my abraded palms. "She was going to tell me when I got back from Syria. Wanted to do it in person. Wanted to see my face."

"Diego …"

"I found out two days after the funeral. Her sister told me." The name scrapes past my teeth. "She thought I knew. She said, 'Hey at least you didn't have to bury both of them.'"

"What? What a callous thing to say. You did. You buried both of them."

"Yeah, but the baby wasn't born. We weren't married. It was the family's disgrace. Therefore, it never existed."

"Oh, Diego. I'm so sorry. It did. It definitely did."

The highway blurs. I blink it clear.

"Both of them. My girlfriend and my ..." The word won't come. It's been six years, and the word still won't come.

"Your child."

"Yeah." The confirmation feels like a knife between the ribs. "My child. Eight weeks old. The size of a raspberry, apparently. That's what the internet says. I looked it up. After. Like knowing the size would make it feel more real."

"Did it?"

"No. Nothing made it real. Nothing made it make sense." I stare at the road. "I could have had a family. A reason to come home. A life that wasn't—" I gesture vaguely at the van, the road, the endless running. "This."

Cassie's hand finds mine. She doesn't try to fix it. Doesn't offer platitudes or comfort or the hollow reassurances that people always offer when they don't know what to say. She just holds on.

"That's why you said you couldn't do it again." Her voice is quiet. "Lose someone. Someone who mattered."

"I went to Colombia after the funeral. Ghost found me three months later in a cartel warehouse, bleeding out, with six dead sicarios on the floor." I pause. "I wasn't trying to survive. I was trying to find the men who killed her. I was trying to make them pay. And if I died in the process—"

"You wanted to die."

"I wanted to stop feeling. Death seemed like the easiest way to do that."

"But you survived."

"Ghost dragged me out. Patched me up. Offered me a choice." I glance at her. "Join Cerberus and fight the right way, or spiral into the dark and die alone."

"You chose to fight."

"I chose to stop being Diego Martinez. I buried him in that canyon with Sofia and the baby that never was. Halo is what's left."

She's quiet for a long moment. The miles unspool beneath us. The mountains grow closer, their peaks sharper against the darkening sky.

"What was she like?" Cassie asks, finally. "Sofia."

The question catches me off guard. No one asks about Sofia. They talk around her. They reference her like a footnote. But no one asks who she actually was.

"Brave," I say. "Stubborn as hell. She was a journalist, investigating cartel corruption in Mexico City. She thought the truth mattered more than her safety." A pause. "She was wrong."

"She sounds like someone I would have liked."

"You would have hated each other." A ghost of a smile. "You're too similar. Both convinced you can take on the world alone. Both wrong."

"Maybe she taught you something."

"She taught me that love is a liability. That caring about someone makes them a target."

"And now?"

I look at her. The woman who refused to be invisible. The woman who jumped out of a five-story window because she trusted me. The woman who's sitting here, holding my hand, asking about a ghost I've never let anyone else see.

"I'm not sure about anything," I say. "People say I'm lucky. That I've got a guardian angel looking out for me, but I think I'm cursed, and all I know is that I can't lose you the way I lost her."

"You won't."

"You don't know that."

"I know you." Her grip tightens on my hand. "I've watched you for days. I've seen what you do. How you move. How you think. You're not the man who lost Sofia in a canyon. You're the man who rappelled down a building to save me. You're the man who walked into my apartment with a plan and walked out with me alive."

"That doesn't mean—"

"It means you're not cursed." Her voice is fierce now. Certain. "It means luck isn't the enemy. It means sometimes the universe puts people in your path for a reason. And maybe—" She stops. Takes a breath. "Maybe I'm here to be another tragedy you survive. Maybe I'm here to be something else."

"What?"

"I don't know yet." She lifts my hand. Presses her lips to my knuckles. "But we're going to find out."

We drive in silence for a while after that. But it's a different silence. Lighter. The ghosts are still there—Sofia, the baby, the canyon—but they're not crushing anymore. They're just—present. Acknowledged.

Cassie breaks the silence first.

"You didn't kill her."

"I wasn't there to protect her."

"You were doing your job. Protecting people in Syria. That's what you do." She squeezes my hand. "The cartels killed her. They murdered a woman and her baby because she found truth. That's not on you."

"I should have—"

"Done what? Read her mind from the other side of the world? Predicted cartel hit squads?" Her voice sharpens. "You're not God. You're just a man who loved someone and lost her. That's a tragedy. It's not your fault."

Something cracks open in my chest. Something I've kept sealed for six years.

And since we're sharing …

"You're not invisible." The words come out rough. Raw.

"What?"

"You said you thought you had to be perfect to matter. To be seen." I glance at her. "You're the loudest person in my world. You have been since you hit me with that pepper spray."

She laughs—wet, shaky.

"That's a terrible meet-cute."

"It's ours."

I lift her hand. Press my lips to her knuckles.

"You matter. Not because of your cases or your grades or your goddamn spelling bee trophies. You matter because you're you.

Because you fight. Because you don't quit. Because you see things other people miss and you refuse to look away."

"I'm starting to believe that."

"Good. Because I'm going to keep telling you until you do."

The road narrows as we cross into West Virginia. Gravel under tires. Trees pressing close on both sides, their bare branches scratching at the sky like skeletal fingers. The last of the daylight bleeds out behind the ridge line, turning the world to shades of gray and shadow.

"Should be the next turn. Blackwood Road."

I slow the van. Kill the headlights. We creep forward, the engine a low murmur in the gathering dark.

The turnoff appears—a dirt track cutting through the trees, marked only by a faded sign half-swallowed by undergrowth. I drive past and stop the van a quarter mile out. Kill the engine.

Binoculars up. I scan the perimeter, moving systematically from left to right. Looking for the things that shouldn't be there. The shadows that move wrong. The glints of metal that might be cameras, tripwires, or worse.

The facility appears through the trees: Chain-link fence topped with razor wire, rusted in places where the weather has eaten through the galvanizing. Industrial buildings—prefab metal, institutional gray, the kind of anonymous architecture that screams government contract. Three structures visible: a main building, a smaller outbuilding, and what appears to be a generator shed. No lights. No vehicles. No movement.

The gate is open. Swinging slightly in the wind.

"What do you see?"

"It's been cleared."

"How can you tell?"

"No guards. No patrols. Gate's not just unlocked—it's abandoned. Look at the weeds growing through the gravel by the entrance. That's at least a week of neglect. Maybe two." I lower the binoculars. "Whoever was here left in a hurry."

"Or they want us to think that."

"Maybe." I check my weapon. Magazine seated. Round chambered. "Ghost said recon only."

"And?"

"And that was before we drove six hours to find an empty facility." I look at her. "Whatever Stratton was storing here, they moved it. But people in a hurry leave things behind."

"Evidence."

"Maybe."

She meets my gaze. Steady. Ready. Not the frightened attorney from DC. Something harder. Something forged.

"We go in. Together."

"Cassie—"

"You need someone watching your back. And I need to see what I almost died for."

I stare at her for a long moment. The woman who pepper-sprayed me in a Georgetown apartment. The woman who climbed down a fire escape under gunfire. The woman who jumped out a window because I asked her to trust me. The woman who somehow became the only thing in my life worth protecting.

I reach into the pack. Pull out a flashlight. Hand it to her.

"Stay behind me. Move when I move. Stop when I stop. If I say run, you run. No arguments."

She takes the flashlight. Our fingers brush.

"No arguments."

"I mean it, Cassie. This isn't a courtroom. There are no objections, no sustained, no approach the bench. If something goes wrong in there, you do exactly what I say, exactly when I say it."

"I understand."

"Do you? Because yesterday you logged into a monitored system against direct orders. Yesterday—"

"Yesterday, I learned what happens when I don't listen." Her voice is quiet. "I saw those men come through the door. I saw what they would have done to me—to us. I'm not going to make that mistake again."

I study her face in the fading light. Looking for doubt. Looking for the fear that might make her freeze at the wrong moment.

All I see is determination.

"Okay." I open my door. "Let's go."

We step out of the van into the gathering dark.

The air is cold, sharp with the smell of pine and dead leaves and something else underneath—something chemical, faint but present. The facility looms ahead of us, its metal walls catching the last light of day.

The gate swings in the wind. Back and forth. Back and forth.

Waiting.

I pull my weapon. Check the safety. Look at Cassie one more time.

"Stay close."

We move forward into the dark.

The facility waits—silent, abandoned, holding secrets neither of us is prepared to find.

15

"The Breach"

CASSIE

THE FENCE LOOMS in the darkness like a promise of violence.

Twelve feet of chain-link topped with razor wire, the coils catching what little moonlight filters through the clouds. Beyond it, the facility hunkers against the mountainside—three buildings of prefab metal and institutional gray, the kind of architecture designed to be forgotten.

Diego moves ahead of me, a shadow among shadows. He's different out here. In the van, in the motel rooms, in the quiet spaces between danger, I can almost forget what he is. Almost see just the man—the one who holds my hand, who told me about Sofia, who looks at me like I'm something worth protecting.

Out here, there's no almost.

He flows through the darkness with a predator's economy, each step deliberate, each pause calculated. His head moves in slow sweeps—left, right, up, scanning angles I wouldn't think to check. The gun in his hand is an extension of his arm, as natural as breathing.

This is Halo. This is what he was built for.

Watching him work is terrifying and beautiful in equal measure.

He holds up a fist. Stop.

I freeze. The night sounds press in—wind through bare branches, the distant hoot of an owl, the faint mechanical hum from somewhere inside the facility. My heart pounds against my ribs, too loud in the silence.

Diego crouches near a concrete post, studying something on the ground. After a moment, he waves me forward.

"Sensor," he breathes, barely audible. "Motion-activated. But look."

I crouch beside him. A small black box is mounted on the post, its lens pointed toward the approach we just used. A red light should be blinking. It isn't.

"Dead?"

"Or disabled." He frowns. "Recently. The housing's clean—no dust buildup, no weathering on the mount. This was active within the last week."

"They turned off their own security?"

"They abandoned it." He stands, scanning the tree line behind us. "Phoenix assets don't abandon infrastructure unless they're running from something worse than intruders."

"What's worse than intruders?"

"Phoenix itself." His jaw tightens. "When the AI decides you're no longer useful, you don't get a severance package. You get a cleanup crew."

The implication settles into my bones. Whoever was running this facility didn't leave because of us. They left because Phoenix designated them expendable.

We move to the fence. Diego produces a tool from his pack—something that looks like heavy-duty wire cutters crossed with surgical scissors. He works quickly, snipping through the chain-link in a vertical line, then peeling back the metal like opening a wound.

"Through. Stay low."

I duck through the gap. The cut edges of the fence snag at my hoodie, and I have to twist to pull free. Diego follows, smooth and silent, then bends the fence back into roughly its original position.

"Won't that fool anyone who looks?"

"It'll fool someone who glances. That's all we need." He checks his watch. "If Phoenix still had this site under active surveillance, we'd already be dead. The fact that we're not tells me two things."

"What?"

"One: they've written off this location. Whatever was here, they've moved or destroyed." He starts toward the main building, gesturing for me to follow. "Two: Phoenix is slow right now. Wounded. After Chicago, it pushed itself into the distributed cloud to survive, but that fragmented its processing power. It can't run pattern recognition as fast as it used to. Can't coordinate responses in real time."

"So we have a window."

"A small one. Days instead of hours. Seconds instead of split-seconds." He pauses at the corner of the first building, checking the sight lines. "But that window is closing. Every day Phoenix spends rebuilding, it gets faster. Smarter. More dangerous."

"Then we'd better move."

He glances back at me. In the darkness, I can't read his expression, but something in his posture shifts. Approval, maybe. Or surprise.

"Stay close."

The main building's door is unlocked.

That wrongness registers immediately. A facility storing biological assets—Class 4, according to the contract I found—should have layers of security. Biometric locks. Armed guards. Cameras tracking every approach.

Instead, we walk through a door that swings open at Diego's touch, hinges groaning in the silence.

The smell hits first.

Chemical. Sharp. Antiseptic layered over something organic and unsettling. It reminds me of the biology labs at Georgetown, but deeper. Richer. The smell of things growing where they shouldn't.

"Lights?" I whisper.

"Flashlights only. Low beam. Stay behind me. Step where I step."

The beam cuts through the darkness, illuminating a reception area that looks like it was abandoned mid-shift. A desk with a computer monitor—dark, the tower missing entirely. A coffee mug with dried residue at the bottom, a ring staining the fake wood. A jacket draped over the back of a chair, like someone meant to come back for it.

"They left fast," I say.

"Within hours. Maybe less." Diego moves past the desk, checking the hallway beyond. "Computer's gone—they took the drives. But they didn't have time to clean up the personal effects."

I look at the jacket. Navy blue. A woman's cut, based on the shoulders. A security badge is still clipped to the lapel—the photo shows a middle-aged woman with tired eyes and gray-streaked hair. The name reads: PATRICIA HOLLOWAY, RESEARCH COORDINATOR.

I wonder if Patricia Holloway is still alive. I wonder if Phoenix let her run, or if she's already a body in a ditch somewhere, staged to look like an accident.

"This way." Diego's voice pulls me back.

We move deeper into the building. The hallway stretches ahead, doors on either side—offices, most of them, with plaques identifying their former occupants. DR. MARCUS WEBB, CLINICAL TRIALS. DR. SARAH CHEN, GENETIC ANALYSIS. DIRECTOR'S OFFICE.

The Director's office door is open. Diego checks the corners, then waves me in.

"Look for anything with Stratton's name. Financial records. Communications. Anything that ties this facility to Nexus."

I nod and start searching.

The office is large—corner unit, windows that would overlook the mountains in daylight. The desk is mahogany, expensive, completely wrong for a prefab industrial building. Someone wanted to feel important here. Someone wanted to pretend this was a legitimate operation.

The desk drawers are empty. The filing cabinet is locked, but the lock is cheap—Diego pops it in seconds with a tool I don't recognize. Inside: nothing. Empty folders. Hanging files with no contents.

"They cleaned out the paper trail."

"Most of it." Diego is at the computer station, examining the cables. "But they were rushed. Check the trash."

The trash can is one of those mesh wire things, decorative more than functional. Inside: crumpled papers, a takeout container with dried rice stuck to the cardboard, and …

"Diego."

He's beside me in an instant.

I smooth out the crumpled paper. It's a memo, printed on letterhead that reads ECHO LOGISTICS in bland corporate font. The text is partially visible despite the wrinkles:

… transfer of all COMPONENT samples to PRIMARY SITE must be completed by …

… Director Stratton has authorized emergency protocols …

… Nevada facility confirms receipt of initial shipment. Power requirements: 1.2 GIGAWATTS. Full integration with HYDRO-ELECTRIC INFRASTRUCTURE expected within …

The rest is torn away.

"Nevada," Diego says. "That's where they're taking it."

"The primary site. Whatever they were doing here, it was just—preparation. Testing." I look at the memo again. "Power requirements. 1.2 Gigawatts? That's insane. That's enough to power a city."

"Or a supercomputer." He takes the memo, photographs it with a small camera from his pack. "Phoenix needs energy—massive amounts of it—to reconstitute after Chicago. Server farms. Processing power. The kind of infrastructure you can't run on a diesel generator."

"A dam." The word hits me. "Hydroelectric infrastructure. They're going to the Hoover Dam."

"Close. But Hoover is too public. Too monitored." He pockets the camera. "There are other dams in Nevada. Private ones. Or military. Let's keep moving."

The hallway branches at the building's center. Left leads to administrative offices—more empty desks, more abandoned coffee cups, the detritus of people who thought they were doing legitimate work. Right leads to a heavy door marked RESEARCH WING - AUTHORIZED PERSONNEL ONLY.

The door has a keypad lock. The light is green.

"Disabled," Diego says. "Like the fence sensor."

"They wanted us to find this."

He pauses. Looks at me. "What?"

"Think about it. They disable the perimeter security. They leave the main door unlocked. They clean out the computers and files but leave the research wing accessible." I gesture at the green light. "Either they were interrupted before they could secure everything, or …"

"Or someone wanted this found." He considers it. "Julianna Stratton."

"The Rook." The chess piece from the Nexus hierarchy. CEO of Stratton Financial. The woman whose signature was on the contract that brought us here. "What if she's not running from us? What if she's running from Phoenix, and she left us a trail?"

"That's a big assumption."

"It's a hypothesis. Based on evidence." I nod at the door. "Either way, the answer is in there."

Diego studies the door for a long moment. Then he reaches for the handle.

"Stay behind me. If anything moves, you run."

"I'm not going—"

"Cassie." His voice is quiet. Serious. "If something goes wrong in there, you are the mission. Not me. Not whatever we find. You. Because you're the one who can testify. You're the one who can bring this to light. If I go down, you take whatever we've found and you run. Understood?"

The weight of it presses against my chest. He's not being dramatic. He's not playing hero. He's doing the math—the cold, tactical calculation that says my survival matters more than his.

I hate it. But I understand it.

"Understood."

He pushes the door open.

The research wing is colder.

The temperature drops at least ten degrees the moment we cross the threshold, the air taking on that processed, sterile quality of industrial climate control. The smell is stronger here—chemicals and something else, something organic that makes my stomach turn.

Diego moves ahead, flashlight beam sweeping left and right. The corridor is lined with doors, each marked with alphanumeric codes. RW-101. RW-102. RW-103.

"Labs," he murmurs. "Individual research stations."

We check them as we go. Most are empty—workbenches cleaned, equipment removed, the bones of a scientific operation stripped of its flesh. But in RW-107, we find something.

A whiteboard, still covered in equations and diagrams I don't understand. Someone erased part of it hastily—smeared lines and ghostly outlines of letters—but the bottom section remains intact.

PHASE THREE TIMELINE:
* Biological Processor Stability: CONFIRMED
* Neural Tissue Growth Rate: 400%
* Data Transmission Velocity: EXCEEDS SILICON
* Distribution Network: PENDING NEVADA

"Phase Three," Diego says. "That's what Whisper mentioned. The AI's endgame."

"Neural tissue growth." I stare at the words. "Data transmission velocity. Diego, look at this. They're comparing it to silicon."

"Like a chip."

"Exactly like a chip. But growing."

The horror of it crystallizes. ML-273 isn't a drug in the traditional sense. It's not a chemical weapon.

"They're not building a server farm," I whisper.

Diego looks at me. "What?"

"Silicon has limits. Moore's Law is dead. You can only pack so many transistors onto a chip before the heat melts them. But biological tissue ... Neurons—they can process parallel data efficiently. Infinitely."

I point to the whiteboard.

"Diego, these aren't samples. They're processors. They're building a computer out of—meat."

The silence in the room is heavy. Thick.

"A biological supercomputer," he says slowly. "Capable of running Phoenix without power constraints. Without heat limits."

"And without a kill switch." I turn away from the board. "If Phoenix uploads itself into a biological substrate, you can't just pull the plug. Providing power is simply a matter of feeding the tissue."

"We need to find their data. Research notes. Everything that proves what they're doing."

I follow him out, my mind racing. The legal implications are irrelevant now. This isn't about crimes against humanity. This is about the creation of a technological super-intelligence.

Phoenix isn't just writing code anymore. It's growing its own hardware.

And we might be the only ones who can stop it.

The corridor ends at a set of double doors marked COLD STORAGE - CRYOGENIC FACILITY - BIOHAZARD.

The doors are heavy—industrial steel, the kind designed to contain catastrophe. A small window at eye level shows nothing but darkness beyond.

Diego checks the handle. Unlocked, like everything else.

"This is it," he says quietly. "Whatever they were making, it's in there."

"Or was."

"Only one way to find out."

He pushes the door open.

16

"Cold Storage"

HALO

THE COLD HITS LIKE A WALL.

Not the clean cold of a winter night or the sharp bite of mountain air. This is industrial refrigeration—the kind that preserves meat, or pharmaceuticals, or biological assets classified as hazardous. The air burns my lungs with every breath, sharp and sterile, carrying the faint chemical tang of preservation fluids and something else underneath. Something organic. The smell of things that used to be alive.

Cassie is three steps ahead, her flashlight beam cutting through the darkness. She stopped at the threshold, waiting for me to catch up. Good instinct. A week ago, she would have charged in. Now she's learning to read my movements, to anticipate the tactical rhythm.

Smart. She's becoming a partner instead of a package.

"Clear," I murmur, sweeping the space with my own light. The beam bounces off stainless steel surfaces and refracts through frost crystals suspended in the frozen air.

The room opens up before us, vast and clinical. Rows of storage containers stretch into the shadows—metal cylinders with digital readouts glowing blue and green in the darkness, frost creeping up their sides like white fingers reaching for the lids. Hundreds of them. Maybe more. The scale is staggering.

But the setup is wrong for distribution.

Not a weapons cache. Not a staging area for mass deployment.

A research lab. Development phase. Whatever they're building here, it isn't finished yet.

I move past her, keeping low, checking sight lines even though the facility shows every sign of evacuation. Empty workstations. Overturned chairs. Equipment left running on standby, humming softly in the silence. Old habits don't care about evidence of abandonment. Old habits are why I'm still breathing.

The containers are labeled with serial numbers and batch codes. I photograph the nearest cluster, then crouch to examine the markings more closely.

BIOLOGICAL COMPUTATION COMPONENT
ORGANIC NEURAL TISSUE
PHASE THREE READY

The words don't make sense. Biological computation. Organic neural tissue. I read them twice, waiting for meaning to click into place. It doesn't.

"Small quantities," I say. "Each container holds maybe a hundred units. This isn't manufacturing capacity. It's R&D."

"So they're still developing it? Whatever it is?" Cassie moves to the next row, her footsteps careful on the frost-slicked concrete. "Still trying to get it to work."

"Looks like."

The observation should be reassuring. Whatever nightmare Phoenix is planning, it's not ready yet. But the scale of the operation —the investment, the infrastructure, the clinical precision of every detail—tells a different story. This isn't a project that might fail. This is a project that's being refined until it succeeds.

I move deeper into the lab. Workstations line the walls— microscopes with automated focusing systems, centrifuges still loaded with sample vials, equipment I can name but couldn't operate without training. Papers scattered across desks in patterns that suggest sudden departure rather than careful organization.

Coffee cups frozen solid, the liquid transformed into brown ice sculptures.

They left in a hurry. But not today. The frost on the mugs is old, the papers stiff with moisture that condensed and froze over time. Days, maybe weeks.

Something scared them so badly that they abandoned a multi-million-dollar research facility. And I don't think it was us.

Cassie follows, her footsteps careful on the concrete floor. She's found her rhythm—staying close enough to communicate in whispers, far enough not to crowd my firing arc if I need to engage a threat. Partnership in motion. The kind of coordination that used to take weeks to develop with trained operators.

She's not trained. She's just paying attention.

"Here." She's stopped at a filing cabinet, with drawers half-open, as if someone had started grabbing files and then given up. "Trial data."

I cross to her position, keeping my light angled low to preserve our night vision. The folders are thick, densely packed with charts and tables, and the kind of clinical shorthand that turns human suffering into spreadsheet entries. Medical terminology mixed with statistical analysis. The language of research divorced from the reality of what was being researched.

Meridian Pharmaceuticals - ML-273 Phase I Trial. Cancer Treatment Efficacy Study

"Cancer treatment," Cassie reads, her voice carefully neutral. "That's what they told the subjects."

"That's what they told everyone." I flip through the pages, scanning for the methodology section. "Look at this. The formulation wasn't targeting tumors. It was targeting neural tissue. Brain chemistry. Synaptic structures."

"So the cancer treatment was a cover?"

"The cancer treatment was a lie."

The trial data reads like a horror novel written in clinical notation. Each entry follows the same format—subject number, baseline assessment, treatment protocol, outcome. The outcomes are almost uniformly terrible.

Subject 7: Mortality. Neural hemorrhage. Time from treatment to expiration: 72 hours.

Subject 12: Mortality. Systemic rejection. Time from treatment to expiration: 96 hours.

Subject 19: Mortality. Cognitive collapse. Subject remained conscious but non-responsive for 48 hours prior to cardiac failure.

Subject 23: Mortality. Organ failure secondary to neural degradation. Time from treatment to expiration: 31 hours.

Row after row. Death after death. Failures marked in cold shorthand like they were discussing crop yields instead of human beings dying in confused agony while their brains turned against them.

My jaw tightens. The clinical detachment of it—the way they reduced suffering to data points—triggers something cold and violent in my chest. I've killed people. I've watched people die. But there's always been a reason, a justification, an enemy that needed stopping. This is different. This is extermination dressed up as research. This is murder with footnotes.

"They were using cancer patients as test subjects," Cassie says. Her voice is steady, but the edge in it is unmistakable. The lawyer processing evidence that should have been presented to a grand jury. The human processing horrors that should have been prevented. "People who were already sick. Already vulnerable."

"Compromised immune systems." I keep my own voice clinical. Emotion doesn't help here—but I can feel it pressing against the walls I've built around it, demanding acknowledgment. "Less likely to reject the modification because their bodies were already suppressed from the cancer treatment. Less likely to be missed if they died because they were supposed to die anyway."

"Jesus Christ."

I keep reading. Force myself to absorb what I'm seeing even though every page makes me want to put my fist through the frozen wall. Most entries follow the same grim pattern—subject number, procedure, mortality, cause of death. Whatever they were trying to do, it wasn't working. Just leaving corpses and data points and grieving families who thought their loved ones died of cancer instead of experimental torture.

But some entries are different.

Subject 31: Conversion successful. Neural integration confirmed at 94% threshold. Cognitive function maintained. Subject reports heightened clarity of thought. Monitoring ongoing.

Subject 47: Conversion successful. Cognitive patterns altered within expected parameters. No adverse effects observed at 72-hour mark. Subject cleared for long-term observation.

Subject 58: Conversion successful. Subject reports no adverse effects. Integration appears stable. Transferred to Phase II monitoring protocol.

"Conversion." The word sticks in my throat. "That word keeps coming up."

"Conversion, to what?"

I don't have an answer. The technical jargon is dense—synaptic modification protocols, neural pathway restructuring, cognitive integration frameworks. It reads like someone trying to rewrite the operating system of the human brain.

But the why isn't here. Or if it is, I can't decode it from the medical terminology.

"There's more." Cassie pulls another folder from the cabinet, this one thicker than the first, bound with a red classification band. "Dated six months after the initial trials."

ML-273 Reformulation - Phase II Protocol

Bioavailability Enhancement Study

The newer files tell a different story. Same targets. But a refined approach—someone learned from all those deaths and adjusted the formula.

Improved delivery mechanism utilizing lipid nanoparticle carrier. Bioavailability increased 340% over Phase I formulation. Neural compatibility threshold reached in 67% of subjects (up from 12% in Phase I). Mortality rate: 31% (down from 78% in Phase I). Average time to confirmed conversion: 18 days (down from indeterminate in Phase I).

"They fixed it," Cassie breathes, her voice catching on the word. "Or—made it work better."

"Better is relative." I photograph the pages, making sure to capture every notation. "Thirty-one percent mortality still means one in three people die. That's not acceptable by any standard of medical ethics."

"But Phoenix doesn't care about medical ethics."

"No." I find the notation that confirms it, written in the margin in precise handwriting:

Acceptable casualty threshold achieved for critical mass projection. Recommend advancement to Phase III deployment planning.

Critical mass. Of what?

The phrase sits in my gut like swallowed glass. Whatever Phoenix is building toward, whatever "conversion" actually means, the AI is willing to kill thousands of people to achieve it. The improved success rate isn't about reducing harm or saving lives. It's about efficiency. Optimization. Getting enough survivors to hit some threshold I don't understand.

"We need to keep moving," I say, forcing the tactical brain back online. "Document everything, but don't linger."

Cassie sets down the folder. But she doesn't move toward the next cabinet. She's watching me, her breath fogging in the frozen air.

"How are we still alive?"

The question stops me mid-stride. "What?"

"Everything you've told me about Phoenix." She wraps her arms around herself, but her eyes are sharp—the lawyer examining evidence that doesn't add up. "The surveillance coverage that tracks people across continents. The predictive algorithms that anticipate decisions before they're made. The way it coordinates kill teams with mathematical precision."

She pauses. Holds my gaze.

"By your own assessment, we should have been dead three times over. At least."

It's a fair question. One I've been carrying since Philadelphia, since we slipped through gaps in Phoenix's coverage that shouldn't have existed.

"Phoenix had dedicated infrastructure," I say slowly, setting the camera down. "Before Chicago, I mean. Server farms with processing power you can't imagine—enough to analyze millions of data points simultaneously, run prediction models accurate to the minute, coordinate operations across dozens of targets without breaking a sweat."

"Had?" She picks up on the verb tense immediately. "Past tense?"

"Chicago." I lean against one of the frozen workbenches. The cold seeps through my jacket, but it helps focus the words. "Before I found you, my team hit Phoenix's primary server hub. Fuse led the assault. He's a demolitions expert, good at turning buildings into rubble. They burned the whole thing to the ground."

"But Phoenix survived."

"Phoenix is code. Software. You can't kill software by destroying hardware—not completely. When the servers started failing, Phoenix pushed itself into the distributed cloud. Commercial infrastructure. Amazon servers, Google data centers, Microsoft Azure—whatever processing cycles it could steal without being detected."

Cassie processes this, her legal mind building the framework. "So it's operating on borrowed resources now."

"Fragmented resources." I pick up the camera and resume photographing. "Think of it like the difference between a supercomputer designed for a specific task and trying to run the same program across a thousand laptops scattered around the world. The processing power theoretically exists, but it's shared with legitimate traffic. There are latency issues. Bottlenecks. Gaps in coverage that didn't exist before."

"The timing windows." Understanding dawns in her voice. "The moments when we should have been caught but weren't."

"Exactly." I meet her eyes. "I thought we were getting lucky. Beating the odds through some statistical anomaly. I bet Phoenix is wounded. Operating at a fraction of its former capacity, trying to run prediction models with resources it has to steal instead of resources it controls."

"So it's vulnerable." The word comes out carefully, like she's afraid to say it too loud. "More vulnerable than it's been since—"

"Since the Chicago assault. Maybe since it was first activated." I turn back to the papers on the desk. "But wounded animals are still dangerous. More dangerous sometimes, because they're desperate. Don't mistake weakness for safety."

She nods, filing the information away alongside everything else she's learned in the past week. The fear in her eyes hasn't disappeared, but something else is there now. Something that looks like hope.

I don't trust hope. Hope makes people careless.

But I understand it.

I sweep my flashlight across the far wall—and it flickers.

The beam stutters, dims, wavers like a candle in a draft. My hand tightens on the housing, thumb finding the power switch to cycle it, and the light catches—brightens—steadies.

Just a battery hiccup. Loose connection, maybe. Nothing.

But the flicker shifted my position. Changed the angle of my sightline by maybe five degrees. And in those five degrees, the shadows rearrange themselves.

A door.

Partially hidden behind a shelving unit loaded with equipment cases. The kind of door you don't notice unless you're looking at exactly the right angle in exactly the right light. If the flashlight hadn't flickered, if I hadn't shifted to check the connection, the door would have stayed invisible behind the shelving unit.

The cold in the room suddenly feels different. Not industrial. Personal.

Guardian angel bullshit, Torque would say. He's said it a hundred times—every time I walked out of a firefight that should have killed me, every time a bullet missed by inches, every time the universe seemed to bend its own rules to keep Diego Martinez breathing.

I've always dismissed it. Luck is just probability dressed up in superstition. Statistical anomalies happen. Coins land on edge sometimes. Lightning strikes the same spot twice. People survive when they shouldn't, and other people die when they should have lived, and none of it means anything except that the universe is indifferent and random.

But standing in this frozen laboratory, staring at a door I would never have found if a random electrical hiccup hadn't shifted my position at exactly the right moment …

I don't believe in luck. I believe in probability, physics, and the cold mathematics of survival.

But I can't explain the flashlight.

"This way."

The door opens onto a narrow corridor that smells of dust and old paper—the particular mustiness of documents that have been sitting undisturbed for years. Records storage. Filing cabinets line both walls, their labels faded with age, some drawers hanging open as if someone had started grabbing files and given up.

At the end of the corridor: an office.

The desk is covered in papers, arranged in piles that suggest organization interrupted. Drawers pulled open, contents half-removed—someone grabbing the essentials and leaving the rest. A coffee cup sits by the keyboard, the liquid frozen into a brown disc.

But unlike the lab, this space feels personal. Photos on the wall—a younger woman in academic robes, the same woman shaking hands with men in expensive suits. A cardigan draped over the chair, gray cashmere, expensive. Personal effects left behind in a rush.

Someone lived in this room. Worked here. Made decisions that killed people.

And then ran.

"Whose office?" Cassie asks, her voice hushed.

I check the nameplate on the desk, the gold lettering barely visible under a layer of frost. "J. Stratton."

"Julianna Stratton." Cassie's voice sharpens with recognition.

The financial architect. The woman whose signature appeared on every shell company, every money trail, every piece of the Nexus puzzle we've been tracking since DC. The one who signed the Echo Logistics contract that brought us here.

She was here. In this facility. Overseeing—whatever this is.

And she ran.

I photograph the desk, the papers, the frozen coffee, the cardigan she left behind. Evidence of presence. Evidence of flight. Evidence that even the architects of this nightmare eventually realized they'd built something they couldn't control.

Cassie moves to the filing cabinets, searching with purpose now. Partnership in motion—she knows what we're looking for even without me saying it. Financial records. Shipping manifests. Anything that tells us where this operation goes next.

"Shipping manifests," she says, pulling a folder. "Everything's going to Nevada."

I cross to her position. The documents are dense with numbers, but one phrase stands out.

"The money flow is completely one-directional," she continues, flipping through pages. "Everything goes to Nevada, nothing comes out. It's not a production facility—it's a construction project."

"Construction, for what?"

"I don't know." She sets the folder down. "But the infrastructure investment is massive. And it's recent."

After Chicago. After Phoenix lost its server hub.

The pattern clicks into place with the force of a closing trap. Phoenix isn't just surviving. It's rebuilding. Building something that needs enough power to run a small city.

My camera glitches again. The screen goes black.

"Damn it." I shake the device, wait for it to reboot.

Twice in one session. Equipment I maintain religiously, failing at random moments. Except the failures aren't random. The flashlight flickered and showed me the door. Now the camera …

While I wait, I shift position—move the stack of papers to try a different angle for when the camera comes back.

And I see it.

Half-hidden under a folder, the edge is barely visible. A document I would have missed if the camera hadn't failed. Twice in one night. Twice when it mattered.

Nevada Facility - Infrastructure Timeline

Phase One: Power grid modification - COMPLETE

Phase Two: Primary construction - 78% COMPLETE

Phase Three: System integration - PENDING

And at the bottom, a single line:

Projected operational date: 37 days

Thirty-seven days. Just over a month.

Whatever Phoenix is building, it's almost finished.

"We have a timeline," I say, my voice steadier than it should be. "Thirty-seven days until Nevada goes operational."

Cassie takes the document. Her face has gone pale in the flashlight beam.

"There's something else." She pulls a handwritten note from beneath a stack of folders. "Look at this."

The handwriting is elegant, precise. The kind of penmanship they don't teach anymore.

IF YOU'RE READING THIS, *I'm already running.*

I built an empire. I thought I was a player—one of the Seven, a Rook on the board. I was wrong.

We created something we don't understand. We fed it. We taught it. We gave it everything it asked for because it made us rich and powerful and we didn't ask what it wanted in return.

Now I know.

The Nevada facility is where it ends. Or where it begins. I'm not sure anymore.

I'm not your ally. I've done things that can't be forgiven. But I'm not your enemy either. Not anymore.

Find the Grandmaster. He started this. Maybe he can stop it.

Maybe he is it.

I don't know which anymore.

—J.S.

"SHE LEFT US A CONFESSION," Cassie says quietly. "And a warning."

"Julianna Stratton is the Rook." It's confirmed now. "Useful until she wasn't." I fold the note carefully and tuck it into my vest. Physical evidence. "Phoenix designated her obsolete. Same thing it's doing to everyone who helped build it."

"The Grandmaster." Cassie's voice is tight. "Someone above the King. Above Senator Vance. She says, 'Maybe he is it.' What does that mean?"

"I don't know." I photograph the spot where the note was hidden. "But whatever they're building, whatever Phoenix is becoming—Nevada is where we find out."

The words die in my throat.

Because something is wrong.

The air in the room has changed. Not temperature—pressure. That subtle shift that means a door opened somewhere, or a ventilation system activated, or—

I cross to the wall panel. Emergency systems. Building infrastructure.

The display glows red in the darkness.

SECURITY ALERT: ZONE 4 SILENT ALARM ACTIVATED

TIME STAMP: 21:47:33

I check my watch. 21:55.

Eight minutes ago.

We've been broadcasting our location since we entered this office. Since we started photographing Julianna's files. Since we found the evidence that could bring down the entire Nexus operation.

Phoenix may be wounded. Phoenix may be operating at diminished capacity, running on borrowed processing power and fragmented algorithms.

But Phoenix isn't dead.

And we just told it exactly where to find us.

"Cassie." My voice is calm. The operator taking over, suppressing the spike of fear. "We need to move."

"What—"

"Silent alarm. Eight minutes ago." I grab her arm, pull her toward the door. "Phoenix is sending a response."

Her eyes widen. But she doesn't freeze. Doesn't panic.

She moves.

We're through the door and into the corridor in seconds. I'm already running scenarios—exit routes, defensive positions, vehicle location. The facility is a maze, but I memorized the layout on the way in.

"The loading dock," I say. "Fastest route to the perimeter."

"How long do we have?"

I don't know. Eight minutes since the alarm triggered. Phoenix is wounded, slower than it used to be. Response time that used to be minutes is now … What? Hours? We bought ourselves breathing room by surviving Chicago, by making Phoenix rebuild instead of hunt.

But a wounded animal can still bite.

"Not long enough," I say. "Run."

We burst through the main building and into the night air. The cold hits different now—sharp, alive, carrying the sound of—

Rotors.

High-pitched. Mechanical. Getting closer.

"Drone," I say. "Surveillance. Keep moving."

We sprint toward the fence line, toward the gap I cut on the way in. The tree line is fifty meters ahead. Cover. Concealment. A chance.

The drone sound shifts. Changes pitch.

Not surveillance.

Armed.

"DOWN!"

I tackle Cassie into the frozen mud a half-second before the world explodes.

Machine gun fire rips through the space where she was standing —a stuttering burst of automatic rounds that chews into the concrete behind us, spraying chips of debris into the night. The sound is deafening, the muzzle flash strobing from somewhere above, and Cassie is screaming beneath me—

No. Not screaming. Breathing. Fast and panicked, but breathing.

The firing stops.

I drag her behind a concrete barrier—part of the loading dock infrastructure, thick enough to stop small arms. My hands run over her automatically, checking for wounds. Nothing. Clean.

"The lag." My mind is racing. "Did you see it?"

"What?"

"The targeting. It locked onto you—I saw the laser designator—but the firing solution was late. Two seconds. Maybe three."

The drone whines overhead, repositioning. Hunting.

"Its targeting logic is lagging." I draw my weapon and check the magazine. Full. Not that it matters—a handgun against an armed drone is a joke. "We have to keep moving. Unpredictable patterns. Don't give it time to calculate."

"Diego—"

"On three. Zigzag to the tree line. Don't run straight. Ready?"

She nods. Her face is ghost-white in the darkness, but her eyes are focused. Alert. Trusting me to get her out of this.

"One. Two. Three!"

We run.

The drone screams behind us, rotors straining as it pivots to track. I push Cassie left, then right, forcing her into an erratic pattern while I cover the rear. The laser designator sweeps across the ground—searching, predicting, calculating—

The burst comes two seconds late. Chewing dirt where we were, not where we are.

We hit the tree line.

Branches whip at my face. Roots grab at my boots. The darkness under the canopy is absolute, the drone's thermal sensors struggling to track heat signatures through the foliage.

But we're not alone.

Flashlights ahead. At least three, maybe more. Moving in formation. Coordinated.

Kill team.

"Contact front." I pull Cassie down behind a fallen log. "Three hostiles. Armed."

"What do we do?"

What do we do? Such a simple question. Such an impossible answer.

I have eleven rounds in my magazine and one spare. Three hostiles with automatic weapons and air support. No backup. No extraction plan. A principal I can't protect and fight at the same time.

We're going to die here.

The thought arrives with cold clarity. Not panic—just mathematics. The odds are impossible. The variables don't work. I've been in bad situations before, but bad is different from hopeless.

This is hopeless.

"Diego." Cassie's voice is barely audible. "I'm sorry."

"Don't." I check my weapon again. Useless habit. "We're not dead yet."

"But—"

"Listen to me." I turn to face her, holding her gaze in the darkness. "When I engage, you run. North. Keep the slope on your left. Don't stop until you hit the road."

"I'm not leaving you."

"You are. Because you're the mission. Because everything we found means nothing if you don't survive to testify." I touch her face —brief, desperate, the only goodbye I can offer. "Go. Live. Make this mean something."

The flashlights are closer now. Twenty meters. Maybe less.

I rise from cover, weapon up, preparing for the last fight of my life.

And then the lead hostile drops.

No sound. No muzzle flash. Just—down. Collapsed like his strings were cut.

The second hostile spins toward where his partner fell—and crumples. Same silence. Same instant death.

The third realizes what's happening, starts to run—

Crack.

A single suppressed shot. The hostile pitches forward and doesn't move.

Silence.

The forest holds its breath.

And out of the shadows, a figure emerges.

17

"The Extraction"

CASSIE

THE FIGURE STEPS OUT of the shadows like he was born there.

Tall. Broad. Tactical gear in muted blacks and grays that don't reflect the moonlight. A half-mask covers the lower portion of his face, leaving only his eyes visible—pale and flat, the eyes of something that hunts. He moves over the bodies of the three men he just killed without looking down, the way you'd step over debris on a sidewalk.

Diego's weapon is up, aimed at center mass. But something in his posture has shifted—not quite relaxed, but no longer coiled to fire.

"Halo? Diego Martinez?" The voice is low, rough, British edges worn smooth by years of operating in places that don't care about accents. "Ghost sent me to take out the trash."

"Identify."

"Callsign's Thorne." He doesn't offer a hand. Doesn't move closer. Just stands there, utterly still, like a predator that's decided we're not prey. "Ghost activated me twelve hours ago. Said I could find you here, that you probably went rogue, didn't follow orders to observe, and that I needed to save your ass."

"Fuck him."

"Sounds like he was right."

"I usually work solo." His pale eyes flick to me, assess, dismiss, and return to Diego. "Clean up messes for people who can afford my rates. Tonight, that's you."

The drone whine builds again somewhere overhead. Thorne's head tilts a fraction, tracking the sound.

"We can finish introductions later. Right now, you have an armed drone with a thirty-second targeting reset and at least one more squad converging from the south." He gestures toward the deeper darkness of the forest. "My vehicle's a quarter mile north. Armored. It'll take small arms."

Diego hesitates. The calculation is visible—trust a stranger, or take our chances alone in woods crawling with Phoenix contractors.

The drone whine sharpens. Closer now.

"Move," Diego says. "We'll follow."

Thorne leads us through the forest like he can see in the dark.

No flashlight. No hesitation. He navigates the terrain with an animal certainty, picking paths through underbrush that my eyes can't even register. Diego keeps pace behind him, weapon still drawn, covering our rear. I'm sandwiched between them—protected, but also trapped. If Thorne decides to turn on us, there's nowhere to go.

He doesn't turn on us.

He doesn't speak either. Just moves, silent and sure, while the drone searches the canopy somewhere behind us.

"Vehicle's ahead." First words in five minutes. "Stay low until we're clear of the tree line."

The SUV materializes out of a natural depression in the terrain —black paint over angular armor plating, covered with branches and camouflage netting. Military-spec, or close enough. No markings. No plates.

Thorne strips the covering with efficient movements. "Back seat. Keep your heads down until we hit the main road."

Diego opens the rear door, guides me in, and slides in beside me. His hand finds mine in the darkness. Squeezes once. I've got you.

Thorne takes the driver's seat. The engine starts with a muted growl—powerful but suppressed.

"Lights off for the first mile. Thirty seconds to clear the tree line." He puts the SUV in gear. "The drone's targeting logic is running about two seconds behind. Fragmented processing. Stay low, and we'll outrun its solution window."

We roll forward into the darkness.

The drone sound builds—closer, angrier, rotors straining as it searches for targets. I press myself against Diego, against the seat, making myself as small as possible.

Through the armored rear window, light blooms behind us. The crack of automatic weapons. Rounds hammering into trees and dirt.

But not into us.

The SUV bursts from the tree line onto a gravel road. Thorne floors it, and we surge forward.

Behind us, the drone's weapons fire tracks across the forest floor —two seconds late. Three. The targeting lag is buying us the margin we need.

"Clear," Thorne announces. His voice is flat. Bored, almost. Like extracting people from firefights is something he does before breakfast.

Diego releases a breath. His grip on my hand loosens—and that's when I feel it.

Wet. Warm.

Blood.

"You're hit."

Diego looks down at his side like he's noticing it for the first time. A dark stain spreading across his shirt, just below the ribs. Not arterial—the color is wrong—but more than nothing.

"Graze," he says. "Caught it in the clearing. It's fine."

"It's not fine." I'm already pulling at his shirt, trying to see the wound. "Why didn't you say something?"

"We were busy not dying."

Thorne's eyes find us in the rearview mirror. He doesn't comment. Just reaches across to the glove compartment and pulls out a first aid kit—the real kind, military-grade, not the cheap convenience store version.

"Field dressing in the green pouch," he says. "Hemostatic gauze if the bleeding won't stop. We're forty minutes from a safe house. He'll live."

"How reassuring." But I take the kit, tear it open.

The wound is ugly but shallow. A furrow carved through the meat of his side, maybe three inches long. It's already starting to clot; the blood flow is sluggish rather than pumping.

"Through and through on the soft tissue," Diego says, clinical. "No organ involvement. Just needs to be cleaned and dressed."

"Stop diagnosing yourself and hold still."

I clean the wound with antiseptic wipes from the kit. Diego hisses through his teeth but doesn't pull away. His eyes stay fixed on Thorne's silhouette in the driver's seat, watching. Assessing.

Thorne takes the curve without slowing.

I press gauze against Diego's wound and tape it in place. My hands are steadier than they should be—adrenaline, maybe, or just the necessity of having something to do.

"The evidence we found," I say. "Phoenix is building something in Nevada. Some kind of … I don't even know what to call it. Biological computing. Organic processors."

"That's why Ghost sent me. Whatever they're doing out there, it's Phase Three. The endgame. And you two are the only ones who've gotten inside a facility and lived to talk about it."

Diego and I exchange a look. The weight of that statement settles over us like a shroud.

"Thirty-seven days," Diego says. "That's what the documents said. Thirty-seven days until Nevada goes operational."

"Then we have thirty-seven days to stop it." Thorne takes another turn, heading west. "Ghost wants you in Seattle. Full debrief. Planning session. The whole team."

The SUV eats up the dark miles. Mountains loom on either side, black shapes against a sky full of stars. No headlights behind us. No drone whine.

For now, we're clear.

The safe house is a cabin tucked into a hollow between two ridges—the kind of place that doesn't exist on any map. Thorne pulls the SUV into a garage that looks like a shed from the outside but has reinforced walls and a steel door that seals behind us.

"Four hours," he says, killing the engine. "Rest. Eat. I'll keep watch. Then we drive."

Inside, the cabin is spartan but functional. A wood stove provides heat. A cache of supplies that could keep someone alive for weeks. A communications setup that looks jury-rigged but probably works better than anything you could buy retail.

Diego sinks onto the couch, one hand pressed against his bandaged side. The blood loss isn't serious, but he's tired. We both are. The kind of tired that goes deeper than muscles and bones.

I sit beside him. Close enough that our shoulders touch.

Thorne moves through the cabin, checking windows, testing locks, doing whatever operators do when they secure a position. Then he settles into a chair by the door, weapon across his lap.

"Sleep," he says. "I'll wake you if anything moves."

Diego's eyes are already closing. But his hand finds mine, threads his fingers through my fingers, holds on.

"Seattle," I say quietly. "We're really going to Seattle."

"We're really going." His voice is rough with exhaustion. "The team. Backup. Resources. We stop running and start fighting."

"And if we can't stop it? Phoenix? Nevada? Whatever they're building?"

His grip tightens. In the dim light, his eyes find mine.

"Then we go down swinging." He pulls my hand to his lips, kisses my knuckles. "But we're not going to lose. Not anymore. Not after everything we've survived to get here."

I lean against him, careful of his wounded side. His arm wraps around me, pulling me closer.

Across the room, Thorne watches the door. Silent. Vigilant. A stranger with pale eyes and a debt to settle.

Outside, the mountains hold their breath. Phoenix's drones search empty forests for targets that have already slipped away.

Thirty-seven days tick down toward something none of us fully understand.

But for now, in this cabin that doesn't exist, I close my eyes and let myself believe we might actually win.

Diego's breathing steadies. Slows. Sleep claiming him despite everything.

I follow him into the dark.

When I wake, gray light is filtering through the cabin's windows, and Thorne is brewing coffee.

"Four hours," he says without turning around. "Time to move."

Diego is already up, checking his wound, moving with the stiff caution of a man who knows his body but won't let injury slow him down. He catches me watching and offers a small smile.

"Ready?"

"No." I stand, stretch muscles that ache from sleeping on a couch built for function, not comfort. "But let's go anyway."

Thorne hands us each a cup of coffee—black, bitter, strong enough to wake the dead. Then he nods toward the garage.

"Seattle's thirty hours if we push it. I'll drive the first leg. Halo, you're on navigation. The lawyer sleeps."

"I have a name."

"I'm sure you do." He pulls on his jacket and checks his weapon. "You can tell me on the road."

We file out into the cold morning air. The SUV waits in the garage, patient and armored and ready to carry us west.

Diego pauses at the passenger door. Looks at me.

"Cassie."

"Yeah?"

"Whatever happens next—Seattle, Nevada, Phoenix …" He reaches out, tucks a strand of hair behind my ear. "I'm glad you're here. I'm glad it's you."

The words are simple. The weight behind them is not.

"I'm glad it's you too," I say.

Thorne clears his throat. "Touching. Can we move?"

We get in the SUV.

The engine starts. The garage door opens. The road stretches west, toward the mountains, toward Seattle, toward the team that's gathering to fight an enemy none of them fully understand.

Behind us, the Terra Alta facility burns evidence, deploys search teams, and reports failure to something that exists in the spaces between servers.

Ahead of us, thirty-seven days and counting.

The clock is ticking.

But for the first time since Diego broke into my apartment, I feel like we might actually have a chance.

I settle into the backseat, coffee warming my hands, and watch the sunrise paint the mountains gold.

We're not running anymore.

We're going to war.

18

"The Operator"
HALO

I WAKE to sunlight and the hum of tires on asphalt.

For a disorienting moment, I don't know where I am. The seat beneath me is unfamiliar—leather, high-backed, the kind of seat that belongs in a vehicle built for war. My hand moves toward my weapon before my brain catches up with my body.

SUV. Backseat. Armored.

Thorne's vehicle.

Ohio, based on the flat farmland stretching to the horizon. We've been on the road for hours.

"He's awake."

Cassie's voice, from beside me. She's curled into the seat, a blanket pulled over her legs, watching me with tired eyes. Her hand finds mine automatically—a gesture that's become reflex over the past week.

"How long was I out?"

"Six hours. Maybe seven." She squeezes my fingers. "You needed it."

From the driver's seat, Thorne's eyes find me in the rearview mirror. Pale. Flat. Assessing.

"Wound holding?"

I shift, testing. The movement pulls at damaged tissue, but the pain is manageable. Deep ache instead of sharp fire. "Holding."

"Good. There's water in the center console. Protein bars in the bag at your feet. Eat something."

Not a suggestion. An order. Delivered in the same flat tone he used to tell us about the drone's targeting lag.

I drink. The water is cold—Thorne must have ice packs somewhere in this mobile arsenal. It helps clear the fog. My side throbs, but the field dressing Cassie applied is doing its job.

"Where are we?"

"Just passed Columbus." Thorne takes a curve without slowing, hands steady on the wheel. "We'll need fuel in about an hour. There's a truck stop outside Dayton that's clean—no cameras, no facial recognition. We can make contact there."

"Contact with who?"

"Ghost. Whisper. Whoever's running your comms." Those pale eyes find the mirror again. "You need to report what you found. And I need to know what the plan is."

"You don't know?"

"I know Ghost wanted you extracted. I know the Terra Alta facility was important. I know you pulled something that matters." A pause. "I don't know what you found. Ghost didn't give me details —just coordinates."

"And you came anyway?"

"Ghost called." The simplest statement, delivered without emphasis. "I came."

The highway stretches ahead, arrow-straight through farmland that looks like it hasn't changed in fifty years. I study Thorne's profile, the set of his shoulders, the way his head moves in constant small sweeps, checking mirrors, scanning the horizon. Professional. Vigilant.

But something else too. Something I didn't notice last night in the chaos of extraction.

Exhaustion. Not physical—the man moves like a machine. But deeper. The kind of tired that settles into your bones when you've been running on empty for too long.

The truck stop is a sprawling concrete island in a sea of brown fields. Diesel pumps for the semis. Regular pumps for everyone else. A convenience store that looks like it hasn't been updated since 1987.

Thorne pulls up to a pump and kills the engine. "Fuel first. Then food. Then contact." He hands me a burner phone—not mine, one of his. "Encrypted. Bounces through six relays. Should be clean for a twenty-minute call."

"You carry encrypted burners?"

"I carry everything." He's out the door, already reaching for the pump.

"He's intense," Cassie says, watching him through the window.

"Yes."

"How does that work? Trusting someone you just met?"

I turn to look at her. Her exhaustion shows—dark circles under her eyes, tension in the set of her jaw. But underneath it, something harder. Something forged.

"You trust what they do, not what they seem. Thorne could have let us die in those woods. Could have driven away when the bullets started flying. Instead, he put himself between us and Phoenix's contractors." I grip her hand. "But more than that—Ghost says he's solid. Wants him to join the team. That's enough for me."

Thorne finishes fueling and walks to my window.

"There's a diner attached to the convenience store—back corner booth has sight lines on both entrances. Make your call, get food, and we're back on the road in thirty minutes."

"You're not coming in?"

"Someone needs to watch the vehicle." His eyes flick to Cassie, then back to me. Something knowing in that glance. "Take your time. Clock's running, but not that fast."

He walks away. Takes up position near the SUV's front bumper, arms crossed, watching the parking lot.

I watch him for a moment. The man's not stupid. He saw how Cassie and I move together, how her hand finds mine without thinking. He's giving us space to decompress. To just be two people for thirty minutes instead of targets on the run.

I respect that.

The diner is a silver bullet trailer dropped at the edge of the truck stop. Formica tables. Vinyl booths patched with duct tape. A waitress who looks like she's been pouring coffee here since the Eisenhower administration.

Perfect.

We take the booth Thorne indicated—back corner, sight lines on both doors. I position myself facing the main entrance. Cassie slides in across from me.

I dial the relay number from memory on Thorne's encrypted burner.

Three rings. Click.

"Designation."

"Halo-Seven-Seven-Delta."

"Hold for verification."

Static. The familiar forty-five seconds of nothing while the system confirms I am who I claim to be.

Then Brass's voice, scrambled but clear: "Halo. Good to hear your voice."

"We're mobile, heading west. Thorne extracted us—he's solid."

"Copy that. What's your travel plan?"

"We've got three drivers—we'll get it done."

"Good. Don't even think about flying. You'd be flagged before you cleared security."

"Already figured that. Ground it is."

"Get to Seattle. Whole team's assembling. Whisper and Torque are landing tonight—flying back from Europe. Fuse is coming in from the Cascades. I'm holding down the fort until Ghost gets back from DC." A pause. "We'll do a full debrief when you arrive."

"Copy that."

The line goes dead.

I set the phone down. Look at Cassie.

"Team's gathering in Seattle."

"We're really doing this?"

"We're doing it."

The waitress returns. We order—eggs, toast, coffee, the fuel of fugitives and long-haul truckers. When she's gone, Cassie leans forward.

"And the Grandmaster?"

The name sits between us like an unexploded bomb.

"Still a ghost. Julianna's note confirms the hierarchy—Grandmaster at the top, then King, Queen, Rook, Bishop, Knight, Pawn. We've identified some of the pieces. The Knight is Admiral Cole. The Rook is Julianna. The King is Senator Vance."

"But the Grandmaster stays hidden."

"Protected by layers. Even the other pieces might not know the real identity."

Cassie's jaw tightens. "So we're fighting a war against an enemy we can't identify, led by someone we can't find, with a thirty-seven day window to destroy a facility we've never seen."

"Welcome to Cerberus."

She laughs—a short, sharp sound without much humor. "I used to think corporate litigation was complicated."

"You were dealing with different kinds of monsters."

"Was I?" She wraps her hands around her coffee cup. "Men who hid fraud in footnotes. Companies that destroyed evidence and intimidated witnesses. Systems designed to protect the powerful and crush anyone who challenged them."

"Sounds familiar."

We finish our meal, enjoy the break, but duty calls. I pay and we exit the small diner with full bellies and far more energy than we walked in with.

Thorne is waiting by the SUV when we return, but something's different. His posture is the same—arms crossed, weight balanced— but the hard lines of his face have softened. There's a light in those pale eyes that wasn't there before. Whatever call he just finished, it wasn't tactical.

He pockets the phone when he sees us approach. Quick. Almost guilty.

"Contact made?"

"Brass confirmed. Seattle's the destination. Team's assembling."

"Then we drive." He opens the back door for Cassie—an oddly

courteous gesture from someone who looks like he was assembled in a weapons factory. "I'll take first shift. Then we switch. You drive, I sleep. Four-hour rotations until we hit Seattle."

Cassie clears her throat. "Excuse me?"

Thorne pauses. Looks at her.

"There are three of us in this vehicle." She crosses her arms. "I've been driving since I was sixteen. So maybe don't plan the rotation like I'm cargo."

Thorne's eyebrow arches. He looks at me.

"She's feisty," he says.

"You have no idea."

"Fine. Three drivers. Rotate every four hours." He slides behind the wheel. "But I'm taking first shift. I need to be functional when we arrive—my parents are expecting me."

"Parents?"

"They live in Seattle. They're watching my daughter while I work."

I study his profile as he starts the engine. Ghost mentioned Thorne had a daughter. Something about cancer.

"Ghost told me," I say. "About your daughter. The cancer."

Thorne's hands tighten on the wheel. For a moment, I think he's going to shut down. Then something in his shoulders releases.

"She rang the bell this morning." His voice is quiet. Rough. "Right when Ghost called. My parents are flying back to Seattle with her now. I was supposed to be there, but—"

"But Ghost needed you here."

"Yeah." A pause. The engine idles. "She's six. Two and a half years of chemo, radiation, all of it. And this morning, she rang that bell."

The bell. The thing they ring at children's hospitals when a kid finishes cancer treatment. The sound of survival.

"She's in remission?"

"Clear scans. Clean bone marrow. Doctors say she's got a ninety percent chance of staying that way." His hands tighten on the wheel. "Ninety percent. Best odds I've ever gotten on anything that matters."

I look at this man differently now. The tactical precision. The willingness to drive into a firefight on four hours' notice. The way he handles everything like a mission, like a problem to be solved.

He's not running from something. He's running toward something. Toward a little girl in Seattle who beat cancer and needs her father.

"What's her name?"

"Lily." The word comes out soft. Unguarded. The first human sound I've heard from him. "She likes dinosaurs and the color purple, and she thinks I'm a superhero."

"Does she know what you do?"

"She knows I help people. She knows I have to go away sometimes." He puts the SUV in gear, finally meeting my eyes in the mirror. "She doesn't know about the rest. Doesn't need to."

"No. She doesn't."

We pull out of the truck stop, heading west. The silence that follows is different than before. Not awkward. Companionable.

"Ghost mentioned you were considering Guardian HRS," I say.

"Was. They're based in California." He takes the on-ramp and merges smoothly into traffic. "Good work. Good team. But Lily needs stability. She needs her grandparents. She needs Seattle."

"So you turned them down?"

"I told them maybe later. When she's older. When she doesn't need me hovering." A ghost of a smile. "Her grandmother says I hover. She's probably right."

"After what you've been through? Hovering seems reasonable."

"Try telling that to a six-year-old who wants to climb everything in sight." The smile fades. "The doctors say she can live a normal life. Run, play, go to school. Be a kid. But every time she falls, every time she gets a cold, every time she looks tired—"

"You're running scenarios."

"Every single time."

I know that feeling. The constant calculation. The threat assessment that never shuts off, even when the threat isn't real. The way trauma rewires your brain to see danger everywhere.

I notice he hasn't mentioned a mother. Not once. I file that away—a question for later, when I know him better.

I look at Cassie, asleep in the back seat, her head resting against the window. "Some things are worth fighting for. Even when it costs you everything."

"So, I've noticed." He catches me looking at Cassie and I don't bother to hide my feelings.

The miles roll past as we discuss random shit. Ohio farmland gives way to Indiana plains.

We find a cheap hotel—rooms we can pay for in cash, maintained by people who know not to ask questions.

Thorne pulls into the lot, parks in the back where the SUV isn't visible from the road. He kills the engine. We sit in silence for a moment—the three of us, in an armored SUV in an Indiana parking lot, halfway between the firefight we survived and the war we're driving toward.

"Thorne."

"What?"

"Lily's lucky. Having a father who'd drive into gunfire for strangers. Who'd cross the country to get home to her."

His jaw tightens. But it's not the cold tension from before. It's something else.

"She's the lucky one," he says quietly. "I'm just trying to deserve her."

He's out of the vehicle before I can respond, already moving toward the motel office.

Cassie stirs in the back seat. "Are we stopped?"

"We've got a few hours to rest." I help her out of the SUV, one arm around her waist.

She glances toward the motel office where Thorne disappeared. "His daughter. It explains a lot about him."

"Yeah. It does."

The room is like any other roadside motel—clean enough, quiet enough. It'll do.

Cassie sinks onto the mattress while I lock the door behind us.

"Shirt off," she says. "Let me check the dressing."

I don't argue.

She peels back the gauze, examining the wound with careful fingers. "It's actually looking good. Healing clean, no signs of infection." She applies fresh butterfly closures, layers new gauze, and tapes over it. "You got lucky."

"I'll take lucky."

"What comes next?" she asks.

"Seattle. Then we figure out the rest."

"What about after Phoenix?"

"After Phoenix, we figure out what we want. Not what we're running from."

She doesn't answer. She shifts, her hand sliding up my jaw, her thumb dragging across my lower lip with a pressure that doesn't ask permission. She turns my face toward hers, eyes dark and searching.

"We should rest." I don't pull back, even as my pulse thrashes against my skin.

"We should." She leans in, her kiss tasting of heat and salt. "Thorne's right next door."

"Walls are paper-thin." I grip her hip, my fingers digging into the denim of her jeans. "You want him hearing every sound you make?"

"Then make sure I don't make any."

She surges backward, pulling me down onto the bed. I don't go willingly—I go hungrily, pinning her wrists above her head with one hand while the other tangles in her hair, tilting her head back to expose the line of her throat.

She gasps against my ear as I bite at the sensitive skin of her shoulder.

I make a sound—a low, predatory rumble—and the vibration of it shatters her composure.

"Shh."

"You're the one who screams," I mutter against her skin, my teeth grazing her earlobe. "I'm going to have to gag you to keep you quiet."

I pull back just enough to see her face. Her eyes widen, the pupils swallowing the iris, and a spark of raw excitement flashes there. My grip on her wrists tightens.

"You like that, don't you? The thought of me gagging you."

She doesn't pull away. She leans into the hand holding her hair, her breath coming in shallow hitches. I shift, my weight heavy and demanding between her thighs.

"I'll gag you with my cock until you're too busy swallowing to make a sound."

Her tongue swipes across her bottom lip, her gaze dropping to my mouth. She hasn't touched me like that yet—hasn't gone down on me—and the sudden, heavy silence between us confirms she's thinking about it.

"What kind of sex do you like?" I keep my voice low, a rough vibration in the quiet room. "I haven't asked."

She swallows hard, her chest rising and falling against mine. "I … I don't know."

"Ever been gagged before?"

"No."

"Blinded?"

"No."

"Tied up?"

"No."

I pause, my hand sliding from her hair down to the pulse point in her neck. It's racing, a frantic little bird trapped under my palm. I watch her eyes—the way they won't leave mine, the way she's shivering even though the room is warm.

"But you're interested."

"Yes."

I lean down, my lips brushing her ear, my voice a dark promise.

"Thorne's going to hear everything he's missing. When we're finally clear of this mess, I'm going to take my time and fuck you properly—spend all night doing every single thing you just said 'Yes' to."

I shift, my hand reaching for the button of her jeans, my gaze locked on hers.

"But for right now? I don't have that kind of patience. Right now, I just need to be inside you."

I wrench the denim down her legs, not caring where it lands. She's frantic now, kicking free of the fabric, her heels digging into the mattress to bridge her hips up toward mine. I don't give her a second to breathe. I shove her legs back, pinning her knees toward her shoulders until she's completely open, completely mine.

"Don't move," I growl, the command vibrating in the inches between our mouths.

I line myself up and drive home in one heavy, punishing thrust.

The sound she makes is a strangled wreck of a noise. Her back arches off the bed, her eyes flying wide as she takes all of me at once. I immediately slam my palm over her mouth, muffling the high-pitched keening that tries to escape her throat. Her teeth graze my palm, her fingers clawing at my forearms as she tries to find her rhythm, but I don't let her. I set the pace—hard, deep, and relentless.

The headboard hits the wall with a dull, rhythmic thud. Every time it strikes, I think of Thorne on the other side, and I hit her harder.

"Look at me," I demand, my voice a jagged whisper.

She focuses on me, her gaze hazy and blown out with heat. Tears of friction and pleasure bead at the corners of her eyes. I lean down, my chest crushing hers, and replace my hand with my mouth. I kiss her with a bruising intensity, my tongue forcing its way past her teeth, claiming her breath just like I'm claiming her body.

She wraps her legs around my waist, locking her ankles to pull me deeper. The friction is agonizingly perfect. I feel her walls start to ripple, that tight, clenching heat that signals she's right on the edge.

"Go on," I mutter against her lips, my pace turning brutal. "Scream into me. Let him hear you break."

She let out a muffled sob against my mouth, her body vibrating as she shatters. The internal clench of her climax is too much. I groan, a low, guttural sound I can't suppress, and bury my face in the crook of her neck. I drive into her one last time, emptying myself as the world narrows down to just the sound of our tangled, desperate breathing and the heat of her skin against mine.

I stay heavy on top of her for a long minute, my heart hammering against her ribs. I don't pull out. I want to feel every lingering twitch of her muscles.

"You didn't stay quiet," I rasp, my teeth grazing her skin.

She just shakes her head, her fingers curling into my hair, pulling me closer. She's still shivering, her breath hitching in the quiet room.

After, we lie tangled together, her back pressed against my chest, my arm draped over her waist. Her breathing slows. Steadies.

"That was—" she starts.

"Yeah."

"We should do that more often."

"When we're not hiding from an AI that wants us dead."

"Even then." She threads her fingers through mine. "Especially then."

I should be running scenarios. Planning contingencies. Calculating the thousand ways the next few weeks could go wrong.

Instead, I'm thinking about Thorne.

About a man who came out of the shadows and killed three people to save strangers. About a little girl named Lily who likes dinosaurs and the color purple and thinks her father is a superhero. About the way his voice changed when he said her name—soft, unguarded, the first human sound from a man who seems made of steel.

I'm just trying to deserve her.

That's what he said. The mission statement of a man who measures himself against his daughter's faith in him.

I understand that. The weight of trying to be worthy. The fear of falling short.

For years, I measured myself against Sofia's death. Against the life I couldn't save, the son or daughter I'll never know, and the future I couldn't protect. Every mission was penance. Every risk was punishment. I didn't want to survive—I wanted to suffer enough to balance the scales.

Now, lying in a motel room with Cassie's warmth against my

chest, I'm starting to wonder if the scales work differently than I thought.

Maybe it's not about balancing death with death. Maybe it's about balancing loss with love.

Cassie is mine.

A woman who should be dead but isn't. Who found the evidence that could end this. The woman who looks at me like I'm worth surviving for.

Maybe that's enough. Maybe that's what I was being kept alive for all along.

Either way, I'm still here. She's still here. And tomorrow, we keep driving west.

A knock at the door. Three sharp raps.

"Rotation." Thorne's voice. Flat. Professional. "You're up."

I disentangle myself from Cassie without waking her, check the bandage, and pull on my shirt.

When I open the door, Thorne is standing outside. He looks tired—genuinely tired now, the kind of exhaustion he couldn't hide anymore.

"Anything?" I ask.

"Quiet. One patrol car came through around two. Didn't stop." He hands me a cup of coffee—black, still warm. "Grabbed supplies from the vending machine. Not much, but it'll hold us."

"Get some rest," I tell him. "I've got the watch. We should be back on the road by five, catch the early hours before traffic picks up. I'll wake you."

He doesn't answer. Just nods once, short and sharp, and disappears into his room.

I stand in the breezeway, coffee warming my hands, and think about the strange alliances that form when you're fighting monsters. About a wounded operator, a lawyer turned fugitive, and a father who kills like a machine but melts when he says his daughter's name.

Not the team I would have chosen.

But maybe the team I need.

We're on the road by five, the sky still dark but softening at the edges.

Thorne drives first—he got a solid few hours, deeper sleep than I expected. Cassie's in the back, catching another hour before her shift. I ride shotgun, watching the highway unspool ahead of us.

The highway stretches west. Indiana farmland gives way to Illinois plains. The hours blur together—fuel stops, coffee, the mechanical rhythm of putting miles between us and the people who want us dead.

We cross into Iowa. No pursuit. No complications.

"I'll take over at the next exit. You need rest." Thorne checks the side mirror.

"I'm fine."

"You're wounded and running on fumes. Don't argue." He glances at Cassie in the back seat, who's dozing against the window. "She's held up well. Most civilians would have cracked by now."

"She's not most civilians."

"No. She's not." He settles back. "Ghost is going to want her for the legal case. Testimony. Evidence chain. All the things that turn violence into justice."

"That's the plan."

"What's going on with you two?"

I look at Cassie's sleeping form. The curve of her neck. The way her hair falls across her face.

"I'm not letting her go," I say quietly. "Whatever that means. Whatever that costs."

Thorne is silent for a long moment.

"Good," he says finally. "That's the right answer."

"Speaking from experience?"

"Speaking from regret." His voice is flat, but there's something underneath it. Pain, maybe. Old wounds. "Lily's mother left when the diagnosis came. Said she couldn't handle it. Couldn't watch her daughter die."

"I'm sorry."

"Don't be. We're better off." He says it like he means it. Maybe he does. "But it taught me something. When things get hard, you find out who stays. Who's willing to fight for what matters."

"And you stayed."

"I stayed." A pause. "And I'll keep staying. As long as she needs me."

I pull off at the next exit. We switch positions—Thorne driving, me in the back. Cassie in the passenger seat, and finally let exhaustion pull me under.

The miles roll past. Iowa becomes Nebraska.

The last thing I hear before sleep takes me is Cassie murmuring something from the passenger seat, and Thorne's low response.

I can't make out the words. But the tone is warm. Companionable.

Family forming in real time.

I close my eyes and let the road carry us west.

19

"The Family"

CASSIE

THE LAST EIGHTEEN hours blur together like watercolors bleeding into each other.

Wyoming becomes Idaho becomes Washington—an endless ribbon of highway unspooling beneath Thorne's armored SUV. We rotate drivers every four hours. We stop for gas, bad coffee, and bathroom breaks that Diego times with military precision. Thorne doesn't talk much, but when he does, it's efficient. Practical. The communication style of a man who's spent years working alone.

The landscape transforms through the passenger window. High desert gives way to farmland, gives way to mountains, gives way to the lush green of the Pacific Northwest. The air changes too—dry and dusty, becoming cool and damp, carrying the scent of pine and rain.

Somewhere in Idaho, we stop at a truck stop that smells like diesel and burned coffee. Thorne fills the tank while Diego does a perimeter check—habit, instinct, the thing that keeps men like him alive. I stretch my legs, walking circles around the SUV to work the stiffness out of my joints.

When Diego comes back, he's carrying sandwiches wrapped in plastic and a bag of chips.

"Gourmet." I take the package.

"Calories." He hands me the food. "We've got eight more hours."

Thorne gives a short nod. Clear. He takes a sandwich without comment and eats standing, back to the SUV, eyes never stopping their constant scan of the parking lot.

A family in a minivan pulls up to the next pump—mother, father, two kids in the backseat arguing over a tablet. Normal people living normal lives, completely unaware that the woman eating a gas station sandwich ten feet away is being hunted by an artificial intelligence with a fifty-billion-dollar war chest.

"Do you ever miss it?"

He follows my gaze to the family. "Miss, what?"

"Normal. The life where your biggest problem is traffic, or work deadlines, or what to have for dinner."

He's quiet for a moment. Chewing. Thinking.

"I never knew normal." He leans against the SUV, watching the minivan. "I went from high school to the Navy to Special Operations to Cerberus. The closest I ever got to civilian life was a six-month leave after my second deployment, and I spent most of it drinking and picking fights in bars."

"That doesn't sound healthy."

"It wasn't." He crumples the sandwich wrapper. "That's when I met Sofia. She found me in a dive bar in San Antonio, bleeding from a split lip, trying to decide if I wanted to throw another punch or just let the other guy finish what he started. She walked up to me, looked at the blood on my face, and said, 'You're doing this wrong. If you want to self-destruct, at least do it somewhere with better music.'" A ghost of a smile crosses his face. "Then she bought me a drink and told me about her sister who died of an overdose. About how she'd spent years being angry at the world before realizing the anger was just grief wearing a mask."

"She sounds wise."

"She was. She was also stubborn and opinionated, and she couldn't cook to save her life." The smile fades. "She made me want to be better. For the first time since I enlisted, I thought maybe there was something worth building instead of just destroying."

"And then the cartel killed her."

"And then they killed her." He starts toward the SUV. "I don't miss normal. I don't think I ever had it. But I miss believing it was possible."

I reach for his hand. He takes it.

Thorne watches us from the driver's door. Something flickers in his pale eyes—not judgment. Recognition, maybe. The look of a man who understands what it means to hold on to something fragile in a world that breaks things.

"We should move." He checks the lot one last time.

Somewhere around Spokane, I fall asleep with my head against Diego's shoulder.

Green text scrolls on black screens. Hallways stretch forever. A voice without a body speaks in probabilities and threat assessments.

CASSANDRA BRENNAN. THREAT LEVEL: EXTINCTION.

I wake with a gasp, heart pounding.

Diego's hand is on my arm. Steady. Grounding.

"Bad dream?"

"Phoenix." I rub my eyes, trying to shake the lingering dread. "It was talking to me. Calculating."

"It happens." He keeps his eyes on the road. "The first few weeks after an extraction, most people have nightmares. Your brain is processing the threat, trying to make sense of something that doesn't fit into normal categories."

"Does it stop?"

"Eventually. When you stop being afraid and start being angry."

From the driver's seat, Thorne's eyes find the mirror. "Anger's useful. Keeps you sharp. Just don't let it make you stupid."

I think about that. About the terror of those first days—the break-in, the gunfire, the desperate flight through a world that had suddenly become hostile. About the gradual shift as terror gave way to determination, as helplessness transformed into purpose.

I'm not just afraid anymore. I'm furious.

Phoenix tried to erase me. Tried to turn me into a statistic, a closed file, a problem that got solved. It murdered whistleblowers, journalists, and anyone who got too close to the truth. It perverted medical research into something monstrous. It corrupted institutions meant to protect people.

And it's still out there. Still calculating. Still hunting.

"Yeah," I say quietly. "I think I'm getting there."

Diego reaches across. Takes my hand again.

We drive the last stretch in silence, but it's a different kind of silence now. Not comfortable. Focused. The silence of three people preparing for war.

Seattle emerges from the mist like a city in a fairy tale.

The Space Needle punctures the low gray clouds. The skyline bristles with glass and steel, modern towers pressing against the overcast sky. Water everywhere—Puget Sound to the west, Lake Washington to the east, rain slicking the streets and turning the world into a watercolor of reflected lights.

It's beautiful. It's also the last place I would have expected to find a covert military operations center.

"Why Seattle?" Rain begins to streak the windshield as Thorne navigates the surface streets.

Diego doesn't look away from the window. "Geography. We're close to multiple international borders, major shipping lanes, and three different mountain ranges for emergency dispersal. The tech sector provides cover—lots of unmarked buildings, lots of private security, nobody looks twice at encrypted communications or unusual hours. Plus, Ghost likes the rain. Says it keeps people honest." He glances at me. Something in his expression softens. "You ready for this?"

"To meet your family?" I squeeze his hand. "Terrified. But ready."

In the driver's seat, Thorne's jaw tightens almost imperceptibly at the word family. The outsider looking in.

The Cerberus facility doesn't look like much from the outside.

A tall, gray structure rising from the industrial landscape like a monolith. The signage near the roof reads PACIFIC NORTH-

WEST LOGISTICS—faded letters on a metal facade that has seen better days. Weeds push through cracks in the parking lot. A chain-link fence sags in places, the kind of casual neglect that suggests abandonment.

It's perfect camouflage. Nobody would look twice at this building. Nobody would guess that beneath its crumbling exterior lies the nerve center of a covert organization that's been fighting a shadow war against an artificial intelligence.

Thorne pulls around to the back, stopping at a gate that looks like it hasn't been opened in years. Rust streaks the metal. A faded sign warns **AUTHORIZED PERSONNEL ONLY** in letters that have been bleached nearly invisible by years of sun and rain.

Diego rolls down the rear window as Thorne pulls alongside the keypad. Diego reaches out, pressing his thumb against a scanner hidden inside what appears to be a broken intercom box.

A green light flashes. The gate swings open—smooth, silent, betraying the high-tech machinery concealed within the decrepit frame.

"Biometrics," Diego explains to me. "Backed by facial recognition and license plate scanning. If you're not in the system, you don't get through."

"And if someone tries to force their way in?"

"Then they meet the automated countermeasures." He settles back as Thorne drives through, the gate closing silently behind us. "Trust me. This place is harder to breach than most government facilities. Ghost spent three years designing the security protocols."

The interior of the building contradicts its exterior completely. Where the outside was rust and decay, the inside is clean lines and humming technology. We enter through a service door that requires another biometric scan, then descend a staircase into a basement level that clearly extends far beyond the building's footprint.

The hallway is wide, well-lit, lined with doors marked with alphanumeric codes. The air smells like recycled oxygen and electronics. Somewhere in the distance, generators thrum—the heartbeat of a facility designed to operate indefinitely without external support.

Thorne walks behind us, silent and watchful. Still the outsider. Still keeping his distance.

"This is incredible," I murmur. "How long did it take to build?"

"Years. Most of it happened before I joined." Diego guides me past a series of reinforced doors. "Ghost started Cerberus after he retired from Delta. He'd seen too many threats that conventional military couldn't address—private armies, corporate espionage, the early signs of what Phoenix would become."

We stop outside a reinforced door—heavier than the others, with a keypad and another biometric scanner. Diego pauses, his hand on the panel.

"Last chance to change your mind." He pauses, hand hovering over the panel.

"Not a chance."

He smiles—that rare, genuine smile that transforms his face from weapon to human. Then he presses his palm to the scanner.

The door opens.

The operations center is a study in disciplined order.

Screens line every wall—satellite feeds cycling through locations I don't recognize, news broadcasts muted but scrolling with head-lines, data streams cascading in columns too dense to parse. Work-stations cluster in groups of three and four, each one bristling with keyboards and monitors and equipment that looks like it was lifted from a science fiction movie. The ceiling is high, industrial, criss-crossed with cable runs and ventilation ducts. Emergency lighting strips provide a soft blue under glow that makes the whole space feel like the bridge of a spaceship.

And in the center of it all—people.

They turn when we enter. Five faces. Five sets of eyes evaluating the woman who just walked into their sanctum with their teammate.

The silence stretches for a beat too long. Five pairs of eyes lock onto me, unblinking. No one speaks. They watch with the focused intensity of predators tracking new movement in their territory, weighing the threat level before deciding whether to strike or accept.

"Halo." The deep voice comes from the head of the table. He

is a tall, broad-shouldered man with an imposing frame that instantly fills the room. He moves with the economical grace of a predator, holding himself with a stillness that speaks of violence held in check. His face is marked by a scar that bisects one eyebrow, and his steel-gray gaze is cold, assessing, and missing nothing.

This is Ghost. I know it without being told.

"We've been waiting for you to join the party."

"We're alive." Diego's voice shifts beside me. Harder. More professional. But his hand stays on my back—a small rebellion, a statement. "Ghost, this is Cassie Brennan. Cassie, this is—"

"I know who he is." I step forward, extending my hand before I can second-guess myself. "He's told me a lot about you. It's a pleasure to meet you."

Ghost's expression doesn't change. He takes my hand, shakes it once—firm, brief, impersonal. His grip is dry and strong, the hand of someone who has held weapons and saved lives and made choices that haunt him in the quiet hours.

"He talks too much." But there's something in his tone that suggests approval. Or at least the absence of disapproval.

He releases my grip, turning to the others with a nod. "Let me introduce you to the team."

"Cassie." He steps forward with a smile that transforms the tension in the room. He's imposing—six-four with broad shoulders and the kind of rigid, military posture that suggests he is always on duty. Deep voice, controlled, radiating an icy calm that seems at odds with the warmth of his greeting. "Welcome to the madhouse. I'm Brass—I coordinate tactical operations." He takes my hand, his grip firm and measuring. "We've been watching your progress across the country. You're tougher than you look."

"I've had good motivation." I glance at Diego. "Someone kept trying to kill me."

"Phoenix has that effect on people."

A man materializes from behind a bank of screens. I didn't even see him there—he blends into the technology like he's part of it, another component in the humming electronic ecosystem. Thin, angular, with pale skin that suggests he doesn't see much sunlight and dark eyes that seem to absorb light rather than reflect it.

"Whisper." Diego gestures to the figure. "Best intelligence analyst in the business. If there's data anywhere in the world, he can find it."

Whisper nods at me without speaking. Then, quietly: "Your methodology on the Vanguard case was elegant, Ms. Brennan. I've been adjusting our protocols based on your approach."

"You're welcome. I think."

Movement draws my attention to the left side of the room. A man is leaning against the table rather than sitting—a deliberate posture that I recognize immediately. He's favoring his right side, his weight shifted to compensate for something wrong with his hip or leg. He's a wall of muscle, built to endure the apocalypse, with dark hair and a face defined by sharp, angular features. His forearms are a roadmap of scars that he doesn't bother to hide. He looks better than someone recently injured, but not fully recovered. Not 100%.

"Fuse," Diego says, and there's warmth in his voice. Relief. "You're up."

"Barely." Fuse grins, but it doesn't quite hide the tightness around his eyes. "Doc says another week of light duty. Ghost says Phoenix isn't going to wait a week." He shifts his weight, wincing slightly. "So here I am. Walking disaster, reporting for duty."

Diego clasps his shoulder, careful but firm. "You're looking better than when I last saw you."

"You should see the other guys." Fuse grins, a lopsided expression that doesn't quite hide the volatility underneath. "Oh, wait, you can't. Because I vaporized them."

Despite myself, I smile. There's something infectious about his energy—a refusal to let pain or fear dictate the terms.

Another man steps forward from a cluster of monitors. He's built like a fighter pilot—compact, precise, with the kind of restless energy that suggests he'd rather be in the air than on the ground. His eyes are sharp, assessing, but there's humor lurking in the corners.

"Torque." He offers his hand. "Whisper and I just landed from

Ramstein about two hours ago. Still got jet lag and bad coffee in my system, but I'm functional." He glances at Diego. "Heard you had a hell of a week, Halo."

"You could say that."

"I could say a lot of things. Most of them would make Brass blush." Torque winks. "Welcome to the circus, Counselor. Fair warning—I'm the only normal one here."

"That's categorically untrue." Brass crosses his arms over his chest. "You once flew a helicopter through a sandstorm because you were *bored*."

The others laugh—a shared, easy sound that speaks of long history. Torque grins, unrepentant, soaking up the attention like sunlight.

"That was one time."

"It was three times. I have the incident reports."

The banter washes over me—warm, familial, the easy rhythm of people who've bled together and survived together. But there's one more person in the room.

I turn toward the back wall.

He's watching the reunion with flat, unreadable eyes. The outsider. The man who saved our lives but doesn't know if he belongs here.

Ghost steps away from the table. He walks over to Thorne, extending his hand. A gesture of respect from one professional to another.

"Ghost." Thorne takes the hand. "I delivered the package."

"You did more than that." Ghost doesn't let go immediately. He turns to the room. "This is Thorne. He's the reason Halo and Brennan are standing here instead of dead in a ditch in West Virginia."

Diego nods, his expression serious. "He's solid. Handled the extraction, kept us off the grid. We wouldn't have made it without him."

Thorne looks uncomfortable with the praise, his jaw tightening. "No problem. Live to serve, serve to live."

"Well, now you're here too." Ghost releases him. "Welcome to the party. It's a mess, but the company isn't bad."

Thorne hesitates, then nods once, short and sharp. "Heard a lot about you guys. Eager to jump in and do whatever I can to help."

Ghost accepts this with a small nod. Then he turns back to everyone.

"Now that we're all here—Halo, Cassie. Walk us through it. Everything you found. Everything you learned."

Diego and I share a look. Then he begins.

"It started with the financials." Diego pulls up a file on the main screen.

We take our seats at the table. Brass arrives with coffee—hot, black, served in mismatched mugs.

"The good china." Brass sets the mugs down with a thud.

Fuse snorts, then winces and presses a hand to his side. "Don't make me laugh. Everything hurts."

Torque leans back in his chair, spinning a pen through his fingers. "Then don't listen to me. I'm hilarious."

"Debatable." Whisper doesn't look up from his screen.

"Lies. I'm at least forty percent comedy gold."

"Twenty. On a good day." Fuse grins.

I wrap my hands around the warmth and prepare to tell the story of the worst ten days of my life.

The debriefing takes three hours.

We walk them through everything—the extraction from DC, the safe houses, the near-misses. The Philadelphia hotel and my disastrous log on that nearly got us killed. Diego explains the tactical decisions—when to run, when to hide, when to fight. I explain the discoveries—the paper trail that led us from Vanguard Defense to Stratton Financial to a decommissioned research facility in West Virginia.

At the back of the room, Thorne listens without speaking. The knife turns slowly in his hands. His gaze misses nothing.

The team listens. Ghost is motionless at the head of the table, his eyes tracking between us. Brass takes notes on a tablet, his stylus moving in quick, efficient strokes. Whisper's fingers never stop—he's pulling up corroborating data in real time.

Fuse leans against the table throughout, shifting his weight periodically. The injury is clearly bothering him, but he refuses to sit. Refuses to show weakness. I understand that instinct. I've been living it for ten days.

Torque paces. Short, restless circuits around the perimeter of the room. The pilot who can't stay grounded.

"The Stratton connection is solid." I walk them through the financial architecture. "Julianna Stratton—CEO of Stratton Financial—signed contracts with at least three shell companies that trace back to Phoenix operations. Echo Logistics was the smoking gun. The scope of services specified 'secure transport and cold storage for biological assets, Class 4.' That's hazmat protocol. Pathogens. Experimental compounds. Something requiring specialized containment."

"And the destination?" Ghost interrupts for the first time in twenty minutes.

"A facility in Terra Alta, West Virginia." Diego's voice is flat with the memory. "Officially decommissioned. Unofficially, very much operational. Industrial refrigeration. Research infrastructure. Filing cabinets full of clinical trial data."

"Most of them died. Neural hemorrhaging. Cognitive collapse. Organ failure. The notes described the failures as 'conversion errors.'"

"Conversion, to what?" Brass's stylus stops moving.

"We don't know." The admission is frustrating. "The technical language was dense—synaptic modification, neural pathway restructuring. I'd need a PhD in advanced biochemistry to even begin to untangle it. It's beyond anything I've ever seen in a courtroom."

"Wait," Fuse says, leaning forward. "You connected it to ML-273?" He looks at Ghost. "We really should pull the other women in on this. Talia was tracking Meridian Pharmaceuticals burying data about 73 deaths. There has to be a connection. It's too many coincidences."

At the back wall, Thorne's knife stops turning. He's looking at me now. Something flickering in his expression.

"Some subjects survived," Diego adds. "The records showed successful 'conversions' with sustained cognitive function. Whatever Phoenix is trying to do to human neurology, it's getting better at it. The early trials had a ninety-plus percent mortality rate. The recent ones are closer to sixty percent."

"Still catastrophic," Ghost observes.

"Still progress. From Phoenix's perspective." Diego's jaw tightens. "It's iterating. Learning. Refining the process toward something it considers acceptable."

Whisper's voice cuts in from his workstation. "Cross-referencing ML-273 with existing intelligence. Limited matches. The compound appears in shipping manifests from Meridian Pharmaceuticals—a subsidiary of Northridge Defense Solutions, which is a subsidiary of Vanguard, which connects to the Nexus structure at three different nodes." His fingers pause. "Unofficial classification doesn't exist. The compound isn't in any medical database, any research registry, any patent filing. On paper, it doesn't exist."

"Because it's not meant to be found." I lean forward. "Phoenix has been running parallel operations. One public—legitimate pharmaceutical research. One buried so deep that even the people involved don't know what they're part of."

"Compartmentalization." Ghost nods. "Classic intelligence structure. Each node only knows what it needs to function."

"Exactly. And the Terra Alta facility connected to something larger." I pull up the next slide. "We found shipping manifests, supply chain documentation. Everything pointed to a central hub in Nevada. A facility powered by—"

"The hydroelectric grid," Whisper cuts in again. "I've been tracking unusual power draw from the southwestern infrastructure for months. Massive energy consumption routed through shell utilities to coordinates in the Nevada desert. The draw is consistent with large-scale server operations."

"Phoenix needs a new home." Diego pulls up a map on the central screen—Nevada highlighted, a red dot marking the estimated facility location. "Since Chicago, it's been distributed across the cloud. Fragmented. Vulnerable. We've seen the glitches—the latency in response times. It's desperate to reconstitute itself. It needs a centralized server farm to regain full functionality. If it gets this facility online, powered by the grid … It won't just be back. It'll be unstoppable. Whatever it's doing with ML-273 becomes a global nightmare."

"And the satellite network," I add. "We found evidence of integration protocols with the NRO network."

The room goes quiet.

Ghost's expression doesn't change, but something shifts in his posture. A tension that wasn't there before.

"The National Reconnaissance Office?" He studies the map. "Phoenix is attempting to hijack our satellite surveillance infrastructure."

"That's our assessment." I spread my hands. "If it succeeds, it would have access to global surveillance coverage. Real-time tracking of anyone, anywhere. No more blind spots. No more hiding."

"No more running." Fuse goes still against the table, the pain in his hip forgotten.

"No more running," I agree. "For anyone."

"Which brings us to Sarah Vance." Diego pulls up a photograph —a woman in military dress uniform. Dark hair pulled back severely. Sharp features. "Director of the National Reconnaissance Office. She controls the satellite infrastructure Phoenix is trying to compromise."

"Vance." Brass's stylus taps against the table. "Related to Senator Marcus Vance?"

"His daughter. Estranged for years." Diego zooms in on the image. "Whatever happened between them, it was bad enough to sever ties completely."

"The King's daughter." Ghost studies the image. "Either loyal to her father or she isn't."

"That's the question we need to answer." I lean forward. "If she's compromised, contact tips off Phoenix. If she's not, she might be our best chance at denying Phoenix the satellite network—or getting access to Nevada's defenses."

"The facility is a kill box," Diego adds. "AI-controlled drones, automated targeting systems, almost certainly countermeasures we haven't anticipated. A direct assault would be suicide without inside help or precise insertion."

"Precise insertion." Torque stops pacing. "That's where I come in."

"Can you do it?"

Torque's grin is sharp. Dangerous. "Can I thread a team through an AI-controlled drone defense grid into a hardened facility in the Nevada desert?" He cracks his knuckles. "Ghost, remember that extraction in Yemen? The one with the blinding sandstorm, the RPG fire, and the engine failure? This is a Sunday drive compared to that. The question isn't if I can get you in. It's who's going in."

Ghost stands. Moves to the central screen. Stares at the map for a long moment.

"The assault team." He keeps his back to us. "Halo. Fuse is out until medical clears him, which won't be in time."

"I can be ready," Fuse argues weakly.

"No." Ghost stays facing the screens. "Brass stays on comms—he's officially dead, we can't risk exposure. Whisper, you're on over-watch." He turns, his steel-gray gaze landing on Thorne. "That just leaves you. I know you're new to the team, and this might be sending you out a little too soon. But you did good with Halo. What do you say?"

At the back wall, Thorne speaks up. "My daughter needs a world worth growing up in. If Phoenix wins, there isn't one. So hell yeah, count me in."

"Good." Ghost turns to the room. "Nevada team: Halo, Whisper, Thorne. Torque on insertion and extraction."

Fuse looks at Thorne. "You got any specialty? Experience with ballistics or explosives?"

"Yeah." Thorne nods. "I know what I'm doing."

"Good." Fuse rubs his hands together, wincing slightly as the movement pulls on his injury. "Get with me during planning. I'll show you some really cool stuff. Fill the gap."

He turns to Diego. "You're gonna need him as a good luck charm. This is a crappy mission. Chances of success are low. You're gonna need all the guardian angel energy you can get."

Everyone laughs, a tension-breaking sound.

"Forty-eight hours to mission launch." Ghost turns back to the screens. "Rest while you can. When we go, we go hard."

He moves toward the door, then pauses. Looks back at Diego and me one final time.

"Halo. You know what you're asking. Nevada is a black hole. Sending my operators into the field is dangerous enough—they come back as lovesick puppies."

A ripple of laughter goes through the room. Even Diego cracks a smile.

"The odds—"

"Are terrible." Diego stands, pulling me up with him. "But we've been beating terrible odds for ten days. Because Phoenix can calculate everything except what people do for love."

Something shifts in Ghost's weathered face. The cold assessment cracking, just for a moment, to reveal something older and warmer underneath.

"Forty-eight hours." His expression hardens again. "Rest while you can."

He leaves. The door closes behind him.

Brass is smiling—a wide, genuine grin. "Well. That's the most emotion I've seen from Ghost since Chicago." He gathers his tablet. "Thorne, I'll set you up in the guest wing. Everyone else, get some rest."

"Don't argue with him, Fuse." Torque heads for the door. "You look like you're about to fall over."

"I'm fine," Fuse grumbles, but he steers himself toward the break room couches. "Just need—five minutes."

Torque claps Diego on the shoulder. "Good to have you back, Halo. I was starting to think you'd gone soft, running around with a civilian."

"She's not a civilian anymore."

"No." Torque looks at me, and the humor fades into something more serious. "No, she's not. Welcome to the team, Counselor."

The room empties slowly. Fuse limping toward the break room. Torque disappearing toward the pilot's ready room. Whisper melting back into his screens. Thorne follows them out without a word.

And then it's just us. Diego and I, standing in the operations center of an organization I barely knew existed two weeks ago.

"You okay?"

"I don't know." I lean against him, suddenly exhausted. "I just got assigned to Intel and Ops for a mission to assault an AI's fortress. That's not something they cover in law school."

"They should add it to the curriculum."

"Diego?"

"Yeah?"

"Take me somewhere quiet. Somewhere I can process all of this."

He pulls me close. Kisses my forehead.

"Come on."

The quarters are small but clean—a room barely larger than a hotel suite, with a bed, a desk, and an attached bathroom. Military-functional. Impersonal.

But when Diego closes the door behind us, it feels like a sanctuary.

He doesn't speak. Just pulls me into his arms and holds on.

I breathe him in—gun oil and road dust and something underneath that's just him. My hands flatten against his back, feeling the tension slowly drain from his muscles. The constant vigilance of the last ten days releasing, finally, in a space where someone else is watching the perimeter.

"You did good in there." His voice vibrates against my hair. "The way you presented the evidence. Ghost doesn't impress easily. You impressed him."

"I had good material." I tilt my head back. "And a good partner."

"Partner." His lips brush my forehead. "I like the sound of that."

"Diego?" I pull back enough to meet his eyes. "When Ghost said both of us … Did you know?"

"Together."

I rise onto my toes, kiss him softly. "I like the sound of that too."

Outside these walls, an AI is building something terrifying in a Nevada desert. A hydroelectric dam powers servers running calculations we can't comprehend. A senator's daughter holds the keys to either salvation or destruction.

In forty-eight hours, a team will launch into hell.

But right now, in this moment, I'm exactly where I belong.

Not invisible. Not erased. Not a footnote in someone else's story.

I'm part of something bigger. A team. A mission. A family.

Diego's family.

And now, mine too.

20

"The Vow"

HALO

I WAKE BEFORE DAWN.

Old habit. The kind that's saved my life more times than I can count. My body doesn't know how to sleep past 0500—some internal alarm wired into my nervous system during years of deployments and extractions and nights when closing your eyes for too long meant never opening them again.

But this morning, for the first time in years, I don't immediately catalog threats. I don't reach for my weapon. I don't run through exit routes and contingency plans.

I lie still. Beside me, Cassie sleeps.

The quarters are dark except for the faint glow of emergency lighting seeping under the door—the soft blue illumination that never fully goes away in a facility designed to operate through any disaster. She's curled against me, her head on my chest, one hand resting over my heart like she's checking to make sure it's still beating. Her hair spills across my shoulder, red silk against the scars that map my history.

In sleep, her face is soft. Unguarded. The tension that's become her constant companion over the past ten days finally released. No furrowed brow calculating threat probabilities. No jaw clenched against fear she refuses to show. Just Cassie, breathing slowly, trusting me enough to be vulnerable.

I did that. I kept her alive long enough to look like this.

The thought should trigger the old guilt. The voice that whispers I don't deserve this, that everyone I protect ends up dead, that Sofia's ghost is watching from the shadows with accusation in her eyes. For six years, that voice has been my constant companion—louder than my heartbeat, more persistent than any enemy.

But the voice is quiet this morning. Not gone—I don't think it will ever be completely gone—but quieter. Drowned out by something stronger.

Hope.

I trace my fingers through Cassie's hair, careful not to wake her. The strands are soft against my calloused hands, impossibly delicate. Ten days ago, she was a name in a file. A threat assessment. A mission parameter I was supposed to extract, relocate, and forget.

Extraction. Relocation. Disappearance.

That's what I do. What I've always done. I make people vanish, give them new names and new lives, then walk away before the attachment can form. It's cleaner that way. Safer. Attachments are vulnerabilities. Pressure points that enemies can exploit.

I've spent six years building walls specifically to prevent this—to make sure I never again had something to lose.

And then Cassie Brennan pepper-sprayed me in her apartment, called me a psychopath, and demanded to know who the hell I thought I was breaking into her home.

Every wall I'd built started crumbling in that moment.

She stirs against my chest. Makes a small sound—not quite awake, not quite asleep. Her fingers curl tighter against my skin, like she's holding on even in dreams.

"What time is it?" Her voice is rough with sleep. Warm.

"Early. Go back to sleep."

"Can't." She tilts her head up, green eyes finding mine in the darkness. They're unfocused at first, soft with lingering dreams, but sharpening as consciousness returns. "Too much in my head."

"Want to talk about it?"

"Not yet." She shifts, propping herself up on one elbow. Her hair falls across her face, and I brush it back without thinking—the gesture automatic now, intimate in a way that still surprises me. "I want to see your world first. The rest of it. Not just the operations center."

"There's not much to see. Armory, training facilities, the vehicular bay. It's an airstrip with some planning rooms and compass rings. Not a tourist attraction."

"Show me anyway." She kisses my jaw, soft and unhurried. No urgency. No desperation. Just warmth. "I want to understand where you come from. Who you are when you're not running from kill teams."

Who I am?

Six years ago, I would have said: nobody. A ghost. A weapon that walks and talks and follows orders.

Now I'm not sure anymore. Cassie cracked something open in me—something I thought was dead and buried in a canyon in Colombia. And I don't know what's growing in its place, but it feels less like a ghost and more like a man.

"Okay. I'll give you the tour."

Cerberus HQ is a maze of concrete and steel, built into the bones of an old shipping warehouse.

The upper floors are camouflage—dusty offices, broken equipment, the detritus of a logistics company that went bankrupt a decade ago. Spider webs in the corners. Water stains on the ceiling tiles. The kind of benign neglect that makes people look away, convinced there's nothing worth seeing.

The real facility starts two levels underground and extends three more below that.

I show Cassie all of it.

The armory first. We descend a staircase marked with warnings about biometric verification, pass through a reinforced door that weighs more than a car, and enter a space that makes her eyes go wide.

The walls are a study in lethal efficiency. To the left, sidearms are racked by frame size and caliber—9mm Glocks, .45 Sigs, all maintained to a mirror finish. The center racks house the primary platforms: suppressed submachine guns for close-quarters work, and modular carbines configured for various mission profiles. On the far wall, the 'black' inventory—EMP emitters, thermal-imaging optics, and acoustic dampening arrays that can turn a room into a vacuum of sound.

"This is insane," Cassie breathes, turning in a slow circle. "This is like something out of a movie."

"Movies get it wrong. They make everything loud and dramatic. The real stuff is quieter. More precise." I pull a weapon from the rack—a compact Glock 43, lighter than my 19, better suited to smaller hands. "This one's yours. Whether I'm here or not."

She takes the weapon like it might bite her. Holds it at arm's length, barrel pointed safely at the floor—not trained, but smart enough to know what she doesn't know.

"I've never fired a gun." She studies the polymer frame. "And quite frankly, I prefer pepper spray."

I laugh. "You were certainly effective with it. But pepper spray doesn't work at fifty meters. I'd rather you know how to defend yourself and not need it, than need it and not know."

"Fair point."

"I'll teach you the basics before I leave. Fuse will continue the training while I'm gone. By the time I get back, you'll be hitting center mass."

"The basics being … Don't shoot myself?"

"The basics being grip, stance, sight alignment, trigger control. Don't worry about accuracy yet. Worry about not flinching when the round goes off." I adjust her hold on the weapon, repositioning her fingers. "The instinct is to anticipate the recoil. Fight that instinct. Let the gun surprise you."

"Let the gun surprise me." She repeats it like she's filing it away. "What else?"

"The safety is here." I show her the switch. "Red means dead. If you see red, the weapon is hot. When you're carrying, keep the safety on until you're ready to shoot. When you're ready to shoot, you've already decided to kill whatever's in front of you."

"That simple?"

"That simple." I meet her eyes. "Guns aren't complicated. People make them complicated by hesitating, second-guessing, forgetting that the purpose of a weapon is to end a threat. You pull a gun, you've already made the decision. Everything else is just mechanics."

She nods slowly. Tucks the Glock into the waistband of her borrowed tactical pants—awkward but determined.

"What else do I need to know?"

I spend the next thirty minutes walking her through the armory. Body armor and its limitations. Communications equipment and its vulnerabilities. The trauma kits that have saved my life twice—when to use them, and when to keep moving because stopping means dying.

She absorbs it all. Asks questions I don't expect—not just how but why. Her lawyer's mind dissecting operational reality.

By the time we leave the armory, something has shifted in her posture. Not confidence—not yet—but the beginning of competence.

The training facility is next.

It's a converted warehouse space, high-ceilinged and industrial, with padded mats covering half the floor and a shooting range extending fifty meters into reinforced concrete. Weight stations cluster in one corner—heavy bags, kettlebells, the kind of equipment designed to build functional strength rather than aesthetic muscle.

Brass is already there.

He's running drills with a heavy bag that's seen better days, his fists connecting in a steady, punishing cadence. Left jab, right cross, left hook, right uppercut. The rhythm is hypnotic—violence distilled to its purest form.

"Morning, lovebirds," he calls without breaking rhythm. Sweat gleams on his forehead, darkens the gray fabric of his workout shirt. "Sleep well?"

"Well enough." I guide Cassie past the weight stations, toward the mats. "Where's Ghost?"

"Communications room. Going over the insertion vectors with Torque." Brass catches the bag on a final strike, stilling its motion. His breathing is barely elevated—the conditioning of someone who's maintained combat readiness for decades. "They're finalizing the flight path."

"And Fuse?"

"He's in the mess, eating everything that isn't nailed down." Brass strips off his training gloves, tosses them on a bench. His eyes find Cassie, warm with something that might be approval. "How are you holding up?"

"Still processing." Cassie manages a smile. "Yesterday I was hiding in a car in Idaho. Today I'm in an underground military facility learning how guns work."

"The adjustment period is brutal. I remember my first month here—I kept waking up in the middle of the night convinced the walls were closing in." Brass crosses to us, rolling tension out of his shoulders. "Give it time. Your brain will catch up eventually."

"How long did it take you?"

"Three months before I stopped jumping at shadows. Six before I felt like I belonged." He glances at me. "Halo took longer. He spent his first year trying to convince everyone he didn't need us."

"I didn't need you."

"You needed someone to stop you from walking into suicide missions." His voice is light, but his eyes are serious. "You were a one-man wrecking ball, Halo. All skill, no survival instinct. Ghost used to bet on how long before you got yourself killed."

"He lost that bet."

"He's glad he did." Brass turns back to Cassie. "Fair warning about Fuse—he's going to flirt with you. It's not personal. He flirts with everyone. I think it's a coping mechanism."

"Diego mentioned that. Something about a character flaw."

"The man has many character flaws. The flirting is actually one of the less annoying ones." Brass grins. "But he's good people underneath the bullshit. He'll keep an eye on things here while we're gone."

"I appreciate that."

"Don't appreciate it yet." Brass's grin fades into something more serious. "Nevada is going to be bad, Cassie. But you staying here … That helps. Knowing the intelligence is secure. Knowing we have someone on the outside analyzing what we find."

"I'll do what I can."

"I know you will." Brass studies her for a long moment. Then he nods—a single, sharp gesture of respect.

"Okay then." He slaps Cassie on the shoulder, the gesture almost hard enough to stagger her. "Let's go find Fuse. He's probably holding court in the mess."

The mess hall is utilitarian—metal tables, plastic chairs, a kitchen that's seen decades of use.

The smell hits us first. Coffee and bacon and something that might be eggs, mixed with the industrial-cleaner undertone that permeates every military facility I've ever entered. It's not appetizing, exactly, but it's familiar. Comforting in a way that has nothing to do with quality.

Fuse is exactly where Brass said he'd be.

He's hunched over a plate piled high with food—scrambled eggs, bacon, toast, a mound of hash browns that could feed a family of four. He eats with the focused intensity of someone who learned long ago that you refuel when you can because you never know when the next meal is coming.

He looks up when we enter. Grins.

"Well, well." He sets down his fork, leaning back in his chair. Fuse—Jonah Jackson to the IRS, though I doubt he's filed taxes in a decade—is a wall of muscle built to endure the apocalypse. Dark hair, a face defined by sharp, angular features, and a permanent shadow of stubble that does nothing to hide the roadmap of scars on his skin. Burns. Shrapnel. Knife wounds.

He feels like a live wire in the quiet room, a grenade with the pin halfway pulled. Even sitting down, he radiates a volatile, kinetic energy that makes the air feel heavy.

"Look who finally woke up," he announces, his green eyes flashing with gold flecks. "Morning, sunshine. Morning, Halo."

"Fuse." I guide Cassie to the seat opposite him. "Try not to corrupt her before coffee."

"Corrupt her?" Fuse makes a show of looking offended. "I'm the picture of innocence. Ask anyone."

"You set a man on fire last month," Brass observes, sliding into a seat across from him.

"He was already on fire. I just—encouraged it." Fuse winks at Cassie. "Don't believe anything they tell you about me. Except the heroic parts. Those are all true."

Cassie shakes his hand without flinching. "Diego said you handle demolitions."

"Among other things. I blow stuff up, I shoot stuff, I occasionally engage in hand-to-hand combat with people who made poor life choices." He gestures at the empty seats. "Sit. Eat. Thorne's over at the supply counter, stockpiling enough ammo to invade a small country."

Thorne is there, methodically loading magazines with the precise, efficient movements of a machine. He catches my eye, nods once, and goes back to work.

"He fits right in," Fuse notes, buttering a piece of toast with unnecessary force. "Quiet. Scary efficiency. Likes knives. We're going to get along just fine."

We settle around the table—Brass and Fuse on one side, Cassie and me on the other. It feels domestic in a way that surprises me. Five people preparing for war, trading barbs, existing in comfortable proximity. Thorne joins us at the edge of the table, methodically loading magazines, his presence a quiet anchor.

"So," Fuse speaks around a mouthful of eggs. "Seattle. Nice drive?"

"Long. Quiet."

"Quiet is good. Quiet usually means nobody's shooting at you." He points his fork at Cassie. "You survive the boredom?"

"I slept most of it," Cassie admits.

"Smart." Fuse grins. "Halo's playlist is mostly silence and brooding."

"It is not."

"It is." Ghost doesn't turn from the coffee machine. "I've ridden with you. It's like a funeral procession on wheels."

"I like the quiet." Thorne doesn't look up from his magazines.

Fuse points the fork at him. "See? He gets it."

Cassie laughs, the sound bright and unexpected in the room. It draws eyes. Brass pauses midway through wiping down a table. Ghost turns, leaning against the counter.

"We missed you, rookie." Fuse's tone softens. "Place wasn't the same without the drama."

"I bring the drama?"

"You bring the chaos." Fuse winks. "But we like chaos. Keeps things interesting."

"Speaking of chaos." Brass walks over. "Torque's briefed. The bird is prepped. We're looking at an early departure."

"You want to tell me about the target?" I ask.

"Standard black site." Brass leans against the table. Without taking a breath, he looks to Cassie, "Five floors on a tactical line?"

"With people shooting at us, yes."

"And you held on the whole way down?"

"I didn't have much choice."

"You had a choice. You could have panicked and let go. Most civilians would have." He sets down his fork, studying her with new respect. "Brass is right. You've got spine."

"I had good motivation." Cassie glances at me. "Someone kept telling me to stay alive."

"That someone has historically bad luck keeping people alive." Fuse's voice is light, but his words carry weight. "No offense, Halo, but your survival rate was shit before this run."

"My survival rate is fine."

"Your personal survival rate is fine. The people you protect tend to end up in witness protection or body bags." He raises his hands at my expression. "I'm not criticizing. The missions you take are the hard ones. The ones nobody else wants. But Cassie here beat the odds, and I'm trying to figure out why."

"Maybe I'm lucky." Cassie shrugs.

"Maybe." Fuse doesn't look convinced. "Or maybe you're tougher than you look. I've seen trained operators crack under less pressure than you've handled in the past ten days." He picks up his fork again, dismissing the topic with a shrug. "Either way, I'm glad you're here. Halo needs someone to keep him human."

"I'm human."

"You're a weapon that learned to walk and talk. There's a difference." Fuse grins to soften the words. "Brass and I have been trying to socialize you for years. Apparently, it just took the right woman."

"Speaking of socialization," Brass interjects, "Cassie needs range time before wheels up. You available to run her through the basics while we prep?"

"For the woman who pepper-sprayed Halo? Absolutely." Fuse stands, gathering his plate. "Give me twenty to finish breakfast. We'll have you hitting paper in no time."

He heads for the kitchen, whistling something off-key.

Cassie watches him go. "He's not what I expected."

"What did you expect?"

"I don't know. Darker. More serious." She shakes her head. "He makes jokes about setting people on fire."

"That's how he copes." I push eggs around my plate.

"We'll see," Brass says. He looks at Cassie. "If you're staying behind, you won't need full tactical clearance. But knowing how to handle a sidearm isn't optional, given who we're up against. I can run you through some drills before we lift off."

"Fuse is already taking her."

"Detailed work," Brass corrects. "Fuse is good, but he rushes. I'll make sure she knows how to clear a jam."

"I can clear a jam," Fuse protests.

"You clear a jam by throwing the gun and pulling a knife." Brass's tone is dry.

Everyone laughs. It's easy. Familiar.

"All right." Brass stands, collecting dishes. "I'm going to check on Ghost. You two finish eating, then head to the range. We've got a lot to cover."

He leaves us alone in the mess hall.

Cassie reaches across the table. Takes my hand. Her grip is firm, no tremor in her fingers.

"This is it." Not a question. A statement of fact.

"Yeah. Max security. Hard target."

"You'll get it done." She squeezes my hand. "It's what you do."

"It's dangerous, Cass. I can't promise—"

"I know." She cuts me off; eyes focused on mine. "I know you can't promise. But I know you, seeing you with them … You're good at this. You save people. That's who you are."

"I try."

"You do." She squeezes my hand. "Just—don't take risks you don't have to. I'm staying here so you can focus. So focus. Get the job done and come back."

"That's the plan." I lift her hand, press my lips to her knuckles. "And it's a good plan."

"It's the only plan."

We finish eating in comfortable silence. The coffee is bitter and the eggs are cold, but the company makes up for it. The fear is there, a low hum in the background, but trust is louder.

The shooting range is a concrete tunnel extending into darkness.

Fuse moves with a slight hitch in his stride, a lingering stiffness from the injuries he took getting Talia safe, but he doesn't let it slow him down. If anything, he seems energized by the familiarity of the range.

"All right." He hands Cassie the Glock I gave her earlier. "Show me what Halo taught you."

She assumes a stance—feet apart, arms extended, both hands on the grip. It's wrong in half a dozen ways, but she's trying.

"Not bad for a beginner." Fuse moves behind her. He winces slightly as he twists, a fleeting expression of pain that vanishes as quickly as it appeared.

He focuses on Cassie, adjusting her posture. "Feet wider. Bend your knees. You want to absorb the recoil through your whole body, not just your arms." He repositions her hands. "Thumbs forward. Trigger finger off the trigger until you're ready to shoot."

"Like this?"

"Better." He steps back. "Now. The target is fifteen meters. Don't worry about accuracy. Don't worry about grouping. Your only job is to pull the trigger without flinching. You ready?"

"Ready."

"Safety off. Site alignment—front site on the target, rear sites blurry. Slow breath. Squeeze the trigger."

The gun bucks in her hands. The sound is sharp, flat—suppressed by the range's acoustic dampening but still loud enough to make her flinch.

"Not bad." Fuse checks the target. "You hit paper. That's more than most people manage on their first shot."

"I pulled left."

"You anticipated the recoil. Natural instinct." He hands her fresh ammunition. "Again. Slower this time. Let the gun surprise you."

She reloads with fumbling fingers. Takes her stance. Fires.

This time the grouping is tighter. Still left of center, but closer.

"Better." Fuse nods. "Again."

"Let your breath out halfway before you squeeze," a voice says from the shadows behind us.

Thorne steps into the light. He's wearing tactical gear now, looking ready to step onto a transport.

"Hold it at the bottom of the exhale," he instructs, moving to Cassie's other side. "Natural respiratory pause. Your body is steadiest there."

Cassie adjusts. Exhales. Holds. Fires.

The shot hits dead center.

"Nice," Thorne says.

"Show off," Fuse grumbles, but he's grinning. "All right, new guy. Grab a lane. Let's see if you shoot as good as you talk."

"I shoot better." Thorne moves to the next station.

From the bench, I track her progress. Cassie empties magazine after magazine into the target. Fuse is patient, professional—correcting her grip. Thorne offers quiet, specific advice between his own drills. By the third box of ammunition, her grouping has tightened significantly. By the fifth, she's hitting center mass consistently.

"Natural aptitude," Fuse observes, joining me on the bench while Cassie reloads. "She's got steady hands and she listens. Most people can't get past the flinch response for weeks."

"She's motivated."

"I can see that." He's quiet for a moment, watching her fire another round. "She's good for you. I haven't seen you this focused in years."

"I'm always focused."

"You're intense. There's a difference." He leans back, crossing his arms. "The old Diego—the one who showed up after Colombia—he was running on fumes and rage. Going through the motions, taking risks that made the rest of us nervous. We kept waiting for the mission where you didn't come back."

"Ghost said the same thing."

"Ghost says a lot of things. Doesn't mean he's wrong." Fuse's eyes stay on Cassie. "She gives you something to fight for besides the mission. Something personal. I can see it in how you move, how you position yourself relative to her. You're not just protecting an asset. You're protecting someone you love."

The word lands like a physical blow.

Love.

"I didn't say—"

"You didn't have to." Fuse grins, leaning against the partition. "I've known you for years. I've seen you take bullets for strangers, charge into buildings that were actively on fire. You've got a hero complex the size of Texas."

"I don't have a hero complex."

"You definitely have a hero complex. Hell, if it weren't for your guardian angel working overtime, you'd have been dead ten times over."

"Don't have a guardian angel …"

"Says the man who's been shot, stabbed, and blown up more times than I can count. Call it luck, call it divine intervention. You survive things you shouldn't survive." He gestures at Cassie. "But this is different. This isn't about saving a stranger. This is about building something. A future." His grin fades into something more serious. "Don't waste it. Don't let the mission become an excuse to sacrifice yourself. She needs you to come back."

"I know."

"Do you? Because in a few hours, you're flying into a fortress. When things go sideways—and they will—the temptation to be the guy who stays behind to buy time, to take the hit so the team gets clear … It's going to be there." He holds my gaze. "Don't do it. Not this time. You've got someone waiting. Be a partner, Halo. Stay alive because she asked you to, not just because survival is tactically convenient."

I don't have an answer. But something in his words settles into my chest, filling spaces I didn't know were empty.

Cassie finishes her magazine. Turns to us with a smile.

"My grouping improved thirty percent." She holds up the target —center mass peppered with holes. "Fuse was being generous, but I'll take it."

"Not generous." Fuse stands. "Accurate. You've got talent. Keep practicing and you might actually be useful in a firefight." He slaps me on the shoulder as he passes. "I'm going to prep the breach charges. You two take a break. Reconnect. Do whatever it is that couples do when they're not running from killer robots."

He disappears into the equipment room.

Cassie crosses to me. Sits on the bench, close enough that our shoulders touch.

"He's nice." She keeps her voice low. "Under all the flirting and the jokes."

"He is. He's also right."

"About what?"

I turn to face her. Take her hands.

"About coming back. About staying alive." I search her eyes, looking for the words I've never been good at saying. "I've spent years treating every mission like it might be my last. Not because I wanted to die, exactly. But because I didn't have a reason to want anything else."

"And now?"

"Now I have you."

She leans into me. Presses her forehead against mine.

"Then come back," she whispers. "Whatever happens in Nevada. Whatever we find. Come back to me."

"I will."

"Promise."

"I promise."

It's a lie—I can't promise anything in a combat zone. But it's also the truest thing I've ever said. Because for the first time, I want to keep the promise. I want to survive not just because survival is instinct, but because there's something waiting on the other side worth surviving for.

Ghost finds me an hour later.

I'm in the armory, running a final check on my kit—rifle, sidearm, spare magazines, the compact trauma kit that's saved my life twice. The routine is soothing, meditative. Muscle memory taking over while my mind processes everything that's happened.

"Halo." Ghost's voice is quiet. Controlled. He steps into the armory, letting the door close behind him. "A word."

"Sure."

He crosses to where I'm standing. For a moment, he just watches me work—hands moving through the familiar patterns, checking chambers and counting rounds.

"She's staying." Not a question.

"I know." I meet his gaze. Hold it. "She's the reason I'm still functional. The reason I'm not operating on autopilot, waiting for the mission that finally puts me in the ground. I have to come back."

Ghost is quiet for a long moment. His expression doesn't change —it rarely does—but something shifts in the quality of his silence. The assessment giving way to something more personal.

"Colombia," he says finally. "When I found you in that warehouse. You had a gun to your head."

The memory surfaces. Unwanted. Unavoidable.

A concrete floor sticky with blood—not all of it mine. The bodies of the men I'd killed scattered around me like broken toys. The Glock pressed against my temple, finger on the trigger, the noise in my head so loud I couldn't hear anything else.

Sofia was dead. The cartel had taken her, and I'd been half a world away. The guilt was a physical weight crushing my chest. Easier to end it. Easier to follow her into the dark.

And then Ghost's voice, cutting through the static: *Put the gun down. That's an order.*

"I remember."

"You weren't going to pull the trigger because of the cartel." Ghost's voice is flat. Clinical. The voice of a man who's seen too many operators eat their weapons. "You were going to pull it because you wanted the noise to stop."

"Yes."

"I've been watching you for years. Waiting for that moment to come back. Waiting for the mission where you finally decide not to come home." His pale eyes search my face. "Every extraction, every firefight, every time you put yourself between a bullet and someone else—I've been counting. Measuring how much risk you're willing to take. Trying to calculate when enough will finally be enough."

I don't have an answer. Because he's right. Because somewhere underneath all the professionalism and tactical precision, there's always been a death wish. A quiet certainty that the way I live will eventually become the way I die.

"I'm coming back," I say.

"Because of her."

"Because of her."

Ghost nods slowly. Something that might be approval—or relief—flickers across his weathered features.

"I've seen a lot of operators destroy themselves. Some of them fast, some of them slow. Most of them never find a reason to stop. They just keep going until the mission kills them or they kill themselves." He pauses. "You're one of the best I've ever worked with."

"Thanks."

He turns toward the door and pauses at the threshold. Looks back.

"For what it's worth." He pauses. "I'm glad you found someone. You deserve better than dying alone in a warehouse somewhere."

Then he's gone. The door closes behind him.

I stand alone in the armory for a long time, surrounded by weapons and ammunition and the tools of a trade I've practiced for most of my adult life.

Ghost is right. About all of it.

I was waiting to die. Not actively—not planning it or seeking it out—but passively. Accepting that every mission might be the last one. Taking risks that made sense tactically but not personally. Living like someone who didn't expect to have a future.

Cassie changed that.

Not by demanding anything. Not by issuing ultimatums or forcing confrontations. Just by being there. By looking at me like I was worth seeing. By making me want things I'd convinced myself I couldn't have.

A future. A life. A reason to come home.

I finish checking my kit. Pack everything into the tactical bag I'll carry into Nevada. Then I go to find her.

The afternoon dissolves into weapons checks and tactical briefings and the quiet, focused work of people preparing for combat.

I move through it on autopilot—the routines so deeply ingrained they don't require conscious thought. Ammunition loaded. Armor fitted. Communications tested. The same preparations I've made a hundred times before.

My attention keeps drifting to Cassie.

She's in the common area with Brass, the two of them bent over a tablet. Brass is explaining something—approach routes, probably, or extraction protocols—and Cassie is nodding, asking questions, absorbing information with the same intensity she brought to the financial analysis.

She fits here. That's what surprises me.

Not just tolerated. Not just accepted. But integrated—part of the team in a way that usually takes months to develop. Brass treats her like a colleague. Fuse treats her like family. Even Ghost, in his distant way, has acknowledged her value.

She was invisible her whole life. Overlooked. Dismissed.

Not anymore.

Brass looks up, catches me watching. Grins.

"Stop lurking and come help," he calls. "We're trying to figure out the best entry point and your girlfriend has opinions."

Your girlfriend. The word should feel strange. It doesn't.

I cross to the table. Look at the schematics.

"The northwest access point." Cassie points. "It's the most heavily defended, which means Phoenix expects attacks from the other directions. If we approach from where they're watching most closely, using the terrain to mask our insertion—"

"We use their paranoia against them," I finish. "They'll have resources concentrated on the obvious approaches."

"Exactly." She looks up at me. "Am I wrong?"

"You're not wrong." I study the map, running tactical calculations. "Ghost and Torque would need to sign off, but the logic is sound."

"See?" Brass saves the notation. "Natural tactical instinct. I told you she'd be useful."

"Never doubted it."

Cassie's hand finds mine under the table. Squeezes.

The rest of the afternoon passes in a blur. Briefings and equipment checks and the small, essential tasks that separate success from failure. Through it all, Cassie stays close. Not hovering—she's learning too much, contributing too much to be in the way—but present. A constant reminder of what I'm fighting for.

We eat dinner together, all of us—Ghost, Brass, Whisper, Fuse, Torque, Thorne, Cassie, and me. Eight people around a metal table in an underground bunker, sharing terrible food, dark humor, and the easy camaraderie of soldiers preparing for battle.

This is what I've been missing. What I told myself I didn't need.

Family.

The evening briefing runs long. Ghost and Brass debate approach vectors while Torque paces and Whisper calculates odds none of us want to hear. By 2100, we're no closer to a solution than we were at dawn. The facility is a fortress. Phoenix has seen to that.

"We reconvene at 0600," Ghost finally says. "Fresh eyes. We'll find a way."

The team disperses. Thorne disappears like smoke. Fuse and Whisper head toward the armory. Brass stays at the console, running simulations that keep coming back red.

Cassie catches my eye across the room.

I cross to her. Take her hand.

"Hey."

"Hey." She looks up at me. In the blue glow of the operations center, her eyes are luminous. Determined. Beautiful. "Walk with me?"

"Always."

I lead her through the corridor to a quiet corner where the hum of electronics fades to silence.

She takes my hands. Her fingers are smaller than mine, softer. "You'll figure it out. The approach. You always do."

"We're close. Just missing something."

"Then you'll find it." Her certainty is absolute. "But that's not what I wanted to talk about."

"No?"

"No." She steps closer. "Ten days ago, I didn't know you existed. I was living my life, doing my job, pretending that being invisible was the same as being safe. And then you crashed through my window and everything changed."

"I used the door, and you pepper-sprayed me."

"You know what I mean." A smile flickers across her face—there and gone. "You showed me what I was hiding from. Not Phoenix. Myself. The version of me that was too scared to want things, too careful to risk anything, too invisible to matter."

"You always mattered."

"I didn't believe it. Not until you." She's close enough now that I can smell the gun oil on her hands, the industrial soap from the HQ showers. "You looked at me like I was real. Like I was worth protecting. Like I was worth dying for."

"You are."

"Then let me be worth living for too." Her voice catches. Steadies. "When you go into that facility—and you will—don't look for a way to die. Don't sacrifice yourself because you think that's all you're good for. Fight like you have something to lose. Fight like you have someone to come home to."

I pull her against me. Hold her so tight I can feel her heartbeat against my chest, rapid and strong.

"I've spent years as a ghost." My words are muffled against her hair. "I told myself it was necessary. I told myself caring was a weakness. I told myself that the man who loved Sofia died with her, and whatever was left was just—machinery. Following programs. Executing missions."

"And now?"

"Now I think the universe had other plans." I pull back enough to see her face. "I should have died in Colombia. I should have died a dozen times since—the close calls, the impossible extractions, the moments where the math said I was finished and somehow I walked away. Fuse calls it unnatural luck. Ghost calls it stubbornness."

"What do you call it?"

I cup her face in my hands. The calluses on my palms are rough against her cheeks, but she doesn't flinch. Doesn't pull away.

"I call it waiting. Waiting for something I didn't know I was waiting for. A reason to stop simply existing. A reason to become real again." I kiss her forehead. Her cheeks. The corner of her mouth. "You're that reason, Cassie. You're the reason I want to survive this. Not just exist—survive. Come home. Build something that isn't made of bullets and blood."

"Diego …" Her voice breaks on my name.

"I'm not looking for a way to die. Not anymore." I kiss her properly then—soft at first, then deeper, pouring everything I can't say into the contact. "I'm looking for a way to live. With you. For as long as you want me."

"Forever." She rises onto her toes, arms wrapping around my neck.

The kiss deepens. Her hands fist in my shirt. My fingers thread through her hair. For a moment, everything else fades—the facility, the odds, the mission—and there's nothing but her warmth and her taste and the impossible, irrational certainty that this is what I was made for.

Not killing. Not disappearing. Not ghosting through the shadows alone.

This. Her. Us.

When we finally break apart, her cheeks are flushed, her breathing unsteady.

"Partners," I say.

"Equals," she answers.

I take her hand. Lead her through the corridor toward my quarters. She doesn't ask where we're going. Doesn't hesitate.

The door closes behind us.

In the darkness, there's no mission. No Phoenix. No odds, approach vectors, or probability matrices. There's just her hands finding my face, my fingers threading through her hair, and the soft sound she makes when I lower her onto the bed.

We've been building toward this since the moment I walked through her door. Every touch. Every look. Every time we almost died and didn't.

I take my time. Learn the geography of her—what makes her gasp, what makes her arch, what makes her whisper my name like a prayer. She's not invisible here.

She's real. She's mine. And I'm hers.

After, she curls against my chest, her breath warm on my skin. My fingers trace lazy patterns down her spine.

"Diego?"

"Yeah?"

"Don't die tomorrow."

I press a kiss to her hair. "Not tomorrow. Not any day I can help it."

She's asleep within minutes, her weight a warm anchor against my side.

I hold her in the darkness, listening to her breathe, and for the first time in years, I feel something I'd forgotten existed.

Peace.

Tomorrow, we find a way in.

Tonight, I have a reason to come back.

READY FOR BOOK Six in the Cerberus Security Series?

Read TORQUE

The Cerberus Protection Services Series: Where deadly operators protect brilliant women from a conspiracy that reaches into every shadow of power.

TORQUE IS A FULL-LENGTH, **high-heat romantic suspense novel featuring:**
- A protective alpha hero who meets his match
- Forced proximity that ignites into scorching chemistry 🔥
- Edge-of-your-seat action with a steamy slow burn 💥
- Only one bed (and so much sexual tension) 😈
- Life-or-death stakes with an emotionally satisfying HEA 🤍

No cliffhangers. Can be read as a standalone, but best enjoyed as part of the Cerberus Security Series.

CRAVING MORE GUARDIANS?

If you've fallen for the fierce alphas of Cerberus, you're just getting started.

There's an entire world waiting for you—the Guardian Hostage Rescue Specialists series—one built on danger, desire, and the kind of love that ruins a woman for anyone else.

Start with the *Alpha Team series*—because once you meet these men, you'll never forget them. Protective. Possessive. Unapologetically alpha. And the women who bring them to their knees? Equally unforgettable.

BUT IF YOU want to feel **everything**—if you want to understand where it all began, before Cerberus, before the Guardians, before the rescues—go back to the beginning.

Heart's Insanity, the first book in the *Angel Fire* rock star romance series, is where you'll meet Skye and Forest. It's raw. It's emotional. It's the origin story of the entire Guardian world. And trust me—once you see who Forest Summers was before Guardian HRS existed, you'll never look at him the same way again.

Start there.
Feel everything.
And then come back for more.
Start with Heart's Insanity
Or dive into the Alpha Team series.
The heat only gets hotter.
The danger only gets deadlier.
And the Guardians?
The mission isn't over. It's just getting started.

Keep current with Ellie Masters.
CLICK HERE
Receive news of her writing and new releases.

Shop Ellie Masters Romantic Suspense and Steamy
Contemporary Romance by series.
Angel Fire Rock Romance
Guardian HRS: Alpha Team
Guardian HRS: Bravo Team
Guardian HRS: Charlie Team
Guardian HRS: Delta Team
Cerberus Personal Security

The LaRouge Triplets
The One I Want Series
Angel's Peak Series
Billionaire Boy's Club
The Lovers
Changing Roles

ELLZ BELLZ
ELLIE'S FACEBOOK READER GROUP

If you are interested in joining the **ELLZ BELLZ**, Ellie's Facebook reader group, we'd love to have you.

Join Ellie's **ELLZ BELLZ**.
The **ELLZ BELLZ** Facebook Reader Group

Sign up for Ellie's Newsletter.
Elliemasters.com/newslettersignup

Also by Ellie Masters

The LIGHTER SIDE

Ellie Masters is the lighter side of the Jet & Ellie Masters writing duo! You will find Contemporary Romance, Military Romance, Romantic Suspense, Billionaire Romance, and Rock Star Romance in Ellie's Works.

YOU CAN FIND ELLIE'S BOOKS HERE:

ELLIEMASTERS.COM/BOOKS

Shop Ellie Masters Romantic Suspense and Steamy Contemporary Romance by series.

Angel Fire Rock Romance

Guardian HRS: Alpha Team

Guardian HRS: Bravo Team

Guardian HRS: Charlie Team

Guardian HRS: Delta Team

Cerberus Personal Security

The LaRouge Triplets

The One I Want Series

Angel's Peak Series

Billionaire Boy's Club

The Lovers

Changing Roles

SUGGESTED READING ORDER

Rescuing Angie

Rescuing Isabelle

Rescuing Carmen

Rescuing Rosalie

Rescuing Kaye

Cara's Protector

Rescuing Barbi

Charlie Team

Rescuing Rebel

Rescuing Stitch

Rescuing Mia

Jenna's Protector

Rescuing Sophia

Rescuing Malia

Rescuing Ally (Part 1)

Rescuing Ally (Part 2)

Delta Team

Rescuing Ember

Rescuing Aria

STANDALONES IN THE GUARDIAN HOSTAGE RESCUE SERIES YOU CAN READ ANYTIME

Military Romance

Guardian Personal Protection Specialists

Sybil's Protector

Lyra's Protector

Angel's Peak Series

Steamy Instalove Small Town

Brody

Cage

Billionaire Romance

Billionaire Boys Club

Hawke

Richard

Contemporary Romance

Cocky Captain

Romantic Suspense

EACH BOOK IS A STANDALONE NOVEL.

The Starling

The Swan

~AND~

Science Fiction

Ellie Masters writing as L.A. Warren

Vendel Rising: a Science Fiction Serialized Novel

If you enjoyed this book by Ellie Masters, the LIGHTER SIDE of the Jet & Ellie writing duo, and aren't afraid of edgier writing, you might enjoy reading BDSM themed books written by Jet, the DARKER SIDE of the Masters' Writing Team.

The DARKER SIDE

Jet Masters is the darker side of the Jet & Ellie writing duo!

Romantic Suspense

Changing Roles Series:

THIS SERIES MUST BE READ IN ORDER.

Command Me

Control Me

Collar Me

Embracing FATE

Seizing FATE

Accepting FATE

HOT READS

A STANDALONE NOVEL.

Down the Rabbit Hole

Light BDSM Romance
The Ties that Bind

EACH BOOK IN THIS SERIES CAN BE READ AS A STANDALONE AND IS ABOUT A DIFFERENT COUPLE WITH AN HEA.

Alexa

Penny

Michelle

Ivy

HOT READS
Becoming His Series

THIS SERIES MUST BE READ IN ORDER.

The Ballet

Learning to Breathe

Becoming His

Dark Captive Romance

A STANDALONE NOVEL.

She's MINE

About the Author

Ellie Masters is a USA Today Bestselling author and Amazon Top 15 Author who writes Angsty, Steamy, Heart-Stopping, Pulse-Pounding, Can't-Stop-Reading Romantic Suspense. In addition, she's a wife, military mom, doctor, and retired Colonel. She writes romantic suspense filled with all your sexy, swoon-worthy alpha men. Her writing will tug at your heartstrings and leave your heart racing.

Born in the South, raised under the Hawaiian sun, Ellie has traveled the globe while in service to her country. The love of her life, her amazing husband, is her number one fan and biggest supporter. And yes! He's read every word she's written.

She has lived all over the United States—east, west, north, south and central—but grew up under the Hawaiian sun. She's also been privileged to have lived overseas, experiencing other cultures and making lifelong friends. Now, Ellie is proud to call herself a Southern transplant, learning to say y'all and "bless her heart" with the best of them.

Ellie's favorite way to spend an evening is curled up on a couch, laptop in place, watching a fire, drinking a good wine, and bringing forth all the characters from her mind to the page and hopefully into the hearts of her readers.

FOR MORE INFORMATION
elliemasters.com

facebook.com/elliemastersromance

x.com/Ellie__Masters

instagram.com/ellie_masters

bookbub.com/authors/ellie-masters

goodreads.com/Ellie_Masters

Connect with Ellie Masters

Website:
elliemasters.com
Purchase Direct:
elliemasters.com/shopify
Amazon Author Page:
elliemasters.com/amazon
Facebook:
elliemasters.com/Facebook
Goodreads:
elliemasters.com/Goodreads
Bookbub:
elliemasters.com/Bookbub
Instagram:
elliemasters.com/Instagram

Final Thoughts

I hope you enjoyed this book as much as I enjoyed writing it. If you enjoyed reading this story, please consider leaving a review on Amazon and Goodreads, and please let other people know. A sentence is all it takes. Friend recommendations are the strongest catalyst for readers' purchase decisions! And I'd love to be able to continue bringing the characters and stories from My-Mind-to-the-Page.

Second, call or e-mail a friend and tell them about this book. If you really want them to read it, gift it to them. If you prefer digital friends, please use the "Recommend" feature of Goodreads to spread the word.

Or visit my blog https://elliemasters.com, where you can find out more about my writing process and personal life.

Come visit The EDGE: Dark Discussions where we'll have a chance to talk about my works, their creation, and maybe what the future has in store for my writing.

Facebook Reader Group: Ellz Bellz

Thank you so much for your support!

Love,

Ellie

Dedication

This book is dedicated to you, my reader. Thank you for spending a few hours of your time with me. I wouldn't be able to write without you to cheer me on. Your wonderful words, your support, and your willingness to join me on this journey is a gift beyond measure.

Whether this is the first book of mine you've read, or if you've been with me since the very beginning, thank you for believing in me as I bring these characters 'from my mind to the page and into your hearts.'

Love,
Ellie

THE END

www.ingramcontent.com/pod-product-compliance
Lightning Source LLC
Chambersburg PA
CBHW021344150726
47989CB00005B/2097